The Blood Bond

Emma Cave is a former publishing editor who is now devoting
herself to full-time writing, after the success of her first book,
Little Angie, which is also published in Pan. She lives with her
husband in Limassol, Cyprus where she is currently writing her
third novel.

Also by Emma Cave
in Pan Books
Little Angie

Emma Cave
The Blood Bond

Pan Books in association with
Heinemann

First published 1979 by William Heinemann Ltd
This edition published 1980 by Pan Books Ltd,
Cavaye Place, London SW10 9PG
in association with William Heinemann Ltd
© Emma Cave 1979
ISBN 0 330 26144 4
Printed in Great Britain by
Richard Clay (The Chaucer Press) Ltd, Bungay, Suffolk

for **Graham,**
and also for **Patrick** and **Wendy**:
summers at Santa, 1958–1964

Again, love and thanks to Margaret and Bill

'That corpse you planted last year in your garden,
Has it begun to sprout? Will it bloom this year?'

T.S. Eliot, *The Waste Land*

part one
1960

one

They crouched in the circle of bushes. With the penknife, he made neat little cuts in their wrists, between the veins. Then, in turn, they pressed their wrists together and, in turn, as the blood merged, stinging, they swore that they would never, never tell.

Esther could feel the sharp small pain now, could hear their voices repeating the words, like a litany, as she stood, astonished, in the smell of incense, staring at Brian.

It was a cold sunny morning at the end of April. Closing the front door behind her, she saw her breath cloud the air. She shivered. There must have been frost during the night, frost not visible on the city pavements. At Mortmere, on a morning like this, when she looked out of her bedroom window across the park, the sun would have melted the frost early, except in those places where the shadows of trees fell on the grass. There, the frost would remain, paling the shade, seeming to reflect each tree as in an old blurred mirror.

But she had renounced all that. The view from the window. The park with its landscaped vistas. The mere where wild duck skimmed the still water.

Two men were heaping empty crates on to a lorry outside the warehouse next door. Though the early morning rush was over now, the district was still full of movement. That was one of the things she liked about Covent Garden, the contrast between the different times of day: the very early bustle, the lively mornings, the still afternoons, the silent evenings. In a few years' time, the Market was going to be moved. She didn't want to think about that, about what would happen to the neighbourhood, about the plans that were being made for towering office blocks.

She knew that protests were already being organized. She really ought to become involved but, as she told herself now, she was concerned with so many other things: meetings about oppression in southern Africa, protests about torture in Latin America, demonstrations against nuclear weapons. Sometimes she felt that none of these activities seemed to produce any

11

visible results; resolutions would be passed, speeches would be made, a leaflet would be printed and distributed to indifferent passers-by, who would glance at it, screw it up, drop it on the pavement. Mightn't becoming involved in community politics, in 'grass-roots activities', be more satisfying? But something about this idea, the closeness, the intimacy of it, perhaps, made her feel stiff and shrinking. And anyway, mightn't the growing restlessness and perfunctoriness with which all her activities had recently seemed to be infected, spread their poison here as well?

Meanwhile, though buildings decayed and windows were boarded up, there was this morning life, there were the crates and trays of blooms in the Floral Hall, smelling of earth, smelling of rain, smelling like the gardens at Mortmere. And there were also little pubs and restaurants, publishers' offices, small arty shops that opened hopefully – often to close a few months later. She passed a shop of this kind now. There were candles, pottery, and old opaque bottles in its window. Her eye was caught by a hanging paper lantern. It was just what she needed for her room, to replace a semi-circular glass shade which cast too harsh, too undiffused a light on the oak table which she had found in one of the disused rooms at Mortmere. ('For heaven's sake, do take what you need,' her mother had said impatiently. Wouldn't it have been wasteful, absurd not to? Surely she wasn't violating any principle. After all, she was only borrowing the things. Nonetheless, she had been modest in her choice. 'Rather a dismal little collection of objects,' her mother had said, eyebrows raised. 'I wouldn't have believed there was such junk in the house. Even in the servants' rooms.' But then, with a quick glance at Esther, a shrug, a measured dose of her famous charm, she had added, 'Oh well, darling, if it's what you want, I'm delighted for you to have it, quite delighted.')

She opened the door of the shop, and went inside. It was small and dark. Paper lanterns hung, on cords of various lengths, from the ceiling. Small objects were crowded on tables. The shop smelled of sandalwood, and she saw that a stick of incense was burning by the till; a little curl of smoke rose from it into the dark air. She had just asked the tousled-looking, long-haired boy behind the counter for one of the lanterns, when a light hand touched her shoulder, a high voice – questioning, surprised – spoke her name. She turned.

He was small and plump, with yellow hair and bright flickering eyes. His clothes were bright too, camp and expensive-looking. Really, he looked just the sort of person she tried to avoid. He was probably the son of some old friend of her mother's, she thought. And then, something clicked in her head. Her stomach lurched as it always did when she was suddenly reminded of that summer. (*Blood welled from the cut in her wrist.*) 'Brian!' she exclaimed. 'Why, it's Brian!', and she was conscious of surprise at the warmth she heard in her voice.

He was looking her up and down. 'Eleven years!' he said. 'And I recognized you *immediately*. Why, Esther, you've hardly changed a fraction. A little tougher, perhaps. Butch? No, too pretty to be that, really.' Though indeed, she reflected, her appearance, in heavy green corduroy trousers, thick cable-knit sweater, and short suede coat, could well be considered to present a positively masculine contrast to his own.

He leaned forward, planted a little peck of a kiss on her cheek, then darted back to survey her once more. 'And what are *you* doing here?' he asked.

'I live just round the corner,' she said. 'I was on my way to work in the library, and I stopped to buy a lampshade.'

'Don't tell me you're a *librarian*,' Brian said.

She smiled. 'No, I'm doing some research.' The boy behind the counter, she saw, had put the lampshade into a paper bag. She paid for it. 'And you,' she said, turning to Brian, 'what brings you here?'

'Filling in time till the pubs open, duckie. No libraries for *me*! But I have found something quite delicious.' He held out a thin little envelope of mauve paper. *Fortune Teller* was printed across the top of it, and *Miracle Fish* across the bottom. In between, a shark raised its head from formal, pointed mauve and white waves.

'What is it?' she asked.

'Patience, darling,' he said. 'Contain your curiosity for just one moment.'

Carefully, he opened the envelope. Delicately, he extracted a fish, made of transparent crimson paper, and decorated with gilt fins and scales. Holding it by the tail, he started to read from the back of the envelope: ' "Moving head – jealousy. Moving tail – indifference. Moving head *and* tail – in love. Curling sides – fickle. Turns over – false. Curls up entirely –

13

passionate. Motionless – dead one." How deliciously the Japanese do express themselves!' He giggled. 'Give me your hand, Esther,' he said. Absurdly, she hesitated. Then she shrugged, and extended her palm. He placed the fish on her hand. Slowly, its head and tail moved together to touch, forming a circle.

Brian consulted the envelope. 'In love!' he exclaimed. 'Isn't that marvellous! You must tell me *all* about it.' But as he spoke, suddenly the fish turned right over, and came to rest, flat on its other side.

Brian peered at the envelope again. 'False,' he said. 'Well, fancy that! Though it's rather more intriguing than "in love", when you come to think of it.'

She laughed. 'I wonder how it works,' she said. 'Something to do with the temperature of the skin, I suppose.' Reproachfully, Brian shook his head. 'Oh Esther, I can see that you've turned into a thoroughly sordid materialist, taking all the lovely mystery out of life.' He lifted the fish, by its tail, from her palm.

'How about *you* having a go, dear?' he said to the boy behind the counter. But the boy looked sullen, and shook his head.

Brian shrugged. 'Oh well, then there's only little me. "Passionate", Esther – that's what it's absolutely *bound* to be.'

He placed the fish on his palm. It lay there, unmoving. Tentatively, he wriggled his fingers, but still it didn't stir. 'Ugh,' he said. '*Dead one*. Really, that is just *too much*.'

Neatly, he replaced the fish in its envelope, which he dropped disdainfully on the counter. 'I've decided I don't want it after all,' he said. Pointedly ignoring a murmur of derision from the shop assistant, he looked at the narrow gold watch on his wrist. 'Opening time at last!' he exclaimed. 'Come, Esther. Let us go and have a nostalgic drink in a delicious pub I know.'

Was nostalgia really the right word? she wondered, as she followed him to the door. Opening it, standing back for her to go ahead of him, he said. 'By the way, have you ever seen Charles since . . . then?'

Blood rose in a thin line in the wake of the blade. 'Charles?' she said. 'No. Never.'

'He's here,' Brian said. 'In London. I saw him the other day. In fact, I often see him. Come,' he repeated, 'and I'll tell you all.'

*

The 'delicious pub' was, as she might have guessed, the Salisbury. Red velvet, dark wood, mirrored walls; polished bronze art-nouveau goddesses bearing cut-glass torches. Although it was so early, a few middle-aged men were already ensconced on the red velvet banquettes, or leaned against the bar, studiedly casual, but perceptibly observant: watching, all the time, the others, the young ones, who ranged from sullen and acne-pitted to sprightly and fragile – she noticed blue shadow on a fair boy's lids.

'One of my favourite haunts,' Brian said. 'Or should I say "hunts"?' He giggled, and squeezed her arm. 'However, as I'm with a *lidy* today, I think we'll sit in the back room.'

There, though the mirrors and the red velvet seats were the same, the atmosphere was different. The tension, the contained frenzy were missing. The room was empty, except for one grey-haired man, sipping a glass of sherry and doing a crossword.

They chose a place on the far side of the room. She sat down, and Brian went back into the bar to fetch their drinks. She had asked for a pint of bitter, and he had exclaimed, 'Darling, how proletarian! But if you insist. Definitely a Bloody Mary for *me*.'

As they walked to the Salisbury, he had told her about Charles. 'He's living in an attic, but a terribly chic one. Just off Jermyn Street. So handy for Fortnum's, you know! The house belongs to that famous cousin of his, Lady Violet – do you remember her?'

'Yes indeed,' Esther had answered, and then she had asked, 'What does Charles do?'

'*Do?* Well, I'm not absolutely clear about that. Something in the City. Though I don't have the impression that he's exactly loaded. However, he's got this girl.'

'Ah, a girl. What kind of girl?' she had asked – coolly, casually. But again – how absurd! – her stomach had given that uncontrollable lurch.

'Mmm, I *knew* you'd be interested in that. You had rather a thing about Charles, didn't you?'

She had laughed. 'I was only a child.'

'We-ell ... But don't let me hold you in suspense. Her name is Clare. She looks as if she's made of very expensive glass, as if she might shatter at a touch, you know. Though glass isn't *quite* right. That pink and white Limoges perhaps? No, too

15

pink. But there's something called milk glass. Yes, that's exactly her – milky but brittle. Glassy kind of hair, too. Like the tails of those birds that people used to put on Christmas trees. And a fragile little voice. She's American, by the way. And she's got money. Everything about her says money – quietly, but oh, *so* distinctly.' As he pushed open the door of the Salisbury, he had added, 'Could that be her appeal for darling Charles? one wonders.'

Now he was back with the drinks. He settled down beside her with a little wriggle. 'Ah,' he sighed, leaning back. 'And now,' he said, 'tell me : do you want to see him?'

'Whom?' she said.

'Whom, no less! Goodness, how grand. I don't know anyone who says "whom". Whom but Charles, duckie. Don't try to play dumb with *this* wise old owl.' And suddenly they were both laughing.

She felt in her bag for her cigarettes, offered them to him. He shook his head. 'So harmful to the lungs, so unbecoming to the teeth, and worst of all, so bad for the breath,' he declared. Lighting one for herself, she said, 'I don't know whether I want to see him or not.'

'But darling, of course you do. I can see that you're quite devoured with curiosity.'

'I'm sure I shan't like him,' she said. 'I find all that sort of thing so boring. Money and smartness and so on, I mean.'

'Oh, isn't she the *blasé* one,' Brian mocked. Then he shook his head. His tone was almost earnest, as he said, 'He isn't, you know. He couldn't be, really, whatever he did.'

'Couldn't be what?'

'Boring. Not Charles.'

She thought for a moment. Then, 'No,' she said, 'I suppose not.'

'It is called Trial by Ordeal,' Charles said. 'All the really important secret societies go in for it. A person has to prove that he is worthy to join. It's not just a test,' he went on. 'It's a kind of purifying, too.'

Sitting around him on the grass, within the Ring, Esther, Brian and Geoff solemnly nodded their heads, Esther wasn't exactly sure what he meant, but all the same, she was fascinated.

'To become a member,' Charles continued, 'a person has to do his very worst thing.'

'Worst?' asked Esther.

'Yes,' said Charles. 'The thing that is worst for him.'

'Or her,' Esther broke in again. 'But how,' she asked, 'does one find out what that is?'

'To do that,' Charles said, 'one has to play the Truth Game.'

A silence had fallen. 'Brian,' she said, 'we've been talking about no one but Charles. What about you? What do you do?'

'*Do*, Esther? What an obsession you've got about *doing*. It's what people *are* that is important, duckie. Surely what they do doesn't really matter?'

Esther believed that it did matter, very much. Ornaments were things of which she disapproved. Certain gilded porcelain figures at Mortmere came into her mind, and she shook her head impatiently.

Brian shrugged, a little petulantly. 'I can see,' he said, 'that you insist on an answer. Well, I suppose I do bits and pieces of this and that. I take quite pretty photographs. I went to art school for two long weary years. I've designed some rather delicious clothes, but just for chums. Of course, I must admit that I haven't been exactly *compelled* to press my nose to the grindstone – thank goodness for that, anyway. Though my papa detested me, he still left me well provided for, blood being thicker than water, as he would certainly have put it – oh, he was a great one for the clichés, was my papa.'

Brian's face had darkened. He shrugged again, and then blinked rapidly, pointing a finger at Esther's chest. 'And what about *you*?' he said. 'Since we've got involved with this excessively tedious aspect of life, let's dispose of it, once and for all. So ... what do *you* do, duckie?'

'I'm at the LSE,' she said, rather stiffly. 'I've finished my degree, but now I'm writing a thesis—'

'Please don't tell me what it's about,' he broke in. 'I'm sure I wouldn't understand even the *title*. Well, well, the London School of Economics – that explains *everything*. The proletarian pint of bitter, those sturdy garments you're wearing, the general importance of being earnest, and so on.'

She burst out laughing. 'Brian, you're quite impossible,' she said.

'Ah, that's what all the boys tell me. And now – I refuse to be put off for another second – what about the reunion? I'm set on it, Estherkins. How often have I said to myself: *"When shall we three meet again? In thunder, lightning, or in rain?"'*

He stood up. 'I shall telephone this minute. It's Saturday, and Charles may well be at home, if he hasn't gone poncing off to some dreary country house or other.'

She put a hand on his arm. 'No,' she said. 'Wait a moment. I want to think.'

'Duckie, there isn't anything to think about. Anyway, one should always act on impulse. It's so bourgeois to *plan*.'

'Oh, all right, then,' she said. 'Go ahead. I'll wait here.'

'But wouldn't you like to speak to him? To give him a surprise?' Brian imitated a feminine voice: 'Charles – guess who?'

She shook her head. 'No, definitely not.' And when Brian still hesitated, she said, 'I don't feel like it, Brian, I tell you.'

'Hoity toity!' he exclaimed but, quite unabashed, he almost skipped as, feeling in his pocket for loose change, he hurried over to the pay telephone that stood near the doorway.

How extraordinary it was that she should feel so disturbed. She lit a cigarette. *Eleven years ago!* What would Charles look like now? Would he still be as beautiful? (That was something she hadn't asked Brian.) And would he still be as ... She hesitated for a word, found 'enthralling' – and deplored it.

It was obvious that Charles was out. Brian had been standing by the telephone (receiver pressed to his ear, coin poised above the pay slot) for what she felt was a ridiculously long time. But, at that moment, he pressed the money in, turned towards the wall, and started to speak. Now he was nodding emphatically. (Did he think that the person he was talking to – probably not Charles, she decided – could see him?) Now he was speaking again, now listening, laughing and nodding, speaking once more, but stopping suddenly. Obviously the person at the other end of the line had rung off.

With one of those little shrugs which she already thought of as characteristic of him, Brian replaced the receiver. With a wave in her direction, he disappeared into the bar. He must be fetching more drinks, and she couldn't face the thought of another pint of bitter – though she approved of beer, somehow she never wanted to drink very much of it.

Either someone else had answered the telephone or Charles

had rejected the idea of the reunion. She felt sure that one or the other had happened. Now Brian was returning with, yes, another great pint of bitter, and another Bloody Mary.

'It's on, duckie,' he exclaimed gleefully, putting the drinks on the table and positively bouncing on to the banquette beside her. 'This evening, as ever is. You can make that, can't you?'

'I don't know,' she said. 'There's a committee meeting I'm meant to be going to.' But, even as she spoke, she knew that she was going to abandon the meeting. As Brian seemed to know too, for he said at once, 'Now don't be naughty. I've played that unattainable-lady role far too often myself to be taken in by it.'

'He took a long time to answer the telephone,' she said.

'Mmm, I could feel you positively quivering behind me.' She allowed herself to giggle. This, she decided, was probably the way to handle things – to treat the subject as an amusing childish crush. Perhaps she'd even be able to make a joke of it with Charles – but, no, something in her shrank from *that* idea. 'He was downstairs with dear Cousin Violet,' Brian went on. 'He's expecting us at six.'

'Did he sound pleased?' she couldn't help asking.

'Well, I wouldn't put it quite as strongly as *that*. But surely you remember that dear Charles was never exactly demonstrative. He hasn't changed in that regard. But I suppose he must have been quite pleased really, or he wouldn't have made a date for tonight, would he?'

'Mmm,' she said, and then, 'well, six o'clock it is, then.' Suddenly she wanted to be back in her flat, wanted to be alone to *prepare herself*. But that was silly – prepare herself for what? Anyway, she wanted to leave. She stood up. 'Brian, I must dash,' she said. 'But you haven't finished your drink,' he said reproachfully. 'Sorry, but I just don't feel like it,' she said. 'What's Charles's address?' she asked. And then, 'Or shall we meet somewhere, and go together?'

'Ah, you want me to cushion the shock of the encounter, do you?' She could envisage Brian's shrewdness becoming rather tiresome, but she smiled, and said, 'That's right.'

'How about the Red Lion in Duke of York Street?' Brian said. 'It's just round the corner from Lady Violet's.' He stood up. 'Since you're abandoning me,' he said, 'I think I'll move into the bar and study the talent.'

The bar was full now, but, as far as she could see, she was the only woman in it. Carrying his drink, Brian came with her to the door into St Martin's Lane. 'The Red Lion, just before six,' he said, and turned back into the bar.

two

She took a taxi back to her flat, which was something she did rarely – taxis were against her private rules. But her desire to be at home, to be alone, suddenly became so acute that, standing in St Martin's Lane, she hailed the first one she saw. And when, at last, she had paid the cab-driver, unlocked the front door, run up the stairs, and let herself into the flat, she leant against the door, breathing deeply, looking around her large room, and trying to see it with other eyes, from another point of view: *Charles's*. But what did she know of Charles's point of view?

The flat had belonged to a designer at the Royal Opera House. Two years before, he had taken a post in Australia, and Esther had bought the long lease with some of the money that her father had left her.

The large room had three windows, looking onto the street. The two side windows had been put in by the architect who had converted the bulding. The central one was long and narrow and came down to the floor. The room, the estate agent had told her, had once been a storehouse for grain, and the long window had been the door through which the sacks had been hoisted. The roof was high, with exposed beams, and the floor was made of sanded and sealed pine planks. She had left the floor bare (the flat was centrally heated), apart from one large kelim in the centre.

The furniture which she had taken from the attics and sculleries of Mortmere (the large scrubbed oak table at which she ate and worked, four upright Bentwood chairs, a Bentwood rocker, a large Victorian wardrobe, and two pine chests of drawers), the double divan she had bought at Heal's (automatically following her mother's maxim that a cheap bed was a false economy – and a second-hand one unthinkable), her red metal filing cabinet, and the bookshelves which covered one wall – despite all these objects the room still had a feeling of spaciousness.

In this room, Esther felt, she had the best of two worlds: the one she had come from and the one she had chosen. After the vast rooms of Mortmere, she found the bedsitting-rooms of most of the people she knew unbearably claustrophobic. Yet, though this room was so large, at the same time it embodied the austerity, the simplicity (qualities conspicuously absent from Mortmere) which she now valued so highly. Not a single ornament in sight, she confirmed now with satisfaction, leaning against the door, letting her eyes travel over the uncluttered surfaces. There weren't even any pictures – only, over her bed with its brown and white striped Mexican cover, a Rivera poster of a peasant bowed beneath a weight of fruit.

On the right, a door – with her bookshelves fitted round it, so that it was an opening in a wall of books – led into a small passage, off which were a kitchen and bathroom, both overlooking the yard behind the warehouse next door. From the kitchen window, in the early morning, she would often watch porters unloading crates of produce, admiring their strength, envying their easy companionship. *Workers*, she would note reverently – though, whenever she actually encountered workers, she invariably found them difficult to communicate with. The common – or did she mean the human? – touch was something which, regretfully, she acknowledged that she lacked. Perhaps, in time, she would develop it. Or was it, as she secretly feared, something inborn: either you had it or you hadn't? But no, she refused to believe that. Wasn't *'one can change'* her deepest conviction?

She sighed. She straightened her shoulders. She decided that she should have something to eat, and went through into the kitchen – so orderly, so spotless, with its pine fittings, its pottery casseroles, its neat row of herbs growing in the window box. Tidiness was something she had taught herself laboriously – *you see*, she addressed the doubter in her head, *one can change*. In her teens, she had been untidy, dropping her clothes on the floor when she took them off, leaving her books and papers in hectic confusion. Changing that, she had felt that she was changing herself. And now, here in the flat, she found disorder unbearable – the people she knew laughed at the *bourgeois* way she constantly emptied ashtrays, straightened chairs, replaced books in their ordained positions on the shelves. Bourgeois? She sighed again. Really one couldn't win.

She made herself an omelette, snipping chives and parsley from the window-box, and chopping them finely. She peeled tomatoes, sliced them, and dressed them with basil, olive oil and lemon juice.

After she had eaten, at the oak table in the living-room, she washed up, and made coffee in her small Espresso machine. Taking her cup of coffee with her, she went back into the living-room. Obeying an impulse, she put the cup down on the floor beside the low divan, and lay down, arms folded behind her head, hands clasping the back of her neck.

She had intended to work in the library all day. But it was already two o'clock, and at five she would have to get ready to go out. *To go to Charles's.* Of course that still left her with three hours free. She should get up, and sit at the table, and make notes on an article in a learned journal which it was necessary for her to summarize. But she didn't feel like it. She sat up and drank her cup of coffee, and then lay down again. She decided that she would regard this as a lost day, and sighed, but luxuriously. *Fate had intended her to meet Brian today –* but of course that was nonsense. At the thought of Brian, she smiled. She really felt that they were old friends – the way they'd talked, the way they'd understood each other. Old friends, close friends – and weren't they?

Brian had reached the far end of the terrace. Facing his audience, he raised himself onto the very tips of his toes. From his lips, with his fingertips, he scattered a shower of little kisses as, still on his imaginary points, he moved a few steps backwards. Then, with a final pirouette, he was gone.

Shattering the silence, the children burst into a great roar. Then, in unison, they began to clap their hands. Gwyneth and the two 'lady helpers' looked around them, as though waking from a trance. Then, simultaneously, they turned their eyes towards Mrs Sidney.

She, behind the trestle table, was convulsed. Tears in her eyes, she gasped, 'Oh, that naughty boy!' Then, once more, she was possessed by laughter.

Brian had certainly come through his test with flying colours, Esther decided. It had been almost as though he had *enjoyed* it. She exchanged a happy, startled glance with Geoff. Then she turned to Charles. But Charles's expression was cold, remote. Charles did not look pleased, and Esther could not understand why.

Brian, she had discovered today, had still the power to charm her. Yet, for so long, she had been so sure (hadn't she?) that she only wanted to know people who were serious and worth while. And now here she was sinking into a vagabond idle enchantment like that which her parents' friends yearned back to when they spoke of their Oxford or Cambridge days.

That, of course, had been one of the reasons why she had applied to neither place, why she had determined so firmly on the LSE. And she had won, despite her stepfather's rantings about Communist cells, her mother's 'Darling, but how unbelievably drab!'

She had won. Just as she had won five years before that, when she went back to Spain at the end of that summer at Glan-yr-Afon and heard the news that her mother and stepfather had decided to return to Mortmere. After all, the war had been over for more than four years. There surely wasn't much danger of 'silly fuss' as her mother called it: danger of being cut by someone smart at the races, or of an outburst from the crusading columnist of the *Daily Mirror*. So Mortmere was to be restored to its former splendour – for it still bore the traces of its wartime function as a military camp. ('They didn't just persecute us; they stole our lovely house and *defaced* it,' her mother would angrily complain.)

Esther had greeted the announcement with her new stony indifference, but one aspect of it had pleased her. The move from Spain would make it easier for her to achieve the objective she had decided upon. What she wanted, she announced, was to go to a good English boarding school. 'Darling, could you really bear to wear one of those terrible felt hats?' her mother had asked. And she had replied that yes, she could certainly bear that. 'The food will be appalling,' her mother had added. Esther had answered fiercely: 'I don't care. And I'm sure if my *father* were alive, he would have let me. After all, you don't have to pay for it. You can use his money.'

Then her mother had looked at her with real dislike. But in fact, that had probably been the moment of Esther's victory – the moment of her mother's realization that, after all, it would be better if she were away from home, at least until she had 'got over this tiresome phase'.

But of course she never had 'got over' it. Though now a truce had been declared. After all, she was *a mature person* now, and nothing *they* did could affect her. So she went down to Mortmere for Christmas and for the occasional weekend, and lunched with her mother two or three times a year in London. In a way, she reflected, these occasions were Trials by Ordeal – but self-inflicted ones.

At school she had been happy. She ate the awful food (her mother had been right about that), attended the boring services in the chapel, slept in a dormitory. She did these things automatically, just as she put on her uniform each morning. They were of no interest to her. What possessed her was a burning desire to learn. And learn she did. Especially, towards the end, from Miss Gessemer.

Most of the girls despised Miss Gessemer for her straggling hair, her beaky nose, the dowdy way she dressed, her German accent. But not Esther who, from the moment she learned that Miss Gessemer had come to England as a refugee from Hitler, became her disciple.

Miss Gessemer taught German and History to the Senior School, and Economics to the two top forms. Esther devoted herself to these three subjects with a particular fervour. And gradually Miss Gessemer responded. She started to give Esther extra coaching for exams, and to ask her to tea in her little sitting-room.

Esther's mother was delighted that she was learning German. Esther smiled a secret little smile whenever she thought about that. For her mother little knew that Esther now thought of German as the language of Karl, about whom Miss Gessemer was telling her so much. Karl was the greatest man who had ever lived. Karl had written the most significant words in human history: *The philosophers have tried in various ways to interpret the world. The important thing, however, is to change it.*

24

And all the good changes that had taken place in the world during the past century had sprung from the teachings of Karl.

Karl, like Miss Gessemer, had come to England as a poor refugee. Karl was a precious secret between Miss Gessemer and Esther – for people like Esther's parents and the headmistress of the school would have been angry if they had known that Miss Gessemer was telling Esther about him.

Red, as Gorki had said, was 'the colour of life itself'. There was a sentence Miss Gessemer sometimes quoted which was 'We'll keep the scarlet standard high.' When she first heard it, Esther didn't associate the word 'standard' with a flag. She imagined it as a standard of conduct, a standard by which she would live, though sometimes this presented difficulties. When she allowed herself to daydream about Glan-yr-Afon and about Charles, wasn't she falling below the level of the scarlet standard? Time solved the problem for her. Glan-yr-Afon and Charles receded into the past – never forgotten, but gradually fading – while, brilliantly glowing, the scarlet standard led her towards the future. Carried – for she had learned that it was a flag, and it now maintained a dual image in her mind – by Miss Gessemer.

She didn't *love* Miss Gessemer. Once, a girl she didn't like had laughed and said, 'Essie got a crush on Gessie' – and had been frozen into silence, for Esther could intimidate people when she wanted to. One evening in Miss Gessemer's sitting-room, Miss Gessemer, passing Esther's chair on her way to fetch a book from the bookcase, had smoothed a slow hand over Esther's hair, had paused, and let her hand linger. Uncontrollably, Esther had stiffened. And Miss Gessemer had taken her hand away, and had moved on, across the room, and everything had been as it was before. Really, Esther would decide later, for her, Miss Gessemer had been more of an idea than a person. When Miss Gessemer died of cancer, a year after Esther left school, Esther had been sorry, but she had not grieved. What Miss Gessemer had given her lived on.

It had been Miss Gessemer who had suggested that Esther should go to the LSE. Even though its best days were over, it was better than Oxford or Cambridge. 'I have never understood, Esther,' Miss Gessemer had said, 'why they call Oxford the home of lost causes. It is the home of no causes. It is the home of nothing. And Cambridge is just the same.' So, bearing the scarlet standard, Esther had set off for the LSE. The idea in her mind was that, when she got there, she would join the Party.

And yet now, five years later, she still hadn't done so, though most of the people she knew were Party members, including Tom.

Tom, with whom she marched, protested, sat on committees. Tom, who laughed a lot, and who drank many pints of beer. Tom, who frequently made love to her. But wasn't his laughter more an expression of 'comradeliness' than of amusement? Didn't he down his pints more as an expression of 'working-class solidarity' than because he really enjoyed them? Wasn't his love-making, despite (because of?) his conscientious emphasis on 'love-play', really more like sex work? Recently, she had found herself asking these treasonable questions more and more often.

Why hadn't she joined the Party? Hungary had shaken her, as it had shaken others – though not Tom. Tom's faith was unshakeable – she admired that. But Hungary wasn't her main reason for not joining. There were other reasons which were more important.

Language was one of them. Party books and pamphlets all seemed to be written in what was literally a dead language. Her eyes would move down a page filled with phrases which all sounded familiar but which conveyed nothing to her mind at all, except an image of a seeping greyness. Always, when she had read something written in this language, she would feel parched. She would go to her bookcase and take out *Tales of Mystery and Imagination* or *Swann's Way* or *The Waste Land* – often *The Waste Land* – and gulp a few pages down.

Again, there was something in her that rebelled against the idea of submitting herself to a group, of abiding by decisions taken by an organization. Secretly, she felt the pull of anarchism – *'Now anarchy is loosed upon the world,'* she would murmur. At night, sleepless, she would imagine everything brought down, the smug buildings of Whitehall laid waste, the stones of Mortmere scattered, birds nesting in its crumbling walls, deer grazing in the ruins of the study where her step-father sat day after day, in his wheelchair, writing his endless memoirs. *Yes, bring it all down.* But she knew – the shade of Miss Gessemer, Tom, her own reason all told her – that anarchism was pointless, hopeless. Yet – oh, *bring it all down*. And she would turn on the light, make tea, read a book – something academic – until she was what she thought of as 'herself' again.

Now in the Saturday afternoon silence, she turned onto her side, facing the wall. She closed her eyes, she thought of Glan-yr-Afon. Behind her lids, Geoff stood frozen against an impossible blue sky, Brian pirouetted across an endless terrace. Within the confines of the Ring, blood welled slowly, merged into wrists eternally joined.

She woke, jerked up into a sitting position, her heart pounding, sweat on her forehead. It took her a moment, eyes darting round the room, to establish where she was. Then she looked at her watch. Ten past five. Filled with panic, she leaped to her feet.

But, standing up, she told herself that she was being ridiculous. There was plenty of time for her to bathe, to dress, to catch the 19 bus to Piccadilly. What should she wear? No, really this was too silly. Grimly she resolved that, when she had had her bath, she would put on the same clothes as she was wearing now.

The Red Lion was almost opposite the Wheeler's restaurant where her mother had taken her to lunch a few weeks before. Grimacing at the memory, she pushed open the door of the pub, which was small and crowded. She looked at her watch. Ten to six – she was always punctual. Would Brian be late?

It was a secret shame of hers that she didn't like sitting in a pub on her own. But no, there he was, waving from the back of the bar, hurrying forward to meet her, pecking at her cheek again. exclaiming, 'Too exciting, duckie! Shall we have a drink before we go?'

'Yes, let's,' she said. Despite her natural punctuality, she wanted to arrive a little late at Charles's.

This time, she didn't ask for beer. She had a large gin and tonic, while Brian drank one of his Bloody Marys. She drank as slowly as possible. It was Brian who said, 'I really think we must move. We don't want Charles to be cross with us, do we?'

Companionably silent, they walked down Jermyn Street. The evening was chilly, and the sky had become grey. They passed a shop which sold more than seventy different kinds of cheese

– *conspicuous consumption,* Esther had thought when her mother told her this after their lunch at Wheeler's. Her mother had gone into the shop to buy some obscure kind of *chèvre* of which Esther's stepfather was particularly fond. She was always considering his tastes. There was no doubt about the fact that she still loved him, or about the fact that she still considered him a great man: 'a prophet in his own country', as she was fond of saying.

Now they passed a shop with richly bound books in its window, and then one devoted to floral essences where Esther's mother had bought soap. Esther hated shopping with her mother, hated her discriminating but casual extravagance and the obsequious deference with which she was treated by the assistants in these expensive shops. When she had made her purchases, on this last visit, she had suggested that they should have tea at Fortnum's, but Esther had drawn the line there, pleading a previous engagement. 'Someone nice?' her mother had asked, immediately alert. Esther knew all too well what her mother meant by 'nice', and had not been able to resist saying, '*You* wouldn't think so.' Now, at the recollection, she frowned. After all, she had made the decision to see her mother. And, if one undertook a duty, one should be able to carry it through to the finish without weakening.

As they turned into Duke Street, St James's, where Charles lived, Brian said, 'Lady Violet's is the only private house left.' Most of the buildings seemed to be occupied by art dealers in whose windows were displayed the kinds of picture that Esther detested: a group of cardinals, quaffing wine in palatial surrounds; a horse, held on a leading rein by a wooden-faced groom; a heap of dead game birds, their feathers realistically stained with blood. At least, she thought, the pictures at Mortmere were *good*.

Lady Violet's was a narrow Georgian house with a black front door. There were two bells, the higher of which Brian now pressed. Esther became aware that her heart was beating faster than usual. She licked her lips, which felt dry. There was silence inside the house. Could he have forgotten that they were coming? Could he have gone out? But now, at last, she could hear footsteps approaching. The door was opened.

The first thing she recognized was those pale grey eyes. She'd never met anyone else with eyes so pale. Then his hands were lightly on her upper arms. He was tall. He was wearing a dark suit, a white shirt, and what was probably a club tie. 'Esther,' he was saying, and then, 'how very amusing.'

'Charles,' she said. 'Charles.'

He drew her towards him, and kissed her cheek. She put her hands on his very broad shoulders, and felt in her fingertips the extraordinary tautness of his body. Now he was drawing back, holding her at arms' length, examining her. 'Esther,' he said, 'you are rather attractive, aren't you?'

She managed to laugh. 'I'm overwhelmed,' she said, as coolly as she could, but a hot blush was rising in her cheeks, and she saw that he observed it. Now he was looking at her clothes. 'But how austere you are,' he said. 'Almost rugged, in fact, wouldn't you say, Brian?'

'*Just* what I said,' Brian piped up.

'Well, don't let's spend the evening on the doorstep,' said Charles. 'Not that we have that much time. You're late, and I have to go to drinks with Violet.'

'I told Esther you'd be cross with us.' As he spoke, Brian was almost simpering, she thought, feeling an irritation which, however, she recognized was really caused by Charles's engagement.

He went ahead of them down the hall. There was a Persian runner on the floor. An elaborate Italian mirror hung over a Regency sofa table.

Through an open door on the left, she could see crystal and silver sparkling on a polished dining-room table. Charles started to climb the stairs. Though his shoulders were so broad, he was very slim.

'This is my cousin Violet's house,' he said.

'I met her at Glan-yr-Afon,' Esther said.

'Oh yes, I'd forgotten that.' They reached a landing, and passed another open door through which Esther glimpsed a drawing-room with gilt French chairs, dark wallpaper, and heavy curtains with braided pelmets.

Now they ascended more stairs to a second landing, from which a smaller, twisting flight of steps led to a white door. 'My little *pied à terre*,' said Charles, opening the door and going ahead of them into a dark little hall. He opened another door into a room on the left.

The room was large, though it had a sloping attic ceiling.

But it was not, she thought, at all the sort of room that the word 'attic' conjured up. There was a pale yellow fitted carpet on the floor. Two high-backed armchairs, covered in cream brocade, a Trafalgar chair with a tapestry seat, and a brown velvet chaise-longue were grouped around a low marble-topped table. On this were a drinks tray and three symmetrically arranged copies of *Country Life*, a magazine towards which Esther had felt a personal antipathy ever since her mother had expressed a wish that a 'studio portrait' of Esther should appear in it. That had been at a time when her mother was still trying to persuade her to be a debutante and to 'do' a season.

Esther wandered over to the chimney-piece. A carriage clock was centred under a marquetry mirror. Next to it, a small stack of invitations was propped against the wall.

Standing with her back to the chimney-piece, searching for traces of Charles, clues to Charles, she found none. Conventional, impersonal, the room returned her gaze with a bland anonymous smile. Pictures? Wherever the sloping ceiling allowed, pale Bartolozzi prints hung on the blue and white striped wallpaper. She wandered over to a small bookcase which stood under the window, and crouched down to examine the titles. There were a few biographies, chiefly of aristocratic statesmen, a few volumes of 'society' memoirs, several military books, recent editions of *Who's Who* and Debrett, a faded copy of the *Almanach de Gotha*, a Shakespeare, and a calf-bound, two-volume edition of Pope's poems.

She stood up, and went over to sit in the Trafalgar chair. Brian had perched on the chaise-longue.

Charles poured out the drinks. There was no beer, and Esther felt a perverse impulse to ask for some. She quelled it, and had the gin and tonic which – oh, why not admit it? – she preferred. Charles came and sat down next to her, in one of the brocade armchairs. Silently, he raised his glass. Charles, she realized, would never say anything so *common* as 'Cheers'. 'Cheers,' she said, rather loudly, as she raised her own. It was with satisfaction that she saw him wince.

But really he was quite extraordinarily good-looking, she thought, observing him now from such close quarters. His skin still had that smooth, even thickness of texture which never seems to react to climate or emotion – and what were Charles's emotions? she wondered. His hair, too, was smooth and thick. His very straight nose, his narrow lips gave his face a regularity which could have been dull – but no, she didn't find it so. And those very pale – really almost colourless – eyes made the whole face extraordinary.

He was leaning slightly towards her. 'Well, Esther,' he said, 'you must tell me how you are occupying yourself nowadays.' His voice, low and even, hardly inflected (not, thank heaven, the upper-class drawl one would have expected), might have been monotonous but for the slight roll, inexplicably French, which he gave to his Rs.

Here we go again, she thought, as she said, 'I'm doing post-graduate work at the LSE.'

'Goodness me. Work on what?'

'On trade union history. Shall I go into details?'

'I'm afraid they wouldn't mean very much to me. But it sounds extremely worthy.'

'By which you mean boring, I imagine.' Now an antagonism between them was out in the open.

'Do I? How interesting to be told what I mean on such brief re-acquaintance. But, leaving aside your subject, tell me, don't you find your fellow workers – or should I say colleagues – very tedious?'

'No,' she said. 'Not in the least.'

'Oh Esther,' Charles said, 'don't tell me that you have become some kind of dreary leftie.'

'Why, yes,' she said, 'that is exactly what I have done.'

'I see. Reacting against your background, no doubt. Somehow, Esther, I never imagined that you would develop so predictably. Brian of course has turned out exactly as one would have predicted. But I expected more originality from you.'

Brian had been looking from Charles to Esther, from Esther to Charles. Like a spectator at Wimbledon, Esther thought. Now his laughter was a little forced.

'So Esther,' Charles went on, 'you're an upper-class rebel in the good old thirties tradition. Don't you wish there were a Spanish Civil War that you could rush off to fight in?'

This was something that Esther had often wished. Her tone was cold, as she said, 'There are plenty of new causes to fight for.'

Charles smiled his smile that was a slight stretching of his lips – his teeth remaining covered. 'I rather like that *grande dame* manner, don't you, Brian?'

Brian giggled – sycophantically, Esther felt.

'So, have you severed all your ties with your family?' Charles asked her.

It was you who started me on that course, she thought. What she said was, 'No. I see my mother in London sometimes. I even go down to Mortmere occasionally.'

'How broad-minded of you. But who could resist the famous Mortmere? Those wonderful pictures, those astonishing *objets d'art*. Tell me, has the wicked stepfather repented of his evil ways?'

'No,' she said. 'He hasn't at all. But he had a stroke two years ago. He's in a wheelchair.'

'Poor old boy,' Charles said easily. Did his tone, his expression never change, whatever he was talking about? *He gives nothing away*, Esther thought – and realized that she found this as fascinating now as she had done eleven years before.

'Another drink?' Charles asked. He looked at his watch. 'Yes,' he said, 'we have just got time.'

'We mustn't keep you, Charles.' Esther made as if to stand up. But he was on his feet, looking down at her, smiling his smile, resting his hand – light, taut – on her arm, to prevent her from rising.

'I shan't let you "keep me",' he said, 'but I shall give you another drink.'

He took her glass, and bent over the tray. How strange it was, she thought, that none of them had said anything about the past. As if he had read her mind, Charles, pouring gin into her glass, said, 'I was at Glan-yr-Afon last year.'

'You were?' Brian and Esther spoke together.

'Yes. I was staying with some charming people who live quite near there, and I drove over one afternoon. The place is falling to pieces. The terrace is crumbling. The Major's cherished drive is covered with weeds, and his rhododendrons have gone to rack and ruin. Actually it was rather a romantic, melancholy scene, I thought.'

He paused. Then, in those quiet, even tones, he started to recite :

'The level'd towns with weeds lie covered o'er.
The hollow winds through naked temples roar.
Black melancholy sits, and round her throws
A death-like silence and a dead repose;
Her gloomy presence saddens all the scene,
Shades every flower, and darkens every green,
Deepens the murmur of the falling floods,
And breathes a browner horror on the woods.'

There was a moment's silence. Then Esther said, 'What's that?'

'Pope – he's quite my favourite poet nowadays. Such dignity, such order.' He paused, then he said, 'They had to close down the hotel a few months after we left, you know. That little accident was hardly a good advertisement for it.'

That little accident. She felt revulsion from the lightness of the phrase, from the indifference with which he uttered it.

Charles said, 'The Major hanged himself, you know, soon after.'

Abruptly she stood up and went over to the window. Brian was saying something, but she didn't listen. *The Major hanged himself.* Staring at the house on the other side of the road, she knew that she couldn't bring herself to think about the Major. She shook her head, and turned to face the others.

'Shall we go down there some time?' Charles said casually.

'Go down there?' Esther repeated.

'Yes. The three of us.' He smiled his smile.

'Ah, the three,' Brian murmured.

'When the weather is a little warmer,' Charles said. 'The doves cooing in the woods, the lilac in bloom. What do you think?'

'Yes,' Esther heard herself say. But it was slowly, almost doubtfully – how strange, when he had been so keen on this reunion – that Brian nodded.

'I shall telephone you,' Charles said. 'Give me your number, Esther.' He wrote it down in a little leather-bound book. 'And now,' he said, 'I am afraid that I shall have to turn you out.'

As they descended the stairs, Esther became conscious of a buzz of voices. When they reached the first-floor landing, it was apparent that it came from Lady Violet's drawing-room. Then, from inside, a husky imperious voice called, 'Charles.' He moved towards the door, but before he had reached it, a woman appeared in the doorway.

Sibylline, she wore a floating purple chiffon robe, and a swathe of the same material wrapped her head, her neck. From this theatrically nun-like drapery, fastened on her shoulder with a blazing diamond and emerald star, emerged, pale as a moon, a tautened, stretched, enamelled mask.

When she had seen Lady Violet at Glan-yr-Afon, Esther had known nothing about her. Now, from illustrations in books, from photographs in newspapers and magazines, she recognized that this was a very famous face. The face of the debutante of a decade, of the brightest of the bright young things, of the great hostess, of the confidante of eminent men.

The sibyl spoke. 'Charles, I have been expecting you.' She nodded to Brian. 'And who' – she gestured towards Esther – 'is this?'

Charles looked almost taken aback. Then he said, 'Violet, this is Esther Farringdon.'

The famous 'azure eyes', still starry enough to rival diamonds, rested on Esther. 'I think,' Lady Violet said, 'that I have met you somewhere before. *Farringdon*. I believe I used to know your mother. Many years ago. Before she married that dreadful man and betrayed her country.' She paused a moment, then went on. 'You're not as pretty as she was, and you certainly lack her dress sense. However, you do not look as stupid.' Her draperies floated round her as she turned, and went back into the drawing-room.

Esther started to descend the next flight of stairs, followed by Brian, followed by Charles, who was murmuring that, 'Violet is becoming a trifle eccentric.'

They were at the front door and, hastily, Charles was opening it. He was smiling, he was saying, 'Remember, we have a *rendezvous*.' The door closed behind them with a click.

On the pavement, Esther and Brian gazed at each other, speechless. Then suddenly, Brian was seized with laughter. And now, Esther, too, began to laugh with an overwhelming sense of release. She leaned forward, resting her head on Brian's shoulder. When she drew away, they both had tears of mirth in their eyes.

' "A trifle eccentric", indeed!' Brian exclaimed. 'An old monster, if you ask me. *"You're not as pretty as she was, and you certainly lack her dress sense."* What a nerve!'

Esther began to laugh again. Brian offered her his handkerchief. 'Come along,' he said. 'If we roll about any longer in this neighbourhood, we shall be arrested for causing a disturbance.'

Slowly they walked up towards Jermyn Street, came to a halt on the corner. 'A drink?' Brian asked.

'No, I don't think so,' Esther said. 'I feel quite exhausted. I think I'd better go home.'

'Yes,' Brian said. 'It has been rather a *draining* day.' He paused. Then he said, 'Odd, wasn't it, Charles spouting all that murky poetry. It really gave me quite a *frisson*. And when he suggested that we should go to Glan-yr-Afon, I suddenly felt that I didn't want to.' He gave one of his shrugs, dismissing the subject. 'I think I shall head for the restful, predictable tumult of the Salisbury,' he said. 'Being such a predictable person – anyway, according to dear Charles.'

Esther said, 'I wonder if he'll telephone.'

'With Charles, who knows? But my guess is yes. Anyway, you and I must meet *very* soon.'

And Esther nodded emphatically. Brian had become part of her life again. A taxi was cruising along Jermyn Street, and she hailed it. (*Two in one day* – she really had *let go*.) 'I'll drop you off at the Salisbury,' she said to Brian. 'It's on my way.'

Back in her room, she found herself pacing from door to window, from window to door. Restlessness possessed her. She felt an acute anxiety. *Her life had been stood on its head.* The doorbell rang.

Charles, she thought, and realized at once that that was impossible. But she hurried out on to the landing, from which she could see the front door, the upper half of which was made of opaque glass. She recognized the silhouette of Tom, standing on the doorstep. Tom – what did she feel about Tom? But the only thought in her mind was that she couldn't imagine anyone calling Charles, 'Charlie'.

She felt an impulse to go back into the flat, to pretend that she was out. She did not want Tom in her bed tonight, doing his ... sex work. She wanted to be alone, to think of Charles, to think about the trip to Glan-yr-Afon. *The Major hanged himself.* Down the stairs she ran. She opened the door. 'Tom,' she said, 'oh Tom, I'm so glad to see you.'

three

At the beginning of May, there were four fine days, and she found herself making excuses to be in the flat as much as possible. But he didn't telephone. Then cold weather set in, and lasted for more than a week. She devoted herself to her work though, often, sitting in the library or at the oak table in her room, she found that her thoughts were wandering, and that her eyes were turning towards the window to scan the grey masses of cloud that hung overhead. When was lilac time? She had never been much interested in flowers.

She telephoned her mother one evening. 'Darling, how nice to hear from you,' her mother said. 'Is something the matter?'

'No, nothing at all. I just wondered how you were.'

'Oh, we're very well. And you?'

'I'm fine. But the weather has been terrible.'

'Here, too.'

'But I expect the garden's looking lovely.'

Her mother laughed. 'You're very chatty this evening, Esther. Yes, it is looking nice.'

'I suppose the lilacs are over.'

'No, as a matter of fact, they're just coming out. Esther, you really do sound rather strange. Would you like to come down this weekend? Though we have some old friends coming whom you'd probably find rather dull.'

'Sorry, but I just can't manage it. I only wanted to say, "Hullo".'

'Sweet of you, darling. I'll give your love to Hugo.'

'Mmm. Well, I must rush. Goodbye then.'

'Goodbye, darling.' Her mother was always more affectionate on the telephone than she was when they met.

Esther rang off. So there was still hope – if the weather changed.

She lunched with Tom nearly every day, and he often spent the night with her. While his lips and hands made their careful journeys over her, her mind went on its own journeys. *To Glan-yr-Afon*. To the terrace where she and Charles would stand, looking down at the river.

36

She would sigh, and Tom would ask, 'Now, Esther? Are you ready now?' 'Yes,' she would say. 'Yes, now.' That meant it would be over soon.

Brian rang up. He came to supper. He sat in the Bentwood rocker, swaying gently. ('It's the granny in me, duckie. All I need now is a nice woolly shawl.') He talked to her about what he called his 'love life'. To Esther, it sounded depressing and dangerous: a series of always brief encounters with sullen and often threatening boys. 'Twice, I've been beaten up, and the second time it was rather nasty. But, there, they say that danger is the spice of life, don't they?'

Ruefully, she shook her head. Oughtn't she to feel that Brian was exploiting these youthful members of the working class? Instead, she felt that they were exploiting him. They were *lumpen proletariat*, she decided, and that made her feel happier.

She had not expected Tom to come round that evening. It was with reluctance that she let him in, and introduced them. But Brian behaved with decorum, and all Tom said, when he had gone, was, 'Rather a weird lad, that. Gay, I suppose?'

People being *gay* was one of the things that – in London, and under Esther's influence – Tom was learning to tolerate. Though she felt that he couldn't help believing that such things were phenomena produced by the effete South, and that, up North, in the mining town he came from, they didn't exist.

Brian telephoned her next day. 'Very *sincere*, our Tom,' he said.

She laughed, and immediately felt disloyal. 'Well, that's a good thing to be, isn't it?' she said defensively.

'Of *course* it is, duckie, and each to her taste. Quite a dish in his way, too, though I've never been one for the beards, myself.' He changed the subject: 'Want to come and see *my* tiny retreat, darling?'

'I'd love to,' she said.

'Tomorrow evening?'

'Yes,' she said, 'that would be fine.'

'Want to bring lover-boy along?'

'No,' she said, and then, 'I'm sure he's got a meeting.' She knew he had, because she was meant to be attending it herself.

Brian's retreat *was* tiny: a doll's house off the King's Road, crowded with art deco, art nouveau – 'Art everything but great,' he said, and added, 'I always find the *very* best rather oppressive.'

They toured the house. In his bedroom, the nude plaster torso of a boy circled under a spotlight when a switch was pressed. 'Gives some of my visitors quite a turn,' he giggled.

'No news of Charles, I suppose,' she asked casually when they were having drinks in the minute drawing-room.

'Nor sight nor sound,' Brian said. 'Pining for him, are you, duckie?'

'No,' she said. 'I'm just interested in seeing Glan-yr-Afon again.'

'Yes, it would be interesting. Almost too interesting, perhaps. Why, I do believe you're as bad as I am, when it comes to embracing the perils of life.'

'Perils?' she said.

'Well ... waking dogs that it might be better to leave sleeping. *Stirring dull roots with spring rain* – as Mr Eliot says, that can be cruel.'

'*Breeding lilacs out of the dead land, mixing memory and desire,*' she murmured.

'Exactly, darling. I couldn't have put it better, myself.'

She left late. At the door, he put an arm round her shoulder. 'They say the weather's going to change,' he said. 'So carry on hoping!'

'They', whoever they were, had been right. On the very next day, the weather changed. The sun was hot. People walked more slowly in the streets, smiled more easily, spoke to strangers at bus stops. A tabby cat basked on the doorstep of a restaurant in Monmouth Street. Esther got up early. She walked through the Floral Hall, soaking herself in its smells and colours.

She had to force herself to go to the library. It was an effort to become absorbed in her work. Time dragged. At five, she hurried home. She felt hot and sticky. She turned on the bath, and went back into her room to undress. She was just opening the wardrobe to take out her dressing-gown, when the telephone rang. For a moment she stood frozen. Then she ran across the room, and picked up the receiver: 'Hullo.'

'Esther?' Yes, unmistakably, it was Charles – as he evidently assumed that she realized, for he did not identify himself. 'You sound out of breath,' he said.

'Oh no, not really,' she said stupidly. Her heart was thumping. She felt light-headed.

'I rang,' he said, 'about our expedition. To arrange a day. I thought that Saturday might do. If we went at lunch time, we would arrive there in the early evening. I shall bring a little picnic, and we can eat it on the terrace. And then we might spend the night at the Angel in Abergavenny – I will book the rooms – and return at our leisure next day.'

'That sounds wonderful,' she said, and then, 'Oh – my bath!'

'You're naked, Esther,' he said. 'Dripping onto the carpet. Or is the bath overflowing?'

'Overflowing. Hang on.'

'No, Esther. I must telephone Brian now. One o'clock at my flat on Saturday. Unless the weather is impossible, of course.'

He rang off, and she dashed to the bathroom to turn off the taps, and to let out some of the water which had almost reached the rim of the bath.

Afterwards, she lay back in the warm water. Perfect happiness. Wednesday now, and only two more days to go. *'You're naked, Esther. Dripping onto the carpet.' 'We might spend the night at the Angel.'* Hotel bedrooms. Anonymous, oddly exciting refuges. Dark narrow corridors. Tiptoeing footsteps. Doors quietly opening and closing. The telephone rang, and she was floundering out of the bath, seizing a towel from the rail, running into the living-room, and just regaining balance as she skidded on the floorboards.

'OMV,' said a voice. It was Brian's.

'OMV?' she said.

'Our Master's Voice. We have been summoned to the blasted heath. Are you thrilled?'

'I am rather looking forward to it,' she said.

'Games of a Summer Night, Esther. So we are going to start playing games again. Statues – where we shall be frozen in strange attitudes, like the mad figures in Ludwig of Bavaria's gardens. Grandmother's footsteps – will Grandmother, as she turns, show us the muzzle of a wolf under her white lace cap? Hide and Seek – but, in the dark, it is hard to tell who is hiding and who is seeking.'

She laughed. 'Brian, don't sound so sinister. It's going to be *fun*,' she said.

'Yes, games *can* be fun, Esther, as long as one doesn't take them too seriously.'

'I don't follow you.'

'No one has ever followed *me*, duckie. Being followed has always been dear Charles's speciality. A positive Pied Piper: *From street to street he piped advancing, and step for step they followed dancing.*'

'You're talking in riddles,' she said. 'Anyway, Brian, I must ring off now. I'm soaking wet. You got me out of my bath.'

'Right you are. See you at Charles's on Saturday. Quite typical, by the way. *We* have to go to *him*. Heil Hitler!' And then, warmly, 'Oh, sorry, darling. I didn't *mean* anything by that.'

'No,' she said. 'I know you didn't. See you on Saturday.'

She was afraid that the weather might change, but it remained perfect. She was up early on Saturday morning, cleaning the flat. Perhaps Charles would bring her back there on Sunday? Perhaps he would come in for a drink? She went out to buy gin – something she had never bought before – and tonic, and a bottle of white wine which she put in the refrigerator. Then she bathed, washed her hair, and extracted from the back of a drawer the bottle of L'Air du Temps which her mother had given her for Christmas. She splashed it on her wrists, on her neck. Really, she reflected, she was behaving in a very bourgeois way. All the same, she put the bottle in her handbag. On Monday, she promised herself, she would return to normal.

What should we wear? She opened the wardrobe, and examined her few pairs of jeans and corduroys, her two or three dresses. She hardly ever wore dresses but, today, she felt an impulse to put one on. There was an Indian cotton, dusty pink, sprigged with brown leaves, which she knew suited her. But suddenly, impatiently, she shook her head. She put on blue jeans and a plain white shirt and dark blue canvas shoes. Then she packed a nightdress (something else she hardly ever wore) and the few other things she would need, in an overnight bag. She was ready.

It was time to go. At the door, she glanced back. How calm

and welcoming her room looked. Ordered, peaceful, designed for a productive life. Suddenly, Brian's words – 'So we are going to start playing games again' – came into her head, and she almost wished that she weren't going. She had believed herself to be so firmly rooted in the real world. And now – wasn't she turning her back on it? Wasn't she moving in reverse, into the past?

Monday, she reassured herself. *Back to normal on Monday*. Quickly she opened the door, closing it behind her with a little jerk, and ran down the stairs.

The hush of mid-day lay on Duke Street, St James's. She could hear her own footsteps on the pavement, as she approached the house. A large white car, with the roof down, was parked in front of the house.

She paused on the doorstep, and then pressed Charles's bell. She wondered if Lady Violet, that purple monster, were lurking, waiting to pounce. The door opened. Charles stood there, in white trousers, a white shirt with the sleeves rolled up. A dark blue silk scarf was knotted round his neck.

'Come in, Esther,' he said. This time, he didn't kiss her, or take her hand. He stood back for her to pass him. 'You know your way,' he said, and she set off, up the stairs, slowly and calmly, determined not to be breathless when she reached the top.

'You're the last to arrive,' Charles said, holding open his sitting-room door for her. There was Brian, bouncing up from one of the brocade armchairs to greet her. 'And this is Clare,' Charles said. Esther's eyes were already fixed on the girl who was lying gracefully on the brown velvet chaise-longue.

She wore a loose dress of natural silk, with a wide band of blue and white smocking – *like a baby's dress*, Esther thought – across the chest. From cap sleeves emerged her thin pale arms. Her little white hands were tipped with long rose-varnished nails. She wore almost invisible stockings, and fragile white sandals on her tiny feet.

Her nose was small – almost flat, like a cat's. Her eyes were large and blue. Her pale blonde hair fell smoothly into the shape of a bell. Her skin was fine; on her cheekbones was a delicate flush. As Charles introduced her, lips, tinted the same colour as her nails, parted to show small perfect teeth. 'Why, hello, Esther,' she said. Her voice was small and high, her accent American. 'Hullo,' Esther answered.

'Clare is coming with us,' Charles said. 'I thought she ought to see something of the country, especially at this perfect time of year.'

'Oh yes,' Esther agreed. 'Everything is looking its best at the moment.' They were words which her mother might have uttered – and as she spoke them she saw Brian's eyebrows rise and a mischievous smile twitch the corners of his lips. But she couldn't share the joke. The day lay wrecked, dismantled, ahead of her. What was Charles doing with this ... baby doll? Why, above all, was he dragging her along today – on this most special day when they – *the three* – were going on their pilgrimage of recovery?

Charles had provided a delicate little lunch: asparagus tips rolled in brown bread and butter, tiny wafer-thin sandwiches with the crusts cut off. (*Dolls' food*, Esther thought. *Just right for a doll like Clare.*) They drank a bottle of flowery-tasting German wine. Sun poured through the window while a breeze gently swayed the curtains. But, for Esther, the food, the wine, the weather were all dry, charmless, sour.

Clare hardly spoke, but she smiled constantly. All the time, she kept her eyes fastened – *like teeth*, Esther thought – on Charles. To everything that he said, she responded with little eager nods. *So this*, thought Esther, *is what is meant by: 'she hung on his lips.'*

'Time to go,' said Charles, and they all stood up. Down the stairs Charles and Brian bore a great wicker hamper and a large deep thermos tin. Coldly, Esther observed Charles's penchant for the grand – the 'posh' as Tom would have called it.

The hamper, the thermos, the luggage – Clare had a soft white leather 'vanity case', as Esther contemptuously heard her call it – were packed into the boot of Charles's big open car. They were off: Clare in the front, next to Charles; Esther and Brian in the back. As the car started, Brian patted Esther's hand, raised his eyebrows in Clare's direction, and grimaced. Feeling slightly consoled – at least she had an ally – Esther wrinkled her brow in answer.

As soon as they had left the sprawl of London behind them,

42

Clare started to exclaim about greenness and beauty. Esther yawned. She had always found the road to Oxford uninteresting. All the same, she couldn't help responding to the sun on her skin, the wind blowing through her hair. Clare had produced a blue silk square from her handbag and tied it over her head. She had also put on sunglasses. It was surprising, Esther thought, that she didn't open a white lace parasol.

After Oxford, in the Cotswolds, Esther felt the old familiar stirrings. Charles turned his head. 'Well, Esther,' he asked, 'are we invited to call at Mortmere?'

'We haven't really got time, have we?' she answered. Charles laughed, and Clare said, 'What's Mortmere?'

'It's Esther's parents' beautiful house,' Charles said.

'My stepfather's house,' Esther corrected him.

Now they were passing the turning. Only two miles to the great iron gates, and beyond them, in the distance, the golden stone Palladian frontage of the house, the mellow red brick of the stables. *Her stepfather propelling his wheelchair along the drive.* But Mortmere was behind them now. She sighed. Partly with relief, partly at the ambivalence of her feelings: the inextricable knot of her love and hate for that beautiful arrogant fastness.

Between Cheltenham and Ross-on-Wye, the country changed. The roads narrowed; they wound and twisted. Riotous growth of green gave a prodigal richness to the hedgerows. Once Monmouth was behind them, there were hills in the distance, with clouds over them, but overhead the sky was deeply blue.

As they drove through Abergavenny, they passed the Angel hotel. But the Angel had lost – hadn't it? – its lure for Esther.

The walls of the old castle in Crickhowell awoke her first memory. She glanced at Brian; Brian glanced back. She felt like a dog rediscovering an old scent. Charles was slowing down; now he turned left, and they started to climb. Up between such great trees, such a diversity of bushes and ferns. There was a rough stone wall on either side.

'Here!' said Brian and Esther together. To the right wound the steep lane up which they had pushed their bicycles so often. Ahead of them was the gate to Glan-yr-Afon.

four

The sun was low in the sky now. In the declining light, the scene had a peculiar desolation. One of the stone balls that had topped the brick gateposts was missing. Ahead, beyond the rusted five-barred gate, receded the drive that Major Sidney had tended so obsessively. Now it was pitted with holes, and was so infested with weeds that it looked more green than grey.

'Open the gate, Brian,' Charles said, and Brian got out of the car. He struggled with a rusted chain that clanked against the gatepost as he undid it, and then the gate creaked open. Revving the engine loudly, Charles started the car, and it seemed to Esther that Brian jumped aside only just in time. There was a dazed expression on his face.

'Stop, Charles,' she called out, but Charles drove on. The car bumped over a deep furrow in the gravel. 'It will do him good to walk,' Charles said.

The rhododendrons were in wild disarray, and bracken grew among them. What had been a neat border of mown grass was thick with weeds. The car rounded the bend in the drive, and there, beyond the circle of gravel, rose the house.

Seeing it now, Esther realized that it was an imitation of an Italian villa. Even in the soft evening light, the almost purple stone of which it was built jarred on her eye. As the car drew up by the stone porch, she saw that almost all the glass was missing from the windows.

'It's quite monstrous, isn't it?' she said, at exactly the same moment as Clare exclaimed, 'What a lovely old place!' 'Not very old,' Charles said judiciously. 'About 1885, I should think.' 'Oh, you Europeans,' Clare fluted, 'you're so snooty. 1885 seems very old to me.'

They got out of the car. Clare looked rather fearfully at the purple walls, the broken windows. 'Are we going inside there?' she asked. 'No, I don't think so,' Charles said. 'It's the garden that we've come to visit.' Esther nodded.

She stared up at the sentinel towers, facing east and west. The hands were missing from the clock on the west tower, the clock that, she now remembered, had marked each quarter hour with a clear gold chime.

Across the gravel, from the drive, Brian trotted towards them. 'Charles, you swine!' he gasped as he reached the car.

'A little exercise won't do you any harm,' Charles said. 'You're getting fat, Brian. Too much dissipation is my diagnosis.'

Brian pouted. 'I think you're an absolute beast,' he said. 'You could have run me over.'

'Ah, but I didn't,' Charles said. 'And now let's move. To the terrace.'

'To the terrace,' Esther echoed.

'We'll take our picnic with us,' Charles said. He carried the big thermos tin – Clare fluttering round him like a white moth – and Esther and Brian took the hamper. As they walked along by the side of the house, the roar of the Usk grew in Esther's ears.

They rounded the corner of the house, and went up the steps to the terrace: the terrace where Brian had danced – Esther's eyes met his. They put down the hamper, and round on tiptoe Brian whirled to the terrace wall, on which he leaned his elbows. Esther joined him. Down below, beyond thick greenery and bracken, the waterfall cascaded into its pool of stillness and of great flat stones. On the facing hillside, beyond scattered trees, Friesian cows grazed in the high sloping meadow.

She turned to face the house, the gaping windows of the dining-room and the library. Then her eyes travelled along the terrace. Weeds grew between the paving stones. Pieces were missing from the mosaics of birds and griffons which were set into the terrace walls. A wooden bench, a wooden table were covered with a powdery greenish mould.

Charles looked at his watch. 'Time for a little drink,' he said. They gathered round the picnic hamper. Charles unfastened its leather straps, and opened it. He took out four champagne glasses which he put on the table. He undid the metal hasp of the thermos tin. Inside, surrounded by packets of dry ice, were three bottles of champagne. 'Champers! Goody-goody,' squealed Brian, clapping his hands.

Charles pointed the bottle towards the edge of the terrace. The cork came out with a satisfying pop. A pigeon flapped from a tree. 'Oo, what a big bang. You frightened the poor birdie,' Clare exclaimed. Esther winced. Charles, filling her glass, observed this, and gave her a small reproving frown.

'To the past,' Charles said, when all their glasses were filled, and 'To the past,' echoed Esther and Brian. 'I think that's a *sad* toast,' Clare said coyly. '*I* shall drink to the future,' and she raised her glass to Charles, and smiled.

Darkness was falling fast. A bat swooped low over their heads, and Clare gave a little scream. 'Oo, I wish I hadn't left my scarf in the car. It might get tangled in my hair.' 'That's nonsense,' Esther said. 'Is it nonsense?' Clare asked Charles. He gave a tiny sigh, and said, 'Yes, darling, absolute nonsense.' The sigh pleased Esther, but the 'darling' did not.

The champagne was beautifully cold, deliciously dry. Too dry for Clare, Esther noticed, seeing her lips pucker, and she thought: *Her tastes are as babyish as everything else about her.*

She went back to the edge of the terrace, leaned her elbows on the wall, and gazed down at the rushing waterfall which showed white in the gathering darkness. A hand lightly touched her arm. 'Esther,' Charles said softly, 'are you sulking?'

She smiled at him coolly. 'No, why should I be?'

'I can't see any reason,' he said. His pale eyes were fixed on her face. 'Come and help me unpack, aloof one,' he said. In the air between them, something grew.

She followed him to the picnic hamper. 'Hand me the things, Esther,' he said. 'I shall put them on the table, and Brian and Clare will arrange them.'

To unpack the hamper, she kneeled on the paving stones, and he stood above her. A folded white cloth lay on top of the food. With a flourish, Brian spread it on the table. Little cries of admiration greeted each item. There were quails in aspic. ('Poor little birdies,' said Clare. 'You feel sorry for them because they are small?' Charles asked her. 'Or are you sorry for turkeys, too?' Esther could not suppress a little laugh, and Clare pouted and shook her finger at Charles.)

After the quails came cutlets, frilled and decorated with rounds of olive and pimento. There was a small salmon trout with a pattern of cucumber on its mayonnaised flank. There was a green salad, with *vinaigrette* in a little bottle. There were crisp rolls and a round pat of butter, stamped with a thistle design. Last of all came white plates and knives and forks. As she passed the things to Charles, their hands brushed lightly. To be kneeling at his feet gave her a strange dizzy sensation.

They were all hungry. Even Clare nibbled away like a voracious kitten. Charles opened another bottle of champagne. Clare covered her glass with her hand. 'Oo, not for me,' she said. 'I'll get high!' Esther lifted her glass to her lips, and drained its contents in one swallow. With raised eyebrows and a faint smile, Charles immediately refilled it, saying 'What a thirsty girl!'

She turned to Brian. 'It's a gorgeous evening,' she said.

Gorgeous it was. While they ate, a great round, almost orange moon had risen over the facing hillside. Brian had finished his food. He put his plate down on the table, and danced across the terrace. 'Moon and June and bingo bango,' he sang in a light high tenor. 'The band was playing a tango, Everyone clapped as we arose, for her sweet face and my new clothes.'

Dipping and gliding, he returned. Suddenly he swooped on Clare, and danced her away. 'It takes two to tango,' he called, and Clare gave her little high laugh. In Esther's ear, Charles whispered – she felt his warm breath – 'Come, Esther. Let's explore.' He took her hand, and they slipped from the terrace. Behind them, she heard Clare call, 'Charles, where are you going?' He didn't answer. They didn't stop. On the far side of the house, they reached the flight of shallow stone steps that led to the lawn. She saw in the moonlight that one of the two heraldic bears that had flanked the steps lay toppled in the grass.

Now they were running through the thick grass that had once been the lawn. She knew where they were going. They were going to the Ring. There it was – the circle of lilac bushes near the fence of the little wood where black sheep had grazed. Now Charles was pushing through the light branches, pulling her after him, and the scent of lilac was overpowering. They reached the centre of the Ring, where now the grass grew tall – concealing, she supposed, the last remnants of the summerhouse. They stood completely still, staring at each other. Charles's pale eyes gleamed in the moonlight.

'Shall we play the Truth Game?' she said. He laughed. He sank down on to the grass, pulling her with him. The scent of lilac was so heavy and her heart was beating so fast. Like a drowner, she reached for Charles's head, dragged it towards her, pressed her lips to his. *What a thirsty girl!* she thought, but his mouth remained firm and unyielding. After a moment he drew away. In a low voice he said, 'Do you fuck, Esther?' She stared at him in astonishment.

'Do you fuck?' he repeated. 'Bitch. Whore.' He started to unfasten the buttons of her shirt. *'Stewed in corruption,'* he muttered, and then again, 'Bitch. Whore.' She didn't understand but she didn't care.

It was a rage, a fury. She wanted it to last for ever, but soon – drained, empty – she lay on the grass. She became aware of twigs pricking her skin. He was standing, looking down at her. *Mine*, she thought, *he's mine at last.* She felt that she had always wanted him. She sat up, and began to put on her clothes. When she was dressed, and standing beside him, she held out her hand to him, but he shook his head. 'You go first, Esther,' he said. 'Say you lost me.'

What was the point of this charade? she wondered. But she nodded coolly. She tossed her hair back, and straightened her shoulders. 'Aloof one,' he said, and smiled. She pushed through the bushes, and made her way up the slope, through the thick grass, smoothing her hair.

On the terrace, Brian and Clare drooped on the bench. There was a whine in Clare's voice, as she asked, 'Where's Charles? Where's he gone?'

'I've no idea,' Esther said lightly. 'Our paths diverged. I think he went into the woods.'

'I hope he won't be long. I'm tired out,' Clare said fretfully.

Brian stood up. 'I'm going to open that last bottle of champagne,' he said. 'I don't want anything more to drink,' said Clare. 'But *I* do,' Esther said. 'And so do I,' said Brian.

Brian was pouring the wine into her glass, as Charles came on to the terrace. 'Champagne?' Brian asked. 'No,' Charles said. 'I've had enough.' 'Me too,' said Clare.

'And how are you, my sweet?' Charles put a finger under Clare's chin, and turned her face up to his. Lightly he kissed her forehead. Esther drank the wine in her glass, and held the glass out to Brian, who refilled it.

'I'm just an itsy bit tired, Charles,' Clare said. 'Come to the car then.' He put an arm round her waist. 'Esther, Brian,' he said. 'Poor Clare is tired. Would you pack up the things, and bring them to the car? They won't be heavy now.' With his arm still round Clare's waist, and bending solicitously towards her, he moved away, down the terrace.

As they disappeared round the side of the house, Brian said, 'What a *nerve*! Leaving poor old us to do all the work. Ickle Clare is tired, is she? Ickle Clare needs a kick up the backside, if you ask me.'

Esther nodded, tried to smile. She couldn't speak. Tears were welling up in her eyes. Again she drained her glass. 'Let's finish it,' Brian said, and poured the remains of the champagne into their glasses. Then he hurled the bottle over the terrace wall. Esther heard it shatter on a stone far below.

He was standing close to her, looking at her shrewdly. He raised his hand to remove something from her hair. It was a sprig of lilac. He sniffed at it disdainfully, and then dropped it on the ground. 'I warned you, didn't I, duckie?' he said. 'Warned me of what?' she asked dully. 'Of the Games of a Summer Night,' he said, patting her hand.

Silently, they packed the hamper. Brian picked it up, and Esther followed him, carrying the empty thermos tin.

In the car, Clare was sitting with her head resting on Charles's shoulder. He was talking softly to her. Brian and Esther put the hamper and the thermos in the boot, and got into the back of the car. Cool air rushed round them as the car started, and Esther shivered. Brian gave her shoulder a little squeeze.

The trees were brilliantly green in the blaze of the headlights. A rabbit loped across the drive, and stopped, dazed. Charles drove straight on. Esther felt the bump as the rabbit was hit by one of the front wheels. 'Charles, how could you?' she said. 'Don't you know,' he said coldly, 'that it's dangerous to swerve?'

He turned slightly towards the back seat. 'By the way,' he said, 'I should mention that when I booked the rooms at the Angel, I booked singles for you two, and a double for myself and Clare. Mr and Mrs Tibbald. In any case, it's near enough to the truth. Clare and I are engaged. We're getting married soon. Of course you must both come to the wedding.'

part two
1963

five

Not until the train was actually moving did she relax, leaning back in her seat, closing her eyes with a deep sigh of release. She was alone in the carriage. As she knew from experience, the train would fill up at Oxford. But until then, she could enjoy a guiltless solitude – at Mortmere, she always felt reproached when she went off on her own.

As usual, in the station yard, her mother had agreed to Esther's request that she should not come onto the platform, had placed her smooth, scented cheek against Esther's, had said, 'Goodbye darling. See you again soon I hope,' as Esther, with alacrity, got out of the car. At the entrance to the station, Esther had turned to wave, and her mother, who was starting the car, had raised her hand in reciprocation.

As she walked along the platform to the iron footbridge, she heard the car drive off. Swinging her bag in her hand, she crossed the footbridge, and walked to the far end of the platform, so that she could get into the first carriage of the London train.

After only a few minutes, the train arrived, and she felt the familiar lifting of her spirits. She got in, the whistle blew, and the train started. Now the visit was really over – *Mortmere was over* for at least another two months. She would probably lunch in London with her mother before then, but that wasn't so bad. And she had managed her departure without having to kiss her stepfather goodbye – how she hated even the idea of touching him. But here she was, free, and still brooding over *them*. Mortmere would, she knew from experience, cast its shadow over her for a day or more, after which she would once more be absorbed into the real world.

The real world. But today the real world had an extraordinary quality of unreality. She opened her eyes, and sat up. She unzipped her bag, which she had put down on the seat beside her, and extracted the newspaper which she had slipped into it before she left.

There they were, staring at her from the front page – the face, the name. And the words: *Battered to death.*

Battered to death. She shut her eyes again, and in the darkness the words merged with the rhythm of the train – *battered to death, battered to death* – until they lost their meaning. She raised her lids and, staring up at her from the newspaper, the words recovered the weight of their extraordinary message. *Battered to death.*

Emotionally, of course, the message signified little to her – except in so far as it would affect *him.* That was what she couldn't calculate; she realized that she had no idea of how he would respond to it. Did she understand him so little? Only three days before, she had thought that she understood him very well. It was Sunday evening now – she found it difficult to believe that only three days had passed since Thursday. For so much had happened since then.

'Essie, can you come around this evening? I thought you might be able to come around.' Clare's voice was rising from plaint to whine. 'I don't know what time Charles will be home, you see,' she continued. 'He never tells me. You'd think he was trying to catch me out in some way.' She gave her little high laugh.

Why did it happen that Clare always telephoned on Thursday? Esther wondered; the one day on which she never accepted invitations. Surely that should have impinged even on Clare's vague consciousness by now?

'Honestly, Essie, there are times when I half think I'm going crazy, cooped up here with only Smoothie for company.' The voice went on and on. 'And really I often feel that Smoothie's no company at all. I don't think I care for cats – they aren't loyal the way dogs are. Yet Smoothie seems to be fond of Charles, even though he never feeds him – it's me that does that. You'd think an animal would respond to the person who feeds it, wouldn't you, Essie?'

She could hardly believe that she'd once thought of Clare as quiet. But that had been a long time ago. It was three years now since she'd first met Clare, three years since they'd driven to Glan-yr-Afon – and two and a half years since Charles's and Clare's marriage.

'I'm sorry, Clare,' Esther said. 'But you know I can never come round on Thursday. You know I've got this committee meeting that I always have to go to.'

54

'Oh yes, of course. That's right. I keep forgetting. You're such a busy person, Essie.'

'Why don't you go out somewhere? To a movie, say? There's that new French film at the Curzon, which is meant to be marvellous. And that's just round the corner from you.'

'But Essie, you know Charles doesn't like me to be out when he gets home. You know he likes me to be here waiting for him.'

Tell Charles to go to hell. The words were on the tip of Esther's tongue, but of course she did not utter them. Instead, she said, 'I could come round tomorrow. How would that be?'

'Why, that would be just fine.' Clare's voice brightened a little. 'Why don't you come to dinner? I don't know what Charles's plans are. But if he's home, I know he'll be pleased to see you, Essie. And if he's out, we can have a hen-fest.'

Esther winced at the phrase, but her tone, as she answered, was warm and friendly: 'That would be lovely, Clare. See you tomorrow, then. I must rush now. There's someone I've got to see before my meeting, and if I don't hurry, I'll be late.'

'Oh, I'm so sorry to have kept you,' Clare said, and then repeated, 'You're such a busy person.'

'Looking forward to seeing you tomorrow. Goodbye for now.'

'Bye-ee,' Clare said, and Esther quickly put down the receiver. Clare was perfectly capable of embarking on some new topic.

She sighed. She had a sudden picture of Clare, sitting on the chaise-longue, turning the pages of the latest Vogue for the third time – Clare didn't read books, she only looked at magazines – while Smoothie, the Siamese cat, paws folded, stared enigmatically at some invisible object. 'The way that cat stares at nothing gives me the willies,' Clare had once exclaimed.

Esther looked at her watch. Half past five. An hour, at least, before he would arrive. If he arrived. Sometimes he didn't. But that was rare and, when it happened, she felt that it was a gesture he was making to himself as much as to her. Was she right? She smiled. She stood up. She raised her hands to unfasten the coil in which her hair was knotted at the back of her head. It had grown considerably in the past three years. Straight and dark and shining, it now fell well below her shoulders.

There were many ways in which she could arrange it, though, most often, with him, she liked to wear it loose – which she never did at any other time. Usually, with her hair pulled back from her face, she looked, if anything, more austere than she had done three years before, when it was short. But when she let it down ... Across her mind passed a sudden fleeting vision of his hands winding it around her throat. She shivered, and again she smiled. She went over to the wardrobe, and pulled open the door.

Large though the wardrobe was, it was hardly large enough to contain the freight of garments which now weighted its rail. Garments of many fabrics, but with a preponderance of chiffon, of satin, of lace, of heavy velvet. Garments of many shades, but with an emphasis on deep rich colours: emerald, crimson, purple, black. They clung together, as she pulled impatiently at the hangers. Should she weed some out, get rid of them? But where? They were hardly suitable for a college jumble sale. And anyway, she realized, she was reluctant to abandon even one of them, when each had been so carefully chosen. And for any one of them, the exact mood, the precise occasion might recur – indeed would be sure to, she felt, the moment she discarded it.

What was her mood tonight? Of course the mood could be changed later, when he arrived – there had been times when he had changed everything. But now what did she feel? She pulled another hanger along the rail. And there was the long, heavy black satin with the plunging neckline and the flowing sleeves. Yes, she decided, she felt *dark* tonight.

She took the dress out of the wardrobe, and laid it on the bed. Then she went through into the bathroom, and turned on the bath. From a shelf crowded with jars and bottles, she took a flask of Arpège bath oil, and sprinkled the water. The rich heavy scent rose to her nostrils with the steam.

At last the doorbell rang. She leaped to her feet from the rocking-chair. Then she willed herself to stand still. 'One, two, three, four ...' she counted aloud. But the numbers were rattling from her tongue like bullets from a machine gun, long before she arrived at the ordained number. She reached it: 'Sixty!' She was out of the flat, and running down the stairs, smoothing the slippery satin over her hips, raising a hand to the frame of the dark glasses which concealed her eyes, the mirror glasses which only offered him his own reflection.

She opened the front door. There he stood, on the top step. Most people, she had noticed, when they rang a doorbell, retreated a step or two – but not he. 'Why, Esther,' he said. 'You're breathless. All this running about! Perhaps you should give me a set of keys.'

As he followed her up the stairs – she moved slowly now – she thought about what he had just said, imagined him appearing suddenly, without warning, in her room. *Out of her control*. The thought was exciting but unnerving. Yes, it frightened her. *She mustn't let him see that*. She said lightly, 'Clare telephoned me earlier. I promised to go round tomorrow evening.'

They were inside the flat now. He closed the door, and she swung to face him, the heavy satin swinging with her.

'A drink?' she asked. But, 'Not now,' he said. He was standing so close to her that she could feel his breath on her forehead. He placed his right forefinger at the V of her neckline, between her breasts, and pressed lightly. And she raised her head, and shook back the hair which clung around her shoulders. He stared into the mirrors of her glasses. Then he propelled her backwards, still with his pointing finger between her breasts, until they reached the bed. Now he increased the pressure, his finger boring into her skin, until she toppled in a swirl of satin. He was over her, on her, his pallor darkened by the glasses which now, suddenly, he plucked from her eyes and tossed aside. 'You can't keep any secrets from me,' he said.

Her eyes were closed, and she could feel him arranging her limbs in the attitude of a figure on a tomb. He pointed her toes stiffly. He crossed her hands on her chest. He folded her hair in two crossed swathes over her throat. He moulded the crumpled satin to her body, drew it in sculptured folds to her ankles. Still as marble, she lay in a depth of darkness.

She heard him going into the bathroom and turning on the shower. Time passed, and then there was the sound of him pacing in the room. She heard him tug at the window curtain, and knew that he was standing gazing down into the silent street. She opened her eyes, and blinked in the soft light. She

57

uncrossed her arms, and stretched them above her head. Then she sat up, on the edge of the bed, groping with her feet for the satin shoes that, long ago, had thudded, one after the other, to the floor. Charles turned from the window to look at her.

'Something to eat or drink?' she asked him.

'Nothing to eat,' he said. 'But yes, some coffee, and a little brandy.'

In the kitchen, she lit the gas under the kettle. While it heated, she showered quickly, and put on a white towelling bathrobe.

She ground the coffee, and made it – very strong, as he liked it – in an earthenware jug. She got out the bottle of Martell Cordon Argent which she kept for his visits. He sat in the rocking-chair, she on the bed. They never touched at these times. Always, it was as if they were strangers. His dark suit was uncreased, his white shirt immaculate, his tie precisely knotted.

He finished his brandy. 'More?' she asked. But he was standing up. 'No, I must go,' he said.

'See you tomorrow, then.'

'Probably. I think I shall be in.' How well she knew his way of never committing himself to anything.

'Don't come downstairs,' he said. 'I'll let myself out.' At the door, he turned. 'What about those keys?' he said. 'Have you got a spare set?'

'No,' she answered quickly. 'No, I'm afraid I haven't.'

He looked at her steadily. 'That's odd,' he said, 'for such a well organized person as you are.' He opened the door. 'Anyway,' he added, 'you can easily get them copied, can't you?' He smiled. 'I shall remember,' he said. The door closed behind him.

With a sigh, she sat down in the rocking-chair. She heard the front door slam. She would have to give him the keys. As he had said, he would remember. And she was sure he had known that she was lying when she had said that she didn't possess a spare set. As a matter of fact, she had two, one in the drawer of the oak table, the other on top of the kitchen cupboard. As Charles had said, she was a well organized person. In every way. Including the organization of her double life.

*

Closing her eyes, resting her head against the back of the chair, rocking gently, she could still feel the precise texture, smell the exact odour of the two weeks that had followed the expedition to Glan-yr-Afon.

The weather had changed again. The days were damp and grey, like the flannel on which she had grown mustard and cress as a child. There were pools of water and wet sacks in the yard behind the kitchen. A trickle of water from a leaking gutter ran down her neck as she stood on the doorstep looking in her bag for her keys. The hall at the bottom of the stairs had a dank smell. The weather wasn't cold; it would almost have been better if it had been. It had a clammy warmth like dirty laundry.

She couldn't work. She walked through grey Bloomsbury squares where beautiful buildings were being torn down and hideous ones put up. She walked through the Market, where everyone was bad-tempered, hunched in raincoats. She walked along Piccadilly, in the slippery rush of traffic, to the sodden park. Muddy water made brown splashes on her legs.

She wanted to exhaust herself; she felt that in that way, she might achieve numbness, a numbness she especially desired in bed, with Tom. She was silent, but her body screamed 'No', screamed 'Charles'.

Of course, her relationship with Tom was doomed, that was obvious to her. But still she lacked the courage to end it, fearing having nobody at all. She had been cowardly – and she had also been cruel. How viciously she had teased Tom. And always, just as he was about to stump off, hurt and baffled, she would change, would soothe and beguile him in a way she despised. But one afternoon, she couldn't even bring herself to placate him. He had tried to resolve an argument in bed, and she hadn't been able to bother to pretend. She had lain rigid, head averted, and when he had finished, she had pushed him away at once, and had rolled over with her back to him. He had dressed and departed, and she had lain there, listening to the rain. And then the telephone had rung.

She could hardly summon up the energy to pick up the receiver, but the ringing continued, and at last she had stretched out her hand. She just held the receiver to her ear, saying nothing. She had an idea that it was Tom, ringing up for a reconciliation. If it were, she decided, she would just ring off; she couldn't face a conversation with him.

'Esther,' a voice said, and she was sitting up, her hand tightening on the receiver. 'Charles,' she said. 'I think we must meet,' he said, and all she could say was 'Yes'. 'I'll come to you tonight. Tell me the address.' She told him, and he rang off.

His engagement to Clare, the night at the Angel – they were irrelevant. All that mattered was that she was going to see him. She got up and went over to the window. The rain was still falling steadily. How wonderful it was to be there, in her room, with the rain falling, like a soft curtain shutting out the world!

He came at eight. That was the first of all the times she counted to sixty before going down to let him in. At last they were inside, together, and Charles was looking round her room. 'Rather Puritan,' he said at last, 'but not unattractive.'

Now his gaze rested on her. And she summoned all her power to return his look, calmly, levelly. 'Aloof one,' he said, and then, 'your gaze is almost insolent,' as he pulled her down on to the rug.

Her enslavement was completed that night. Down, down, down she went into darkness. Next day she was like a sleep-walker, her limbs so loose and heavy, her mind so tranced.

She determined to keep this area of her life as a separate, closed compartment. Though sometimes the sealed chamber leaked, and its essences seeped into the everyday. She would find herself staring blankly at a book in the library, her nostrils pricking for a memory of his smell. She would find herself watching the lips of a lecturing professor while her ears strained after an echo of another voice.

Yet, really, her work suffered very little. She completed her thesis. She was offered a junior lectureship at London University. Conscientiously she prepared her lectures, crisply she delivered them, punctiliously she corrected her students' essays. *She was in control.*

But wasn't something perhaps missing – something that had been there before? A phrase she had heard Tom use about an ageing statesman came back to her. Had 'the fire gone from her belly'? And particularly as far as her political life was concerned? Of course, her break with Tom – which she had made the day after Charles's first visit – hadn't helped; he was no longer at her elbow to sustain her political drive. Even so she continued with many of her political activities. After all – there was Mortmere, there were her mother and stepfather. She wouldn't, couldn't stop fighting that, stop fighting them. But sometimes she wondered if another, less acceptable motive were also involved. Wasn't her political commitment an element in her game with Charles, an aspect of the challenge she offered him as 'aloof one', as 'upper-class rebel'? Even while he disparaged it, didn't it intrigue him? And intrigue him she must. Intriguing him was one thing which she felt certain that Clare wasn't capable of.

Charles and Clare had been married in November, six months after their engagement – about which, Brian told Esther, Lady Violet had at first been furious. 'I hear,' he said, 'that she calls Clare "that dreary little nobody". Perhaps she has come to regard Cousin Charles as her personal property – it would certainly be a mistake for *anyone* to do that.' And he had given Esther a sharp glance. He was the only person who knew about her and Charles. She hadn't been able to resist having someone to confide in – though she hadn't told him very much. There were moments when she regretted having told him anything at all. Smoothly she had said, 'Oh, I *do* agree, Brian,' and, rather reluctantly, he had smiled.

Lady Violet had relented. 'Dear Charles's fatal charm,' said Brian. 'Though perhaps all that lovely money played some part, as well. I have a feeling that Lady Violet has had to stump up for Charles once or twice. Some of his financial ventures have been distinctly risky, one hears.'

Whatever her reasons, Lady Violet had been almost overpoweringly gracious at the wedding reception, which was held in her house. Swathed in coffee-coloured chiffon, and wearing a vast hat of matching straw, she had quite overpowered Clare's mother, a tiny garrulous widow, with pastel-pink hair and a tight little mouth, who apparently was also rather intimidated by Charles. 'Poor Momma is quite scared of you, I think,' Esther had heard Clare exclaim to him with wonder in her voice. For, in her mother's presence, Clare became almost drugged with passivity, fetching and carrying, nodding and shaking her head like a puppet, perpetually murmuring, 'Yes, Momma.'

'I doubt if Charles will be too keen to have *Momma* around

for long, after the wedding,' Brian observed. 'I don't think he cares to have quite such a formidable rival for Clare's devotion.' Brian was proved right. Very soon after the wedding, Clare's mother, who had been talking about spending the rest of the winter in London 'to be near those dear children', was on her way back to Georgia. 'The Confederacy has been routed again!' Brian declared.

At the wedding reception, Esther had placed her lips against Clare's cheek. With the blood mantling under her transparent skin, with her blue eyes glittering, Clare, in white lace, had looked almost improbably bridal. Moving on to Charles, Esther had smiled, had pursed her lips. Lightly, for an instant, she rested them against Charles's chin. 'Two weeks on Thursday, Esther,' he had murmured in her ear. She had smiled, she had passed on, and he had turned to the next guest.

Was it ever quite so wild as it had been on that Thursday after his honeymoon? Down, down, down, she sank into darkness. She clutched, she clung. His skin had a searingly vivid taste of stolen fruit; exotic fruit, plucked by stealth from an enemy's tree.

An enemy? It had been on his second visit that Charles, drinking his coffee, had said, 'I've decided that you and Brian must be friends with Clare. There won't be any difficulties. You'll find that, if you're nice to her, she will respond.'

So it had turned out. Quickly, eagerly, Clare had taken Esther and Brian to her heart. After all, weren't they Charles's old friends? Hadn't they been his friends ever since that wonderful holiday they had spent together, when they were hardly more than children, at that quaint old Glan-yr-Afon?

Brian became fond of Clare. Esther, from the sidelines, watched it happening. 'She's got a good heart,' Brian said, and Esther nodded.

Brian and Clare chattered and gossiped. Together, they bent their heads over the pages of *Vogue*. 'She knows how to dress,' he said to Esther. 'Oh Brian,' she answered, 'rather Little Miss Muffet, isn't she?' 'Ah,' he said, 'and you hope a big spider will come and frighten her away, hmmm? She has her own style. Stronger clothes would swamp her. But perhaps you'd like that? Esther, I'm *fond* of Clare. Aren't you?'

Esther stretched. She gave a little yawn. 'Why yes,' she said. 'I expect I am. Why not?' she smiled.

'You know, Esther,' he said, 'sometimes I think you're potentially quite *wicked*.'

She laughed. 'I can't imagine what you mean,' she said.

What did she really feel about Clare? Certainly, she obtained a curious pleasure from her company, whether Charles were there or not. Though was 'pleasure' the right word. Wasn't 'fascination' more exact? Yes, it fascinated her to watch Clare, to listen to her, to smile while, deep inside herself, she cherished her marvellous secret. When she was with Clare, she usually wore her dark glasses – on the pretext that her eyes needed rest.

Clare would nod sympathetically: 'Oo yes, I'm sure your eyes must get tired, Essie, reading all those great big books.'

The large drawing-room of Charles's and Clare's flat in Hill Street had the same impersonal quality which she had noticed in Charles's flat at Lady Violet's. It was a room without cherished objects. At first it had contained a large collection of spindly glass animals, which Clare called her 'pets', but these had soon been consigned by Charles to the bedroom. Smoothie, the Siamese which Charles had given to Clare – 'He'll be company for you when I'm out' – stalked or brooded, occasionally giving a little cawing cry.

Clare would curl on the chaise-longue which had accompanied Charles from Duke Street, St James's. Esther would sprawl on a great new sofa, and listen to Clare talk about Charles. About his wit (which Esther didn't really feel was one of his strong points). About his perfect taste (which Esther found dull). About, above all, his wonderful protectiveness (which Esther was interested to hear of).

'You know, Essie, sometimes I feel he really doesn't like me to set foot outside the door. He's always telling me to get things delivered from Fortnum's. And he's always phoning me during the day – "just to make sure you're all right" he says. If I weren't here when he got home, I really believe the skies would fall.'

Sometimes, when Clare described this state of affairs, she would assume a tone of mock petulance. But usually she didn't try to disguise her belief that Charles's watchfulness was a supreme proof of his love. And, apparently, there was another, equal proof.

This had been revealed by Clare after she had known Esther

for over a year. One evening Clare, contrary to her usual abstemious practice, had taken three glasses of the sweet sherry which was the only drink she really liked. Charles was late. Esther, who had been invited to dinner, had filled Clare's glass whenever she replenished her own gin, saying, 'Clare, you can't let me drink alone.' And Clare, probably motivated by some dim desire to observe the code of hospitality, had acquiesced.

'You know, Essie,' she had said suddenly, lurching a little as she re-arranged herself on the chaise-longue, 'Charles is so wonderfully considerate. You'd hardly believe it, but he never bothers me at all *that way*. Do you know what I'm talking about?'

'I think I do,' Esther had said cautiously.

'Yes, I guess you do. You're so respectable, Essie, and yet you're so sophisticated – I admire that. So I expect you do know what I mean when I say he never *pesters* me. It's so wonderful of him. Momma always told me that it was something wives just have to put up with.' (My God, Esther thought, and then was suddenly assailed by the memory of herself and Tom.) 'Well,' Clare continued, 'Momma was certainly wrong as far as Charles is concerned. We don't want children. Essie, my hips are so narrow, just like Momma's. She nearly died when I was born. I've heard that terrible story so often. And Charles just couldn't bear me to go through an experience like that.'

'There are ... precautions,' Esther heard herself saying.

'Oh, Essie, don't talk about those sordid things. Charles says they're just too awful. Anyhow, don't you think it's just wonderful of him?'

'Oh yes, wonderful,' Esther said. And she felt it was. *It's only me he wants!* That was what she thought. What she said next was, 'It certainly sounds most unusual. I'd never have guessed. Why I remember ...' She hesitated. Then she asked, 'What about that night at the Angel in Abergavenny?'

Clare giggled. 'Fancy your remembering that,' she said. 'Oo, Essie, were you shocked? Yes, I can imagine you were. I don't know how it was I didn't tell you – but of course I didn't know you then. In fact, I had the impression you were hostile towards me. But that was your English reserve, I understand that now. Anyway, I never would have agreed to it – to sleeping in the same room with Charles when we weren't even married yet.

Except that I knew it was all quite innocent. And I knew – just between ourselves, Essie – that Charles just can't bear to sleep alone. He has these terrible dreams, you see.'

At that moment, Smoothie jumped down from the chaise-longue, on which, unusually, he had been sitting at Clare's feet. He trotted to the open door into the hall, slipped through it. And Esther heard the front-door key turn in the lock. So did Clare, who was standing up, putting a finger to her lips.

'Essie,' she said, 'of course, all that was just between us girls.' She smoothed her bell of hair, glanced at herself in a gilt-framed mirror, hurried after the cat to greet Charles in the hall. Esther closed her eyes.

It's only me he wants.

Now, as so often before, she repeated those words in the stillness of her room. She stood up. She took the coffee cups and glasses into the kitchen, and washed and dried them. She replaced the brandy bottle in the cupboard. In the bathroom, she put the discarded satin dress in a bag to take to the dry cleaner.

She went to bed with the thought that she would be seeing Charles at dinner next day.

She was awakened by the telephone. Dazed, she sat up, looking at her watch. Ten past eight. She picked up the receiver. 'Hullo,' she said.

'Essie, you sound quite dopey. Did I wake you up? I guess I must have. I'm so sorry. But I have to leave soon. Something terrible has happened.' There was a note of hysteria in Clare's voice.

'Calm down, Clare. What's happened?' *Charles?* she wondered, gathering herself together, and blinking the sleep from her eyes.

'It's Momma, Essie. She's very ill. She's had a heart attack. I have to go to the States today. Charles says I should wait for more details, but I just can't do that.' Beneath the hysteria, Esther heard an unfamiliar touch of steel. 'So I'm catching a plane this morning,' Clare went on. 'I nearly asked you to look after Smoothie – Charles is out so much – but I know how busy you are.'

'I suppose I could. When will you be back? The only thing is that I'm going away tomorrow for the weekend.'

'Are you going home?'

'To Mortmere.'

'That's what I meant. To your momma's. Anyhow, Essie, it's quite all right. I called Brian, and he's coming around for Smoothie right away. I don't know when I'll be back. As soon as I can, of course. I just wanted to let you know that I'm sorry to have to cancel our date this evening. You do understand, don't you, Essie?'

'Of course I do,' Esther said, and then, 'I'm sorry about your mother. I do hope she'll be better soon.'

'Oh, Essie, I pray she will—' Clare broke off. 'There's the doorbell,' she said. 'That'll be Brian. So I must run. Take care of yourself, Essie dear. Oh, and look after Charles for me. Perhaps you'd ask him around for a meal sometime?'

'Of course. And I'll be thinking of you, Clare.'

''Bye then, Essie.'

'Goodbye.'

After she had rung off, she lay back on the pillows. She wondered whether, with Clare away, she would see more of Charles. Really, she wouldn't have minded looking after the cat. It would have been – a link. Was Charles fond of the cat? Certainly it was fond of him. She remembered it hurrying to meet him, with little growls, butting its head against his ankles. It liked to sit on his lap. Sometimes he pushed it off, but she remembered that, at other times, he would stroke its smooth, creamy coat. Once he had noticed her watching his hand, and a little smile had appeared on his lips. She had blushed, and had stood up abruptly and gone over to the window, to look out, so that Clare wouldn't notice. Though Clare never seemed to notice anything.

Esther imagined Charles, in her rocking-chair, slowly stroking the cat's soft fur. Did he like fur? she wondered. That was something she had never worn for him. She disapproved of killing animals for their skins. But the thought of his hand, stroking fur, lingered. It was a pity that fake furs were so tatty.

Getting up, making coffee, she wondered how Charles was reacting to the prospect of Clare's departure. She was sure that he wouldn't be pleased about it. For she realized that, in some unknown way, he depended on Clare. There had been a time when she had tried to persuade herself that it was only Clare's money that concerned him, but she had been forced to recognize that that wasn't the case. No, for some reason, he *needed* Clare. Why else his insistence that she should always be there, at home, waiting for him?

She remembered Clare saying that Charles couldn't bear to sleep alone. She herself had no direct knowledge of that, for – it was extraordinary, she supposed – Charles had never fallen asleep in her presence. There had been times when she had longed to drown in slumber, had dozed, had started awake to hear him moving in the room. Once she had slept deeply, and had woken to find him gone. Ever since, she had always dragged herself back from the brink of unconsciousness.

Would Charles reconcile himself to sleeping alone while Clare was away? she wondered, pouring out her second cup of coffee. How she wished that she weren't going to Mortmere next day. Should she ring her mother up, and put it off? But the weekend, as usual, had been arranged far in advance. This, she knew, was in order that encounters which might be 'unfortunate' could be avoided. Esther must not be invited at the same time as various friends of theirs who visited them frequently. Thinking of those friends now, she hunched her shoulders in a little gesture of revulsion. She remembered a desiccated Frenchman, a weary Italian, a heavy German with a duelling scar on his cheek, a portly Spaniard. The Spaniard had had a special air of complacency; his country alone had preserved a regime of the kind they all believed in – Franco (*El Caudillo*) still clutched the reins in his blotchy old hands.

Round the dinner table at Mortmere, they and their expensively dressed wives had sat, like dreadful old spiders, spinning out political threads, convinced that they were weaving not cobwebs but nets of steel. Their pouched eyes would brighten as they re-lived vanished triumphs: Vichy, Ethiopia, Nuremburg, the fall of Madrid. Her stepfather had looked almost his old self, as he recollected that great rally in the Albert Hall ... how fond had been her mother's look as she watched him. (Didn't she ever get sick of those old stories?)

Anyway, after two occasions on which Esther had clashed with them, the old friends were not seen at Mortmere during her visits. Was this for their comfort or for hers? She didn't really care. But she decided that she had better not cancel the weekend. Besides, Clare had probably told Charles that Esther was 'going home', as she persisted in putting it. So, if she stayed in London, it would be evident that she was staying because of him. And that – wouldn't do. No, she would go to Mortmere.

She cleaned the flat, she showered, she put on a shirt and blue jeans. She had no lectures that day, but there was a pile of essays on her table, waiting to be corrected. She sat down, and willed herself to concentrate. Soon she was lost, frowning occasionally at woolly thinking and careless language, writing comments in the margins in her small neat writing. (She was, she knew, somewhat notorious among the students for her pre-occupation with grammar and style. However, they basically approved of her because she was 'politically all right'.)

The stack of corrected essays on her left grew steadily; the heap in front of her diminished. She sat up with a start when the telephone rang.

Charles, as usual, spoke without preamble: 'You know that Clare has gone away. I'm sure it's a false alarm raised by that dreadful old mother of hers. But all the same, she would go.'

'She told me,' Esther said.

'I thought I might be able to come round tomorrow evening,' he said. 'We could go out to dinner somewhere.'

She had never been 'out to dinner' alone with Charles. The idea intrigued her. She had to take a grip on herself in order to say, 'Oh Charles, I'm so sorry, but I'll be away. I'm going to Mortmere.'

'Oh really,' he said, and yet she felt quite sure that Clare had told him that she would be going.

'Yes,' she said. 'It was arranged a long time ago.' There was a pause. She guessed that he was waiting for her to say that she would change her plans, but she didn't say anything. At last, it was he who spoke. 'I see,' he said. 'Well, I shall obviously have to find some other diversion.'

Panic rose in her. 'I shall be back quite early on Sunday evening.' She tried to keep her tone casual, but was not sure that she had succeeded.

'I see,' he said again, and then, 'But I shan't be free on Sunday.' His voice lightened: 'However, Esther, I do want those keys. You'll get them copied today, won't you? I'll drop in to collect them at about six. But I'm afraid I won't be able to stay. I have an engagement.'

'Very well,' she said. There was a click as he rang off.

Game to Charles, she thought, and smiled. But then she realized that there was nothing to smile at. The sentence which she had been trying to forget ever since he uttered it rose, unsubmergeable, to the surface of her mind: *'I shall obviously have to find some other diversion.'*

Surely it wasn't too late? She could telephone him, and then her mother to make some excuse for putting off the visit. Her hand was on the receiver. Then she snatched it back. She imagined Charles's voice, saying, 'I see.' And he was quite capable of announcing that he was no longer available, that, unfortunately (yes, she could hear his very intonation), he had just made 'another engagement'. No, she couldn't take the risk of that. She would have to go to Mortmere – and already she was registering her decision as another black mark against it, against *them*. (Did she go to Mortmere, she suddenly, uneasily, wondered, to perform a duty or to nourish a hate?)

Even the fact that she would be seeing Charles in only a few hours failed to cheer her. For he was coming only to take possession of her keys, those keys which she felt profoundly reluctant to give him.

She glanced towards the essays awaiting her on the table. Suddenly the thought of them oppressed her. She turned back to the telephone. She picked up the receiver, and dialled Brian's number.

'Duckie!' he exclaimed, as soon as she had said 'Hullo', it's been centuries since we've had a chat ... at least a week, anyway. But honestly, life has been positively action-packed lately. Have you heard about my tiny feline lodger? Yes, our Clare probably told you before she flew away to her old Kentucky home.'

'She comes from Georgia, I believe,' Esther said.

'Georgia, Georgia, my whole life through,' Brian sang. Then, 'Yes, I think you're right,' he said in his normal tone. 'But what's the difference? I would have thought that, in either place, there'd be some lovable old black mammy who could tote the weary load, and nurse Momma back to health. Dear Charles, of course, is convinced that she's suffering from nothing more than a fit of the vapours. Charles is very sulky *indeed*. There he sat like a thundercloud, positively exuding menace, when I darted in to collect the kitty. Incidentally, why Charles can't minister to the animal himself I don't know. But Clare evidently thought the beast would starve to death, and that she'd be greeted by a catty corpse on her return. What she *said* was that it might tie him down – and who shall gainsay her? I feel positively in bondage already. Yes, Esther, the cat is very cross – almost as cross as Charles. At the moment, he has taken refuge behind the sofa – the cat, I mean, not Charles – and there is nothing I can do to lure him thence. I've put down a dear little Rockingham saucer, filled with *cream* – but I haven't been rewarded by so much as the twitch of a whisker. Perhaps *I* should get cross too, but that leads to ugly frown lines – the *last* thing one wants.' Brian broke off, and Esther could hear him calling, 'Kitty, kitty, kitty.' Then, 'No,' he said, 'not a flicker of response. Anyway, sweetie, enough of *my* woes. How are you? Are *you* feeling cross?'

'Not exactly cross. A bit depressed.' Brian wasn't having his usual tonic effect on her. 'I'm going to Mortmere tomorrow.'

'Ah! Never one of your favourite outings, I know. And I would have thought that perhaps ...' He paused, and then went on: 'That perhaps dear Charles might have been seeking solace from you this weekend, in his hour of need.'

This was one of the times when Esther wished that she'd never told Brian anything about herself and Charles. 'I wonder what could have given you that idea,' she said lightly.

'Esther, are you being coy, by any chance?'

'I've never felt less coy in my life,' she said coldly.

'Goodness, how touchy we are today!'

She softened. 'I'm sorry, Brian. I suppose I'm in a bad mood.'

'Poor sweetie!' As ever, his sympathy was instant. Really, she thought, he was a dear, was one of her closest friends. *Almost the only one, nowadays*, said a voice in her head. 'Well,' he went on, 'my advice is to pour yourself a great big drink and have a nice hot bath. That's the way I always wash *my* troubles away.'

'Perhaps I'll do that,' she said. 'Well, anyway, have the bath.' Hot, soothing, scented water – yes, the idea did appeal to her. 'And now I mustn't moan away to you any longer, dear Brian.'

'Oh, that's all right,' he said. 'Auntie Brian always lends a willing ear. I suppose dear Charles will be round this weekend, telling me his troubles.'

'Does he?' she asked. 'Tell you his troubles, I mean.'

'Oh, from time to time,' Brian said airily.

'Mmm,' she said, and then, casually, 'Brian, what *are* his troubles?'

'Oh – this and that, you know. Usually we get drunk.'

'Get drunk?' Esther said. 'Goodness, I've never seen Charles drunk.' Yes, she was jealous. Of Brian! 'What does he do when he's drunk?' she asked.

'Oh well, to begin with he gets quieter and quieter and paler and paler. And then, all at once, he starts to talk a lot. And then, quite suddenly, he lurches to his feet, and goes home.'

'How extraordinary,' she said. 'But what does he talk about – when he talks a lot?'

'Oh, his childhood, and so on.' Brian was really being irritatingly vague. But she felt that it would be undignified to press for further details. And certainly she wouldn't ask him the question which suddenly filled her mind: *Does he ever talk about me?*

'Well,' she said, 'I think I'll go and soak in that bath you recommended. I'll ring you when I get back from Mortmere, and tell you all about how awful it was.'

'Come, come, Esther – don't be defeatist. *That*'s not the spirit that made you captain of the hockey team.'

'Heaven forbid that I should ever have been any such thing,' she said.

'Another illusion shattered. Why, Esther, I've always pictured you pounding around in your gym tunic, chopping savagely at all the other girls' ankles. Well, anyway, when I first met you again, in that shop, I thought you were rather like that. But actually, since then, I think you've changed.'

'Oh really. In what way?'

'Well ... how shall I put it? I think I feel that perhaps you do not gaze quite so frankly on the world as you once did.'

'I see. Well, Brian, I really must ring off now. Goodbye.'

'Goodbye, duckie. And cheer up. Perhaps Mortmere will be fun after all.'

Fun! she thought fiercely, putting down the receiver rather hard. She stood up, and went to turn on her bath. In the bathroom, she went over to the mirror, and stared into it. Bared by her swept-back, neatly coiled hair, her face stared back at her. Sunburned skin. Short neat nose. Decisive chin. Her eyebrows, which had once been too heavy, were now plucked into smooth curves. Beneath them, wasn't the glance of her brown eyes cool and level? Surely it wasn't true that she no longer gazed frankly on the world? Brian had been talking nonsense. Briskly she shook her head. Anyway, tonight, there would be no roles, no disguises. No games would be played on this particular summer night.

He had arrived; he had left. She had been tempted to bring him upstairs to fetch the keys – in the hope that he might, after all, linger. But her pride had prevailed; the battle had been won. When the doorbell rang, she had gone down with the set of keys from the kitchen cupboard. 'Right,' he had said, putting them in his pocket, turning immediately, and moving towards his car, which was parked at the edge of the pavement. 'Have a nice weekend,' he said, as he got in. Abruptly she pulled the front door shut.

six

Battered to death, battered to death, battered to death, said the wheels. How extraordinary it was that she should have learned the news at Mortmere.

At half past six, on Saturday evening, she had joined them in the library. A wood fire was burning in the grate. Even in midsummer, an evening chill descended on the rooms of Mortmere.

They had, as usual, changed for dinner. Her stepfather had put on an old velvet jacket. Her mother wore a long tweed skirt and a white blouse. Esther's dress was a narrow tube of black wool, sleeveless but with a high polo neck.

'Why, Esther, how splendid you look,' and 'That's a very nice dress, darling,' came, simultaneously, from her stepfather's and her mother's lips. With the painful deliberation which had characterized all his movements since his stroke, her stepfather put down his book on the little table next to his wheelchair. Her mother paused in her mixing of 'Hugo's cocktail', as she always called it, though she invariably shared it with him – for her, it was usually the only drink of the day. The ingredients were brought in, on a silver tray, at quarter past six each evening.

'Cocktail, Esther?' her mother asked, and 'Yes, please,' Esther answered. The cocktail, a potent mixture of gin, lemon juice and Cointreau, might, she hoped, do something to revive her from the state of passive apathy which, at Mortmere, seemed to be her only alternative to rage.

'You must be taking more interest in your clothes, these days,' her mother said, and Esther wondered why she had to take back with one hand what she offered with the other. Her compliments always came with an undertow of criticism. But wouldn't her mother's voice, clipped, clear and hard, have turned anything she said into something unacceptable to Esther?

'Perhaps she's in love, Sarah.' Her stepfather – it was impossible for her to call him Hugo in her mind, and she never said the name unless she had to – gave his abrupt barking laugh. *If they could have seen her last time she had worn this dress!* The skin on her arms prickled. A slow smile quivered on her lips – cut off immediately she became aware of her mother's sharp observing glance. 'No, I'm not in love,' she said flatly, and her stepfather sighed. *How dull the poor girl is,* she could feel him thinking. *So unlike her mother. No sparkle.*

Now her mother placed her stepfather's drink, in its small, trumpet-shaped glass, on the little table at his side. Esther stepped forward to take her own glass, and went to stand by the fire. As she put the drink down on the marble chimney-piece, she glimpsed her wavering reflection in the dark watery glass of the great gilt mirror, topped by an eagle, that hung above it.

'Your health, Esther,' her stepfather said, raising his glass – so slowly, so carefully – to his lips. And Esther and her mother lifted their glasses, and sipped from them.

'Well, Esther,' her mother said briskly, 'amuse us.' (What an impossible instruction!) 'Tell us all about your gay life in London. Put us in touch with what's going on. Have you seen any good plays lately?'

'I used to love a good play,' her stepfather said. 'But nowadays there seems to be nothing but this kitchen-sink drama. And I'm damned if I know why all the actors have to talk in those hideous north-country accents. But perhaps you appreciate that sort of thing, Esther?'

'I haven't been to the theatre for ages,' Esther said.

'What a pity,' said her mother, 'when you're there on the spot. The theatre, the ballet, and of course the opera are the things I really miss, living in the country. Even if there aren't any amusing plays on, there's usually something at dear old Covent Garden. Just round the corner, too, from that extraordinary place you live in.'

Could her mother possibly have forgotten Esther's frequently expressed distaste for opera? She disliked opera in the way she disliked *ornaments*, she thought now, flashing a hostile glance at a cabinet in the corner which contained porcelain figures.

'I've been working very hard,' she heard herself say.

'Funny,' her stepfather said, 'when you were a young girl, I never would have expected that you'd become a school-marm.' The temptation to say, 'I'm not. I'm a university lecturer,' was acute, but she resisted it. On a previous occasion, she had yielded, and her stepfather had said, 'My dear Esther, either one's a don at a proper university – Oxford or Cambridge – or, as far as I'm concerned, one's a schoolmaster or, in your case, a school-marm.'

She took a large swallow of her drink – the trouble with cocktails was that they were too small – but it didn't make her feel any more cheerful.

'Why,' her stepfather said, 'you used to be such a game little thing. D'you remember when I taught you to shoot? You took to it like a duck to water. I wonder what happened to that little Beretta I gave you. Somewhere around the place, I suppose.'

She felt a little flicker of triumph: *a well-kept secret, that.*

'What an eye you had,' he went on. 'You were a natural. Do you remember?' he repeated.

'Yes, I remember,' she said and, yes, she remembered. The hot Spanish sun, and a faint breeze from the sea, and the keen joy as the bullets thudded, time after time, into the petrol tin.

But keener still the joy of her stepfather's hand patting her shoulder, the joy of his exclamations of surprise and praise. Yes, she remembered, though she did not want to.

'But I suppose you never do anything as lowbrow as shooting nowadays?'

She shook her head.

'All work and no play makes Jill a dull girl, you know,' he went on. 'You don't want to overdo things. Now just look at you this afternoon – we'd hardly finished luncheon before you were running off to correct essays, of all things.'

It was true that, as soon as they had drunk their coffee, she had escaped on the pretext of the essays which she had brought with her. But as soon as she was in her room (some of her old clothes still hung in the wardrobe, and a Spanish doll named Carmen sat in a small chintz-covered armchair), she had hurried over to the bookcase to search among the familiar titles. *The Cuckoo Clock* – yes, that was the one she felt like reading. In a moment, she was lying on her stomach on the bed, having failed to take off the counterpane – she had a tendency to revert to old untidy habits at Mortmere – and was eagerly turning the pages. Later, she had fallen asleep, waking at five to tiptoe out through a side door for a solitary walk in the park.

'You missed tea, so I expect you must be hungry,' her stepfather said.

Her mother looked at her watch. 'Seven o'clock,' she announced. 'Well, we mustn't keep the servants waiting.' For they dined nowadays, when it was 'just family' at 'this uncivilized hour', as her stepfather put it. 'The servants like to go off and watch that damn television,' he would explain. And Esther would imagine old Deal, the butler, and old Lettie, her mother's maid, nodding in front of the television in the servants' hall. The Spanish couple – she cooked, and he looked after Esther's stepfather – had their own flat upstairs. 'You couldn't wish for a nicer flat,' her mother would exclaim. 'In London, it would cost a fortune. Their own bathroom, and everything! Really, servants expect the earth, these days.'

Now her mother held open the door for the wheelchair to pass through, and followed immediately behind it, leaving Esther to dawdle in the rear. She found herself regressing to a schoolgirl's sulky slouch, and straightened her shoulders.

As she and her mother took their places, on either side of her stepfather, at the end of the long mahogany table. Esther had a sudden vision of herself and Charles sitting side by side on a velvet banquette in a small dimly lit restaurant. She sighed.

'Buck up now, Esther,' her stepfather admonished her. 'You look like a dying duck in a thunderstorm.' She felt her lips stretch across her teeth in a parody of a smile.

With trembling hands – he was getting shakier every time she came down – Deal put plates of pale *consommé* in front of them. Her mother, Esther foresaw, would taste little else apart from this soup; perhaps a morsel of meat or chicken and a spoonful of green vegetable. She was always dieting – why, Esther couldn't imagine; if anything, her mother was slimmer than she was – and at the end of each meal she took a vitamin pill from the little Battersea enamel box which always stood beside her place at table.

'A glass of wine, Esther?' her stepfather asked. 'That would be lovely,' she said, and he looked pleased at her enthusiasm. 'Deal,' he said, 'what are we eating tonight?' 'Chicken, sir.' 'Hmm, bring up half a bottle of the 1955 Chablis, would you?'

As Deal tottered out on his mission, Esther wondered how early it would be possible for her to escape to bed.

As things turned out, it was earlier than she could have expected. After dinner, back in the library, her mother had switched on the news – the only television programme that was watched at Mortmere. However, she caught the end of a documentary about West Indians arriving in Britain. Suddenly, Esther heard a sort of growl emerging from her stepfather's throat. She glanced towards him. With his left hand, he was pounding on the arm of his wheelchair. 'Black apes from the jungle,' he was gasping. 'Pouring into our country, diluting the purity of the race. A nation of half-breeds, of mongrels – that's what we'll become.' Shaking with anger, Esther was on her feet. But then a fit of coughing seized him. He sank back in his chair. The coughing subsided, and was replaced by deep rasping breaths.

Esther's mother, in three swift steps, was over by the television, switching it off. Now she was by his chair, stroking his arm, murmuring: 'Darling, please, you mustn't upset yourself. You know what the doctor said. You must keep calm. Remember the Memoirs – you don't want anything to interfere with your health.' Gradually the flush faded from his cheeks; the rasping died away.

'I know it's awful, perfectly awful,' her mother went on. 'But that's what you must tell people in the Memoirs. You must explain it all there.'

His head slumped; his chin rested on his chest. 'You're quite right, Sarah. I'm sorry. But it makes my blood boil . . .'

'I know, darling, I know,' Esther's mother interrupted, while her hand continued its rapid, soothing motion on his arm – as if she were trying to mould him into stillness, Esther thought. Now he was still, but his face had taken on a yellow, chalky look.

'Time for bed I think, darling,' her mother said. She went over to the fireplace with those quick decisive steps of hers, and tugged at the bell-pull of braided silk that hung next to it. Esther heard a faint, far-away jangle. She realized that she was still standing with her arms stiffly at her sides, her fists clenched. She forced herself to sit down. She picked up her bag, and fumbled inside it for her cigarettes. As she lit one, she saw that her hands were trembling as badly as Deal's.

The young Spaniard appeared in the doorway.

'*Lleva al señor a su habitación, Manuel. Se siente muy fatigado. Necesita descansar.*' Esther's mother's Spanish was fluent but always sounded very English. Esther was surprised that she herself could still understand the language. For so many years now, she had felt an aversion to it.

Manuel inclined his head. '*Sí, senora,*' he murmured. He went round to the back of the wheelchair – Esther's stepfather was obviously in no condition to operate it himself. 'I'll be with you very soon, when Manuel has got you ready for bed,' her mother said, stooping towards the slumped figure.

'Yes, my dear. And thank you.' His face still had its chalky look. As he was wheeled past Esther, he nodded, muttered, 'Good night.' 'Good night,' she said, turning her head away slightly. Manuel wheeled the chair out into the hall, and closed the door.

Her mother was still standing by the fireplace, and now, for a moment, rested her forehead against the edge of the chimney-piece. Then she straightened up, and turned round. Esther met her look, which was hostile.

'Your stepfather is a great man, Esther,' she said, 'a very great man. The most brilliant man of his generation, and the most misunderstood. Oh, he has been treated shamefully, and by people who were supposed to be his friends.' Esther was waiting for her next words, and now they came: 'A prophet without honour in his own country.'

She paused, as if expecting Esther to comment, but Esther said nothing.

'Sometimes,' her mother said, 'I think you have no heart, Esther.' Was she deliberately trying to provoke? Esther believed so, and was determined not to give her the satisfaction of succeeding.

'Anyway,' her mother went on, 'even if you haven't got a heart, you are supposed to have a brain. When you read the Memoirs, you may understand him a little better.'

Again, there was a silence, broken by her mother, who said, 'Well, I'm going upstairs now.'

'I'll stay down here for a little,' Esther answered. 'Good night.'

'Good night then,' her mother said curtly. Briskly she crossed the room, and went out, closing the door behind her with a sharp little click.

Alone – at last! – Esther stood up, went over to the fireplace, leaned her forehead against the marble as her mother had done. She looked down into the fire, which was dying. Suddenly she shivered. She stooped to put another small log on the embers, and jabbed at it with the poker. Sparks rose.

If her stepfather's outburst this evening were anything to go by, she thought, then the intellectual contents of the Memoirs were unlikely to be impressive. But perhaps, when he wrote, he was more rational. She couldn't help remembering how many people – though mostly long ago – had described him as brilliant, original, extraordinary. Say the Memoirs were good – now *that* really was a depressing prospect, for then people might be taken in by them.

Restless, she wandered to the drinks tray, looked it over, finally picked up the decanter of whisky, and poured a little into a glass. She went back to her chair, and put the glass down on the table next to it. She sat down, and lit another cigarette. Her stepfather's distorted face reappeared before her eyes. Suddenly she remembered how she had once peered into a cage in the reptile house at the zoo. There had been nothing in it but a twisted branch. And then – the branch had *rippled*. Despite the intervening barrier of glass, she had sprung back with an instinctive shock of revulsion. That was exactly what she had felt tonight; that was what her stepfather could always make her feel. She would be lulled – bored – into thinking of him as just a tiresome old man. And then – the shock: the sudden recognition of evil. What an emotive, what an illogical word that was. And yet it was the only one she could find.

How could her mother defend him, support him, actually appear to admire him? Well, she thought she knew the answer to that. Not to do so would be to declare twenty-five years of her life null and void; her divorce from Esther's father, her imprisonment, her exile. Esther supposed that she should sympathize – but she didn't.

She raised her glass, and drank. She grimaced. She had never liked the taste of whisky, but the glow that now ran right down to her stomach was comforting. If she lived at Mortmere, she would probably take to drink, she reflected grimly. But Mortmere was the last place in the world she would ever choose to live. And yet – it pulled at something in her. Wasn't she already planning how, in the morning, she would get up early, and go across the park to the little classical folly that topped a small artificial mound on the other side of the mere? Mortmere. The dead lake. *'The sedge is withered from the lake, and no birds sing,'* she murmured aloud.

Abruptly she stood up, and took her glass over to the drinks tray where, after a moment's hesitation, she put it down. This time tomorrow, she would be at home, at her *real* home. And Charles – perhaps he would come round after all? *'I shall have to find some other diversion.'* But firmly she thrust *that* out of her mind.

The log which she had put on the fire hadn't caught, the embers were turning to ash. A chill was settling in the room. There was gooseflesh on her arms. It was time to go to bed.

She had set the alarm of her little travelling clock for seven, but she was already awake when it rang. Well, half awake; in a state between sleep and waking in which she felt that she had spent the whole night, a state in which she had been unable to tell if she were thinking or dreaming. Charles had been in her thoughts – or dreams. So had her stepfather and her mother. At one stage, she had been in her stepfather's study, reading the Memoirs, and they had been extraordinary; their resonance had echoed in her head like chimes. That, anyway, she realized, sitting up in bed, had been a dream.

Should she get up, and go for the walk she had planned? There was a greyness, left over from the night, in her head. But she didn't feel like staying in bed. She got up, went over to the window, and drew back the curtains. Her first impression was of clouds. But then she saw that it was only a morning mist, behind which she could sense the sun's immanence. Her mood lightened a little. Quickly she washed – at Mortmere, reverting to childhood, she always bathed at night – and dressed. She padded quietly along the corridor and down the staircase into the hall. She could hear Deal, in the dining-room, laying the table for breakfast.

She went along the flagged passage behind the hall, to the side door that she always used. She walked along by the side of the house, and then crossed the terrace, with its great stone urns from which leafy plants trailed, and ran down the steps to the gravel. She passed the stables with their round archway, beyond which was a cobbled yard. There was only one horse in the stables now; an old chestnut mare which her mother sometimes rode. Esther had loved riding, as a child. Perhaps she might still enjoy it. But she didn't intend to find out. Riding was one of the things that had been poisoned for her; it was part of *that* way of life.

She went through the iron gate beyond the stables, and turned left into the park. Now the stables were between her and *them*. Suddenly she felt free.

The sun was breaking through the mist. Ahead of her, the water of the mere glimmered. Beyond it, the stone columns of the folly were gold in the early light. She quickened her pace. On an impulse, she pulled the pins from her hair, and put them in the pocket of her shirt. She shook her head, and her hair tumbled down around her shoulders.

She circled the edge of the mere. A heron, standing in the reeds, flapped away at her approach. She climbed the little mound, created two hundred years earlier by a landscape gardener, and entered the folly. She inhaled its familiar smell of damp stone. On the wall at the back, under the little dusty window, she had carved her initials when she was fourteen. She had carved them small, and low on the wall – she crouched down and traced the letters with her finger, now – but her mother had noticed them. 'Really, Esther,' she had said, 'how very common of you. Just like some tripper!' Standing up, Esther angrily shook back her hair at the memory.

She sat down on the wooden bench with curved wrought-iron arms, which, ever since she could remember, had stood between the Doric columns. On their wartime walks, Esther and her nanny had sometimes brought a picnic tea there.

A dove was cooing in the trees that were grouped behind the little temple. In the distance, the soft pink brick of the stables was in perfect accord with the golden stone of the house which, beyond them, glowed in such serene, such confident perfection. The rage which the memory of her mother's contemptuous remark had stirred in her overflowed now to encompass that perfection. *Birds nesting in its crumbling walls. Deer grazing in the study.* She closed her eyes. The sun's warmth stroked her eyelids. One dove answered another, coo-coo-cooing.

She sat up with a start. Immediately, she looked at her watch. The time was nearly half past nine. She jumped to her feet, and set off at a run. She was panting by the time she reached the house. When she entered the dining-room, she saw that they had almost finished breakfast – well, her stepfather had; her mother didn't eat breakfast, only drank a glass of orange juice and a cup of black coffee.

'Sorry,' Esther said as she sat down, 'I fell asleep in the folly.'

'Fell asleep?' her mother said. She made it sound as if Esther had admitted the practice of some sordid minor vice. She had a puritanical streak where anything that could be classified as 'self-indulgent' was concerned. Esther could still remember her mother's disgust when, aged eleven, she had eaten a box of sweets, brought to her by some visitor, in a single afternoon. Eating between meals, scratching insect bites, coughing, lying in bed late in the morning: these, like hot rooms, closed windows and 'doing nothing' (reading novels came into this category) were, she indicated – that word again – 'common'.

'But surely,' she said now, 'you had only just woken up?'

'I didn't sleep well last night,' Esther said. To which her mother replied, 'You smoke too much.'

'That's a mysterious statement. I don't really see the connection,' Esther said, and heard a touch of shrillness in her voice. She nearly added, 'I hardly smoke at all in London.' Instead, she buttered a piece of cold toast with a scraping sound.

'Of course, at the moment, your hair's very untidy, but on the whole I think it is better *down*,' her mother said. 'I don't know why you always scrape it back. It makes you look like a skinned rabbit.'

Her stepfather's teaspoon clinked against his saucer. Then he said, 'Ah, the papers. That damn boy comes later every Sunday.'

Looking out of the window, Esther could see a youth dismounting from his bicycle on the gravel, and approaching the door which opened, under the terrace, into a stone passage that led to the kitchen and servants' quarters. A few minutes later, Deal came in with the papers folded on a silver salver: the *Express* for her mother, the *Telegraph* for her stepfather – the Sunday counterparts of their weekday papers. (*The Times* and the *Sunday Times* had long been discontinued as too 'red'.)

No one thought of offering a paper to Esther. Not that she wanted either of those Tory rags, she thought angrily. But it would have been pleasant if the gesture had been made. Defiantly she pulled her packet of cigarettes and matches from the pocket of her jeans. She lit a cigarette.

It was at that moment that her mother said, 'Hugo, how extraordinary! Have you seen what has happened to Violet Ferney?'

'Old Vi?' Her stepfather scanned the front page of the *Telegraph*. 'What? Oh yes, here it is.'

'*What* has happened?' Esther asked. As neither of them answered, she stood up, and went round behind her mother's chair to peer over her shoulder, which, she noticed, made her mother straighten the newspaper irritably.

Lady Violet, her face blown-up, hazy, stared at Esther from the front page. FAMOUS MAYFAIR HOSTESS BATTERED TO DEATH screamed the headline.

'*Discovered last night* ...' – now her stepfather was reading snatches from his paper. 'Hmm, hmm, hmm ... *poker next to the body* ... hmm ... *body found by her maid* ... *robbery* ... hmm, hmm, hmm ... *Thought to be missing is the famous*

Colgong Star, a present to Lady Violet from her late husband—' he broke off. 'Damn hooligans,' he said. 'Ever since they abolished the birch—'

'I must get back to London,' Esther said. 'When's the next train?' she asked her mother.

'Get back to London?' Her mother looked up from the paper. 'Esther, what are you talking about?' She frowned over the frames of the large hornrimmed reading-glasses which she always wore perched near the tip of her nose, as if to disclaim any real dependence on them.

'It's a friend of mine,' Esther said, 'a great friend. He knew her very well. He'll be terribly upset.'

Now she had her mother's full attention. 'Goodness, I never imagined that you knew anyone in such respectable circles, Esther,' she said. 'Who is this "great friend"?'

Esther hesitated. Then she said, 'His name's Charles Tibbald.'

'Tibbald . . . Tibbald – it strikes a chord of some kind. Hugo, who do we know called Tibbald?'

'Hmm,' Esther's stepfather said. 'Just a moment. Ah yes, I've got it. That would be Vi's cousin's son. Yes, of course – the offspring of Bad Belinda. She was always called Bad Belinda. Oddly enough, her brother was married to another Belinda, and she was known as Good Belinda.'

'Why was she called Bad Belinda?' Esther asked.

'Because she *was* bad. A thoroughly bad lot. Some scandal with an Italian chauffeur when she was only eighteen or so. And then the family married her off to Tibbald, in a hurry. The only chap who was willing, I suppose. Seemed an obvious queer to me. But I could have been wrong about that. Anyway, he was a snobbish little fellow – I'm sure that was why he married her. Couldn't resist the title. Your friend Charles was born about six months after the wedding. There was some other shady business later. Drink, I seem to recollect, and a car crash.'

'Yes, I remember now,' Esther's mother said. 'Violet Ferney brought the boy up. She used to have him to stay in the school holidays, and so on. Esther, you are a dark horse, aren't you?' For once her mother actually sounded pleased with her. 'Why don't you bring this Charles down here some time, if he's such a "great friend"?' she asked. 'Or wouldn't we get on with him?'

83

Unfortunately, Esther could imagine Charles getting on with them wonderfully. 'He's married,' she said, and then added quickly, 'He and his wife are both great friends of mine.'

'I see,' her mother said. Once more she aimed that sharp blue stare at Esther over the rims of her glasses.

'Anyway,' Esther said – she had moved back to stand behind her own chair, and she realized that she had picked up her table napkin, and was twisting it between her fingers – 'I really feel I should get back to see if there's anything I can do for them.' To mention Clare's absence, she decided, was quite unnecessary.

'But, darling,' her mother said, 'mayn't you be a little *de trop*? It must have been a tremendous shock for them. And I suppose there will be policemen scurrying about all over the place.'

'Policemen?' Esther said stupidly.

'Yes, interviewing relations, and so on. Don't they always do that? No, really, I'm sure you should go back on the half past four, as usual. Anyway, there's only one train this morning, and that leaves in half an hour. I'd never be able to get you to the station and be back in time for church.'

Church! Another of her mother's conventions, which Esther had often wondered about. Her mother had never shown any signs of being religious, except that she always went to the village church on Sunday. Her stepfather had never gone, even before his stroke. But whenever she visited Mortmere, Esther was aware that her mother was annoyed that she did not go.

No, it wasn't worth pressing to return to London now. Anyway, perhaps her mother was right. After all, how did she know that Charles would want to see her? No, she'd stick it out. 'Oh well,' she said, 'I might as well stay.' Her mother's raised eyebrows registered precisely how ungracious she sounded.

The train would reach Paddington in another ten minutes. Now the waste land of factories and junk yards was being superseded by the backs of row upon row of grey terraced houses. Washing hung from their windows. The strips of garden behind were weedy and forlorn, crowded with the detritus of years of makeshift living. Yet at least such houses were on a human scale, unlike the vast new tower tenements that loomed above them. She knew which she would choose. Or she thought she did. For that was a choice, she imagined, that she would never have to make. After the Revolution, perhaps? Who knew?

Suddenly before her eyes, blotting out the terraces, the towers, arose the figure of the purple sibyl. And then it was struck down. Red and purple now. A hand tore the Colgong Star from blood-soaked chiffon.

She tried to replace that fearful image with a picture of Charles, tried again to imagine his reaction to what had happened. But, summoning up his face, she could not make it express an emotion, could not envisage his pallor flushed with anger or grief.

Bad Belinda – she had wanted to ask her mother and step-father more about *her*. But she hadn't been able either to think of a natural-sounding way of reviving the subject or to face the prospect of another of her mother's piercing stares.

She realized that she had never heard Charles mention his parents. Somehow she had formed an impression that they had both died when he was very young, and that that was why he had been brought up by Lady Violet. ('Old Vi' – she couldn't help smiling at the incongruity of that.)

She wondered if Brian knew more than she did. If he did, she was surprised that he had never mentioned it. She determined to probe next time she saw him.

When the train pulled into Paddington, she was waiting in the corridor. As it stopped, she opened the door, was out on the platform. The station was loud with the hiss of steam and the slamming of carriage doors. She decided to take a taxi home. As soon as she arrived there, she would telephone Charles to express her sympathy. It was only common courtesy to do that, and – he might want to see her, after all. She was glad that she had forced herself to finish correcting those essays after lunch.

seven

As the taxi drew up, she saw that Charles's car was parked outside the house. Quickly she paid the driver, opened the front door, and ran up the stairs. As she reached the top, she heard voices inside the flat. She paused, key in hand. Whom had Charles got with him? Then she thrust the key into the lock.

Brian was perched on the edge of her bed, and Charles was sitting in the rocking-chair.

'Charles,' she said. 'Charles, how are you?' He looked just as usual – as pale, as calm.

'I'm quite well, Esther,' he answered.

'Hullo, duckie,' Brian said, but not with quite his usual exuberance. 'How are you? Renewed by the magic of Mortmere?'

She put her coat and her travelling bag down on the table. 'If you knew!' she said. 'I can't tell you how wonderful it is to be back.' But wasn't she being frivolous? 'Charles,' she said. 'I'm so sorry about Lady Violet. How terrible it is.'

'Yes,' he said, but his face, his voice didn't change.

'Charles is more shocked than he realizes,' Brian said gently. 'It's been a terrible day. He spent most of the afternoon with the police.' He added, lightening his tone, 'Charles stayed with me last night. So you see – he has an alibi.'

She smiled perfunctorily. But what she was thinking was: *So he didn't 'find some other diversion'*. He had just stayed at Brian's. How happy she felt! But she must not show it.

'Have you been in touch with Clare?' she asked Charles.

'I spoke to her on the telephone this morning,' he said. 'Of course she was horrified to hear about Violet. But apparently *Momma*' – he put the word in italics – 'is really quite seriously ill. Or so Clare is wholly persuaded. She has to stay there, she insists, for the present.'

'*I* thought,' Brian said, 'that we three should go out for a quiet little dinner tonight. To cheer ourselves up a bit after our dreadful day. And I know how you always feel when you get back from Castle Deadlock, Esther. Just like a limp rag, don't you, duckie?'

She nodded. So coming round to see her had been Brian's

idea. Anyway, what did that matter? Charles was there – that was the important thing. And after dinner? Perhaps Brian would tactfully vanish, and Charles would come back with her? Perhaps he would stay all night?

'I do think, Esther, that you might offer us a tiny drink.' Brian's tone was plaintive. 'I could certainly do with one,' he went on. And indeed, observing him more closely, she saw shadows under his eyes, a quiver at the corner of his mouth. He really did look exhausted. 'I said to Charles,' he went on, ' "Well, you may have the key of the door, dear, but have you got the key of the drinks cupboard?" Just as important, as far as *I*'m concerned.'

She felt herself blush at the mention of the door key, and she moved quickly towards the kitchen. 'I don't keep the drinks locked up,' she said. 'You should have helped yourselves. What would you like?' she asked, from the doorway.

'What have you *got*, duckie?' Brian asked.

'Brandy and gin,' she said, 'and there's a bottle of white wine in the refrigerator.'

'A very large brandy for me,' Brian said.

'I'll have a brandy too,' said Charles.

She poured three generous measures of brandy. Brian took a gulp of his. 'Perhaps that will bring back the roses to my cheeks,' he said.

They drank in silence until, putting down his glass, Charles said 'Well, shall we go and eat?'

'I feel that spaghetti's the answer tonight,' said Brian. 'A large comforting plate of spaghetti with some plonk to wash it down.'

Charles shrugged indifferently. 'That sounds lovely,' Esther said. She tried to speak brightly, but there was a heaviness, a dullness in the atmosphere, which weighed her down. All she wanted was to be alone with Charles, to forget everything: Mortmere, her mother and stepfather, Lady Violet. She wanted to consign them all to oblivion, wanted, herself, to drown in darkness. *He would wind her hair around her throat.*

'There's quite a nice little Italian place just down the road,' she said. 'It's open on Sunday.'

'If it's so near, we won't take the car,' said Charles. 'We'll have a quick meal and then an early night. Brian, I can trespass on your hospitality again, can't I?'

'But of course, Charles,' Brian said.

Depression descended on her. Suddenly she wanted to say that she wouldn't go with them, that she felt too tired. But what a blatant revelation of her pique that would be. She straightened her shoulders. 'I'll just go and wash my hands,' she said. 'I won't be a moment.'

In the restaurant, gloom persisted. It was empty, and a listless waiter registered dissatisfaction when they entered. They sat in silence. Brian abandoned his spasmodic attempts to chatter. *The shadow of Lady Violet is lying over us*, Esther thought. The spaghetti felt thick and greasy in her mouth. She put her fork down. 'I don't think I can eat any more,' she said. She noticed that Brian had eaten hardly anything either, though, restlessly, he continued to twist and untwist the limp, tomato-red strands around his fork. Only Charles ate steadily, winding up the spaghetti with perfect neatness, raising his fork to his mouth, with never a stray end protruding from his lips, never a drop of sauce staining his chin. For some reason, this made her feel even more depressed; there was something robot-like, mechanical, about his movements, something almost somnambulistic. She felt that he was miles away. Where? Was he mourning Lady Violet? Was he missing Clare? A wave of jealousy washed over her mind. How degrading, she thought, to be jealous of that dead old woman, to be jealous of that ninny, Clare.

'Coffee?' Brian asked, when Charles's plate was empty. 'What?' Charles grunted, raising his head. Yes, she had been right. He had been somewhere quite other. Brian repeated his question. 'No,' Charles said, 'no coffee for me.' And Esther, finishing her glass of wine – she and Brian had drunk the whole bottle; Charles's glass was almost untouched – shook her head.

'Well, my dears,' Brian said, visibly gathering himself together, 'it seems to me that bed's the place for all of us.' He grinned suddenly. 'Not the *same* bed of course – or do you think that would be cosy?' But Charles's face was stony, and Esther didn't even try to smile.

Outside, dusk was falling. The street was warm and empty. They walked to Esther's door in silence. Outside it, Charles stirred from his trance. 'I shall probably be seeing you, Esther,' he said.

As she went slowly up the stairs, holding on to the banister – yes, she was weary – it was that 'probably' that gave her hope. If he had just said 'I'll be seeing you,' the prospect would have seemed more remote. He would come, as usual, on Thursday, she told herself, as she opened the door of the flat. She was determined to believe it – if only to brighten the days that stretched between.

The three empty glasses on the table made the room feel emptier. How silent everything was! She had always disliked Sunday evenings. They were sluggish; they left a trail of slime.

She took the glasses into the kitchen, and washed and dried them. She came back into her room, and unzipped her travelling bag.

There, on top, was the newspaper. She avoided looking at it again. She folded it up small, and crammed it into the waste-paper basket. Suddenly the flat seemed very lonely. *Battered to death.* She went over to the wardrobe, opened it, slid her hand to the back of the top shelf on which she kept her jerseys. She groped for, she found the familiar object, wrapped in an old grey pullover she never wore. There it was: the well-kept secret that she had smuggled back from Spain so long ago (feeling that by doing so she had scored some kind of victory over *them*), had hidden at Montmere, had taken with her to London. As always, touching it made her feel safe and strong.

'Somewhere around the place, I suppose.' That was what her stepfather had said yesterday. But he had been wrong. She smiled.

On Thursday evening, she wondered what to wear. She felt – she smiled briefly at the idea – that it would be somehow in bad taste to put on anything too extravagant so soon after Lady Violet's death.

In the end, she chose a striped kaftan which, she decided, she could quite well have worn if she had not been expecting anyone ... and, after all, she wasn't really expecting Charles, was she? She fastened her hair in its everyday, neat coil. *He will unwind it*, she thought – and then: *if he comes.*

At eight, she was sitting in the rocking-chair, holding a book. But she found herself turning the pages without being aware of what she read; soon she put it down in her lap – she would raise it to her eyes when she heard him opening the front door.

It was at twenty past eight that she heard him. But what slow, heavy footsteps mounted the stairs. They sounded so different from Charles's usual light, firm tread that she put her book down on the floor. She half stood up, her hands on the curved arms of the chair. She heard the jangle of keys. It must be he; she willed herself to sit down again, to snatch up her book, as the key turned in the lock.

He stood there. But he looked altogether different. He was wearing old twill trousers and a sweater. Under his arm he was carrying a creased paper bag. He had a stooped look. She stared at him, astonished.

'Esther?' he said, and then again, 'Esther?' His voice was tentative, questioning. He seemed wholly preoccupied. She could see that he didn't notice what she was wearing, what she was doing; it was of no interest to him whether she were reading or waiting. No, none of that meant anything to him.

She stood up. 'Charles,' she said, 'what's the matter?'

'I didn't go to work today,' he said. (Was this meant to be an answer to her question?) Then, suddenly the words jarred from his mouth: 'Oh, Esther. My God. Esther.' He took four stumbling steps towards her, and then he was resting his head on her shoulder. The paper bag he was carrying dropped to the floor, unheeded.

Stiffly, she raised her arms from her sides. Tentatively, she placed her left hand on his arm, hesitated, and then raised her right hand to his head. She started to stroke his smooth hair.

This new form of proximity to him confused her utterly. It was – *different in kind* from anything she had ever experienced with him, before. After a moment she slid her body up against his. He raised his head. Blank, dazed eyes stared into hers, and suddenly became clouded. Slowly, he took a step back.

What was coming now? Of habit, she raised her chin, straightened her shoulders, would have swung her hair except that, she remembered now, it was fastened up. Should she let it come tumbling down?

She took her hand from his head to effect this. But 'Esther, oh Esther,' he exclaimed. He put his hands on her shoulders, and pressed her down into the rocking-chair. His hands felt different today; they seemed to be seeking to draw something

90

from her, rather than to impel her, and as she sank back in the chair, down he came to the floor. He rested his head in her lap. Then he started to rock backwards and forwards, and she and the chair rocked with him. Suddenly a grating sound came from his throat, and his shoulders began to shake.

'Charles,' she said, and heard the unease in her voice. But, tentatively, she raised her hand and, with a kind of distrust, as if she were touching something unknown, she stroked his head again; she had to will herself to do it.

'Can I bear it?' he muttered now. 'I miss her so.' *Whom* did he miss: Lady Violet or Clare? she asked herself coldly. Meanwhile, her hand continued its mechanical movement over his hair, down to the nape of his neck.

At last he raised his head. His cheeks were flushed. His eyes were reddened, moist. She felt it was ... an outrage, as he looked at her from those blurred eyes. *This isn't Charles*, she thought. He murmured, 'Perhaps this is how we were always meant to be.'

No, no, said her mind. *We were never meant to be like this.*

Now he stumbled to his feet, almost dragged himself over to the window, stood there, staring out at the darkening street. She stayed in the chair, rocking just slightly, her hands resting on the curved arms.

Charles had pulled a handkerchief from the sleeve of his jersey. With his back to her, he was dabbing at his eyes. When he turned, his face was almost normal. But the step with which he came towards her was slow, faltering, and when he reached her, it was slowly, falteringly – she had never seen him clumsy before – that he groped for the paper bag on the floor. He picked it up. He placed it in her lap. 'Esther,' he said, 'Esther, be pure for me tonight.'

For a moment, she regarded the crumpled paper bag. As she looked at it, her curiosity revived. Charles was almost himself – *his real self*, she told herself – again. 'Be pure for me tonight' – what strange new game might not that foreshadow?

She opened the bag. She looked inside it. There was a garment there, she saw, with a lifting of her heart. She pulled it out, and shook it.

It was the dress that Clare had worn on their expedition to Glan-yr-Afon. How clearly she remembered the creamy silk, the blue smocking. *A baby's dress*, she had thought then.

'And what,' she said to Charles – her voice was cool and even – 'do you want me to do with this?'

'Do with it?' he said. 'Why, just put it on, and be quiet with me for a little.'

She stood up. 'Sit down,' she said, 'and shut your eyes while I change.' Obediently, he sat down in the rocking-chair.

As she moved around the room, opened the wardrobe, prepared herself, she cast occasional glances at him. He lay back in the chair, his eyes closed, his face once more pale and calm. She went through into the bathroom, to the mirror. When she came back, he had not stirred. Positioning herself in front of him, she said, 'You can look now.'

She was so much taller than Clare that the dress came only to the middle of her thighs. And she had slit it, straight up the centre to the smocked border. Beneath the dress, she was naked, except for black mesh stockings, held up with black rosetted garters. On her feet were high-heeled black sandals.

She had brushed her hair so that it fell in a black curtain over her left eye. What could be seen of her face was a mask of dead-white make-up. Her lips were crimson, and her eyelids were dark with purple shadow.

She had splashed on so much Arpège that she felt as if she were drowning in its heavy sweetness.

'Am I *pure* enough for you now?' she asked him. He started to his feet, and involuntarily she stepped back.

His fists were clenched at his sides. 'How could I have expected understanding from a filthy whore?' he shouted. 'Enseamed with filth. Stewed in corruption. You're all the same. All but her.' He took a step forward, and again she shrank back. Then he thrust past her, was across the room, at the door. Violently he pulled it open, crashed it shut behind him. She heard his footsteps clattering down the stairs, and then the slam of the front door. She sank down on the bed, buried her face in the striped cover.

Later, she kicked off the high-heeled sandals, and wandered through into the bathroom. She washed the make-up from her face, took off the garters, the stockings.

She bundled the mutilated dress into the dustbin. Would Clare miss it? she wondered, not caring. She put on her bathrobe, and went to sit in the rocking-chair.

The icy rage that had possessed her had ebbed away now,

and, of course, she hadn't expected that he would react as he had. She had gambled on her long-held power to arouse him, had imagined that he would once more become 'himself'. Not this other who had come to her for – had it been *comfort*? The idea repelled her.

The Charles she wanted was the statue which, like the Commendatore's in *Don Giovanni*, descended from its pedestal to deliver her into darkness. Had she lost *that Charles* for ever now? If she had, what was there to put in his place? Meetings and lectures? Weekends at Mortmere?

She woke with the feeling of being in a void. It persisted. It was there as she walked to college, worked in the library, drank coffee. In the canteen she saw Tom with an earnest puddingy girl. She smiled, and gave him a little wave. His eyes lit up. She knew how easy it would be to recapture him. But that knowledge did not fill one single inch of the void.

Alone in her flat, that evening, she thought of telephoning Brian. But Charles might still be staying with him. She was absolutely determined to do nothing which could be interpreted as pursuing Charles.

She ate a tin of chilled *consommé* with lemon juice and black pepper. With it, she drank a glass of white wine. Afterwards she felt an impulse to go on drinking wine. Firmly, she replaced the cork in the bottle.

She went to bed, and slept till morning. When she woke, the void was still there, but she felt that she might be able to cope with it. When she had dressed and drunk coffee and eaten a piece of toast, she sat down at her table and worked on a book review she was writing for a left-wing semi-academic journal.

She finished it, and looked at her watch. Ten past one. What was she going to do with the rest of the day? she wondered. She decided that she would go to a film that evening. (Should she ring Tom, and ask him to go with her? *No*.) Beyond to-night, Sunday loomed. Sunday morning was never too bad. In the afternoon she would go to the National Gallery, and perhaps to another film in the evening. She was looking at the cinema programmes in the paper when the telephone rang.

'Esther,' he said, 'you must be at home for me tonight.'

'Charles,' she exclaimed. Then she controlled her voice. 'Yes,' she said. 'Yes, I think I can manage that.'

'I want you to wear a mask for me tonight,' he said. 'A velvet mask, Esther. Black, with little ribbons fastened under your hair. Arrange that, Esther. I want you to be wearing it when I arrive.' And he rang off.

She put down the receiver. *That* had been an aberration. If he could forget it, then so could she. She crunched the newspaper into a ball between her hands. She must buy velvet; she must buy ribbon. She picked up her bag, and she was off. How light her feet felt as she ran down the stairs.

At eight, she was ready, sitting in the rocking-chair, which she had turned so that it faced the door. She had put on a dress of crimson velvet, full, loose, heavy. She had coiled her hair, low on her nape; it looked as smooth, as glossy, as if it had been japanned.

She wore the mask of black velvet, stiffened with thin cardboard. It rose to butterfly points on her temples. The satin ribbons were fastened under her hair. The eyeholes were narrow and slanting. She had spent nearly two hours making it. Now she raised her hands, and stroked the slanting eyepieces. She loved the mask.

She sat, rocking gently. The *New Left Review* lay, unopened, in her lap. She didn't feel impatient. She didn't doubt for a moment that he would come, and, just after half past eight, she heard the front door being opened.

There was the sound of hurrying, almost scuffling feet on the stairs. The key turned, her door was flung open. And there was Charles. He was leading a girl by the hand.

She was so plump, she was so soft, in a drawstring peasant blouse and a brown, woven skirt, gathered at the waist. She was a young cow; she was a little white heifer. Her round firm legs went straight down into her sandals, with no indentation at the ankle – even her feet were like little hooves. Great strings of coloured wooden beads hung round her neck; yes, she was a small white heifer, garlanded. And from her full pink lips, there now issued a sound of astonishment: a moo.

Charles pushed the door shut behind them. 'Esther,' he was saying, 'Esther, I want to introduce Sue. Isn't she pretty? Isn't she sweet?' Raising the girl's hand, he spun her round. *A little white heifer on show*.

Esther was standing up. She was fiddling with the bow that

fastened the ribbons of the mask under her hair. And then, because her hands were shaking so, she gave that up, tugged at one of the butterfly points, tore the mask from her eyes.

'Our Esther,' Charles said to the girl, 'has her eccentricities.' His voice was slightly slurred, and suddenly she realized that he was drunk, observed that his pallor was almost waxen. 'Here she sits,' he went on, 'reading what I am sure is some impeccably left-wing journal' – he gestured to the *Review* which, when she stood up, had fallen, unheeded to the floor. 'And she wears a mask to do it, a black velvet mask. Isn't that amazing?'

'Em-moo' came from the pink mouth. And then the girl made a visible effort. 'Hullo, Esther,' she said. 'Isn't this man perfectly crazy?'

'Oh, absolutely.' She heard her own voice, clipped and cool – why, she sounded exactly like her mother. 'Can't I get you a drink?' she asked the girl.

The girl's round, ruminant eyes, with their curling cow lashes, were circling the room – from the bookshelves to the bed, and back to Esther, standing with the black velvet mask dangling from her fingers. Now her gaze shifted to Charles, became questioning. It was he who must decide whether they should have a drink with this strange woman who spent the evening reading, wearing a red velvet robe and a black mask.

'A drink?' Charles said. He appeared to reflect. 'Yes, perhaps just one, before we go. Sue and I are going on the town tonight, as the Americans say. We're going to paint it red, aren't we, Sue? Though red is really more Esther's colour. So perhaps we'll paint it a royal shade of blue.' He led Sue over to the bed, sat down on it, and pulled her down next to him. 'Let's have some wine,' he said. 'Esther always has a nice cold bottle of wine in her refrigerator, don't you, Esther?'

Levelly she smiled at them, and, in that cool, clipped voice, she said, 'Yes, let's have some wine, by all means.'

Safe in the kitchen, she paused by the window. The disorder of the deserted yard outside jarred on her nerves. She ground her teeth together. The mask still dangled from her hand. She opened one of the kitchen drawers, and pushed it inside.

With extreme deliberation, she moved about the kitchen, taking glasses from the cupboard, putting them on a tray, opening the bottle of wine. She carried the tray through into her room. On the bed, Charles was whispering into Sue's ear.

Sue giggled. She drew a little away from him, as Esther came in.

'Charles tells me you're a lecturer, Esther,' she said in a polite little-girl voice. 'You must be very clever.'

'Yes, Esther is a very clever girl,' Charles said. 'Are you a clever girl, Sue?'

Sue giggled again. 'Me clever? Goodness, no! I could never pass any exams at school, except Art.'

'Sue is an art student,' Charles said to Esther. 'Isn't that charming?'

How did one answer a question like that? Esther nodded and smiled.

Charles stood up, and came over to the table to fetch two of the glasses of wine which Esther had poured out. As he took them over to the bed, Esther raised her own glass to her lips, and drained it. *This has happened before*, she thought. Yes. On the terrace at Glan-yr-Afon. *Clare all over again*. But no, there was a difference. Sue might be little-girlish, but she exuded sex. Sue was rounded, pouting, juicy. Esther poured herself another glass of wine.

Charles, too, had finished his drink quickly. Now he stood up, and came over to the table. He swayed a little, as he poured more wine into his glass. His eyes met Esther's, and what she saw in them, unmistakably, was triumph. She kept her face absolutely expressionless.

Taking a gulp from his glass, he turned towards Sue. 'We must go now,' he said. 'We mustn't keep Esther from her studies any longer.'

Obediently, Sue put her glass down on the floor, and stood up. She came over to stand at his side, by the table. 'Thank you so much for the drink, Esther,' she said. 'It's been so nice to meet you.' Again, Esther smiled and nodded. 'Esther's very quiet tonight,' Charles said.

He put down his empty glass. His right hand went into his pocket, and came out with Esther's keys. He jingled them in his palm. Esther couldn't take her eyes off them. A moment before he did it, she knew that he was going to drop them on the table. How loud the sound was, as they fell, and the silence afterwards was absolute.

Then, 'Come along, Sue,' he said. 'Esther, thank you so much. So nice to see you.'

He had taken Sue's hand again. And now, again, he raised it, and spun her once, spun her twice, over to the door. He opened it, and spun her a third time, ahead of him on to the landing. Quietly he closed the door. She heard their laughter on the stairs.

When lovely woman stoops to folly and
Paces about her room again, alone—

She supposed that the words came into her head because that was what she was doing, pacing from the bed to the table, from the table to the bed.

On the table lay the keys. As she stared at them, they seemed to take on life, to vibrate before her eyes. She blinked. Again she paced over to the bed, where Charles and the girl had sat, where he had murmured into the girl's ear. She picked up the glass from the floor – the drink was hardly tasted. Esther half raised the glass to her lips, and then – suddenly, violently – threw it from her. It shattered against the door.

eight

Days passed, and she plodded through them – or perhaps 'waded' was a better word, for they seemed to drag at her like wet heavy sand.

She woke. She made coffee. She dressed. She went to the college. She lunched in the canteen. She stayed in the library until the evening, when, reluctantly, she would walk slowly home. For she didn't like being in the flat. For the first time, it felt like a prison, rather than a refuge.

Each evening, she forced herself to cook a little meal. She didn't feel hungry, but she forced herself to eat. Really, she decided, everything she did she had to force herself to do. A continual exercise of will power was necessary. *The Triumph of the Will*, she thought, and made a little grimace of distaste,

97

remembering that this was the title of her stepfather's favourite film, the Leni Riefenstahl film of the Nuremburg Rally. She had protested when a college film society had decided to show it in the previous year, and she had been accused of favouring censorship. 'I believe in censoring Fascist propaganda,' she had said. But she had lost; the film had been shown – and she had gone to it. The great square, the ranting murderer surrounded by his henchmen, the flickering torches. She knew that her stepfather had been at the Rally, and had looked out for him, but he had not been caught by the camera which dwelt so lovingly on blank blond faces, on raised arms. Had her stepfather described the Rally in the Memoirs? she wondered.

Always, in the flat, she was listening. But for what? For the telephone to ring, she supposed. It was useless, now, to listen for the opening of the front door, for steps on the stairs, and the jingle of keys.

The Thursday after Charles's and Sue's visit was the worst night of all.

She was running across the park to the little temple. She did not know what she was running from, but she knew that when she reached the temple she would be safe. She gave the mere a wide berth; there was something in the water that would try to drag her down. At last – running, running – she had circled it. Above her, at the top of the mound, was the temple. But there, between the Doric columns, he sat waiting – her stepfather, in his wheelchair. And now he was propelling himself forward. Completely silently, the wheelchair came down the slope, gaining impetus till it was hurtling towards her. And she was frozen; she couldn't move from its path. Now it was on her – he was on her. She woke, hearing her strangled scream in the silence of the flat.

It was three in the morning, and she couldn't get back to sleep. When she got out of bed, at eight, she felt as though she had been drugged. Her eyes were hot and heavy. She was thankful that she had no lecture on Friday. Today, for the first time, she felt unable to move from the flat, unable to move at all. Even making coffee seemed an endeavour beyond her power. She sat on the edge of the unmade bed in her white bathrobe, which, during the past week, she had been wearing all the time, when she was at home. It was looking distinctly grubby, she noticed now, fingering one greyish cuff, but she couldn't face the task of washing it. Anyway, what did it matter if it was dirty? There was no one to see her. But what an admission that was; she was slipping, slipping. She looked round the room, and noticed dust and disorder, last night's supper dishes still on the table. She had thought she had been exerting so much will power; she hadn't realized how much she had let things go. She must pull herself together. Suddenly she felt a pressing need to talk to someone.

Why hadn't Brian telephoned her? She hadn't seen him since the evening she had got back from Mortmere. Could Charles still be staying with him? She determined to risk it. If Charles answered the telephone, she would ring off. She dialled Brian's number.

The ringing went on and on. She was just about to put the receiver down, when Brian answered 'Hullo?' He was breathing heavily. 'Hullo, Brian,' she said.

'Esther! my goodness, aren't you the early bird!' he exclaimed. He sounded peevish. She looked at her watch. The time was half past eight.

'I'm sorry,' she said. 'I didn't think of it being early. Did I wake you up?'

'I must admit you did.' But his voice was friendlier now. 'I had a *very* late night – well, to be accurate, a very early morning. I've been extremely *occupé*, of late. I don't know ... I've been depressed, and I've just wanted to forget about everything. So I've been living dangerously, duckie. Drowning my sorrows, and so on. That's why I haven't been in touch.'

'What's been the trouble?' she asked. 'Why were you depressed?'

'I've had a bit of a problem on my mind. But let's not talk about that now. Perhaps when I see you. I don't know.'

'All right,' she said. Carefully casual, she asked, 'Is Charles still staying with you?'

'Charles?' he said. He paused, and then went on: 'Oh no indeed. I've been busy with quite other matters. Though I've still got that cat on my hands. But Charles is back at his flat.'

'You haven't seen him, then?' she asked. She couldn't stop herself.

'Well ...' Brian was sounding his vaguest. 'I did pop round there the other day ...'

All at once, she understood: *He's got that girl with him. At*

99

the flat. And Brian didn't want to tell her. That was why he was sounding so strange. She said, 'Any news of Clare?'

'Yes, as a matter of fact there is. Apparently the old dragon is much better. Clare will be back on Wednesday next week, unless anything untoward occurs. And about time too, if you ask me.'

'Why do you say that?' she asked.

'Quite the little inquisitor, aren't you, this morning?' Again, his tone was edgy. She thought: *He's only trying to protect me.*

Brian said, 'It's just that I feel Clare is a good influence on our Charles.' His tone was a little grim. Then, 'Must see you soon, duckie,' he said. She had a feeling that he was trying to end the conversation.

Feeling desperate, she said, 'That would be nice. Perhaps I could come round this evening.'

After a moment, he said, 'Well, perhaps not this *very* evening. I have a *guest*' – now he was sounding positively coy – 'who just *may* still be here.' Again he paused. Then he said, 'But I'm sure tomorrow would be all right. Yes, Esther, it would be delicious to see you tomorrow. Actually, I have been quite *distrait*. I think I really would like to talk to you about what's on my mind.'

'How mysterious you're being,' she said.

At the other end of the phone, a male voice shouted something in the background. '*Must* go now,' Brian said hastily. 'Tomorrow, then, About half past six for tiny drinkies. And perhaps a bite to eat, later.'

'Lovely,' she said.

'Bye-bye till then, duckie,' Brian rang off.

She put down the receiver. *Brian's love life,* she thought, with a little shrug. Anyway, talking to him had cheered her. She was looking forward to seeing him. Somehow, she would get him to talk about Charles. She wondered what it was that he wanted to discuss with her.

She could feel vigour and energy returning. Looking round the room again, she frowned and straightened her shoulders. Now she felt capable of dealing with the mess. She rolled up the sleeves of her bathrobe – she would wash *that* when she had finished cleaning.

As she stripped the sheets from the bed, made it again with clean ones, she wondered how she should approach Brian.

Perhaps he might talk more freely if she could manage to make him feel that Charles's affairs were of purely academic interest to her. But wasn't he too perceptive to be deceived in that way? What if she told him that her relationship with Charles was definitely, finally over? After all, that was the way things seemed.

But from the moment he had dropped her keys on the table, her desire for him had been all-consuming.

Punctually at half past six, she was standing on Brian's doorstep. The sky was blue. The sun shone on the window-box, filled with bright pink geraniums, on the glossy white door with its brass knob and letter-box flap.

She pressed the bell at the side of the door, and heard it ring. She waited, but there was no sound of movement inside. Perhaps Brian was upstairs? She took a step back, and looked up at the first-floor windows. One of them was open. She pressed the bell again.

Surely he couldn't have forgotten. He would have let her know if he had had to change his plans. She lifted the flap of the letter-box, and stooped to peer inside. Nothing stirred in the hall, but the glass-panelled door at the end of it, which led into the tiny back garden, was open. She could see a bright green patch of lawn.

She straightened up. He wouldn't have gone out leaving the back door open. Not in this smart, burglar-conscious little street. Unless he had run out of gin or tonic or something, and had gone round the corner for a fresh supply. Perhaps that was it? She looked at her watch. Nearly twenty to seven. He would probably appear at any moment.

She looked down the street. Nothing moved except a cat, which hurried across the road, jumped on to a brick wall on the corner, and was gone. She turned to the door again. Half-heartedly, she gave the brass door-knob a twist. It turned, and the door opened.

She hesitated for a moment. Then she went inside, pulling the door shut behind her. 'Brian,' she called, standing in the hall. Her nostrils pricked, becoming aware of an unfamiliar, distasteful smell. Suddenly she felt that something was wrong, terribly wrong. She wanted to turn and run. She had her hand on the door-knob when she told herself that she was being absurd. Light streamed into the hall from the garden and from the open door of the little drawing-room at the back, which looked onto it. Quickly she walked down the hall, and went through the drawing-room door.

The smell was dreadful. There was a buzz of flies. They hummed and circled around Brian's face, which was clotted with make-up, clotted with blood. His body was huddled at the end of the sofa. It was dressed in a lace and chiffon nightdress, coffee-coloured, stained with dark blood. She could see little golden hairs curling on his chest in the deep V of the neckline. His right hand, a bloody, broken, shapeless thing, was raised, as if he had tried – how hopelessly! – to protect his head with it.

She stood and stared. The sun shone full on to the body. Brian's left arm dangled over the arm of the sofa. She noticed that his fingernails were painted exactly the same colour as his blood. She heard a movement in the far corner of the room, and whirled round.

Its spine arched, a high cry coming from its stretched mouth, the cat, Smoothie, was backed against the wall. She took a step towards it. In a rush, it was past her, and through the door into the hall.

Her heart was pounding. Irresistibly, her eyes were drawn back to the sofa. But something was different now. A shadow had fallen right across Brian's body, a shadow that seemed as tall as a tree.

She could not turn. *She must.* She did. There, outside the window, the shadow loomed, but it was solid; the sun was behind it. A face was pressed against the glass.

part three
1949

nine

'I'm sure that you four are going to be the greatest friends,' Mrs Sidney gushed. 'Being so close in age, and so much older than my other guesties.'

Charles's lids descended for an instant. 'Flinching', Esther decided, was just too strong a word to describe the way in which he showed his contempt. She herself remained impassive. Brian rolled his round blue eyes, and giggled, Geoff looked from Mrs Sidney to the other three with an eager doggy friendliness. If he had possessed a tail, he would have wagged it, Esther thought. His likeness to a dog had struck her several times during the past few days.

'I'm sure you're all going to have a wonderful time,' Mrs Sidney went on. 'Such delightful countryside. Simply super for walks and bicycle rides, and all sorts of jolly things. And there's bathing in the river, of course.' She gestured towards the terrace wall. 'Though it's one of our rules that guesties can't go swimming without a grown-up person. We don't have many rules at Glan-yr-Afon, but we do expect chaps to stick to the ones we have. And chapesses too, of course,' she added, with an arch glance at Esther. 'Anyway,' she concluded, 'one of my two young lady helpers will always be keen for a dip when you want one.'

'Don't you feel that *we* are old enough to swim on our own?' Charles asked, though really it sounded more like a statement than a question, Esther thought. The look Mrs Sidney gave him was uncertain, but just a little timid. Charles did talk in such a very grown-up way.

'Well,' she said, after a moment's hesitation, 'I'm not quite sure about that. I shall have to discuss it with the Major. You're all good swimmers, are you?'

'Oh yes,' chorused Esther, Charles and Brian. Only Geoff hesitated. Then, seeing the cold glances of the other three, he nodded vigorously.

'Well, we'll see,' Mrs Sidney said. 'And now I shall leave you to get to know each other. There are so many things to do, you know, when one takes in guesties. And of course it's not something I've been accustomed to until very recently. I often wonder what my dear mother would have thought about it. But really, when the Major retired, he needed an interest in life. So here we are, don't you know?'

'Yes,' Esther said politely, though she wasn't quite sure what she was agreeing with. Geoff nodded, Brian giggled and Charles inclined his head.

'What a perfectly frightful woman!' Charles exclaimed, as soon as she had left them on the terrace. 'Unbelievably suburban under all that jolly-hockey-sticks stuff. *Guesties*, indeed. *Delaiteful* countryside. As for "discussing it with the Major" – imagine calling one's husband "the Major" anyway! – I'm sure he's completely under her thumb. He drinks. You've only got to look at his skin.' He turned to Brian : 'Did you see his hands shaking on the steering-wheel when he drove us back from the station?'

Esther, Brian and Geoff all laughed rather nervously. *He's very sophisticated*, Esther thought, impressed by the speech, but even more by its cool delivery. She felt that life at Glan-yr-Afon was beginning to develop possibilities. The week she had spent alone – well, with only the Sidneys, the dreary 'lady helpers' and a mob of little kids – had been so horribly boring. How could Mummy and darling Daddy have done it to her? She had begun to feel that she would never be able to trust them again, even though she knew it had been necessary for them to go to Argentina – the reason was something to do with money. 'It will pass in a flash, Esther,' Daddy had said, ruffling her hair. 'You'll have the greatest fun, darling,' Mummy had said more briskly. 'I've had an excellent recommendation of this children's hotel.'

'But I'm not a child. I'm fourteen,' Esther had muttered rebelliously.

'Don't be silly, darling,' Mummy had said sharply. 'I told you that Mrs Sidney said that there would be other people of your age.'

'Esther will cope beautifully when the time comes,' Daddy had interposed soothingly. 'She always does.' And Esther, though reluctantly, had smiled, thawed by the warm sun of his affection.

'Hugo, we must go and change for dinner,' her mother had said. 'It's a long drive to the Marquesa's.' As they went through the french windows that led from the patio into the house,

Esther had heard her add, 'Really, Hugo, you do spoil that girl.' *She's jealous*, Esther thought.

It was an idea which had occurred to her increasingly often, lately, and it gave her an odd feeling of satisfaction. On the other hand, there were disadvantages attached to it – she was sure it was the reason why her mother had decided that Esther should not go to Argentina with them, but should be sent, instead, to the despicable children's hotel.

'Horrible, horrible, horrible hotel,' Esther had muttered to herself again and again, during that first week. And the three days after Geoff's arrival hadn't been much better – Geoff was really pretty stupid, she had decided, and she was irritated by his stammer and the way he followed her about. But these two new boys – Charles, anyway; she wasn't sure about Brian, with his perpetual giggle – were more interesting.

They were all leaning on the terrace wall. 'I suppose we might as well look round the place,' Charles said now.

'There's a t-t-tennis court,' Geoff said eagerly.

'Hard or grass?' Charles asked.

'G-g-g-grass,' Geoff finally got out. His stammer, Esther had already observed, was unpredictable. Sometimes he could talk for ages without any trouble at all. At other times, he could hardly utter two words.

'G-g-g-grass, g-g-grass – it's much softer on your arse,' Brian sang out suddenly. Geoff roared loudly – Brian's mimicry of the stammer hadn't been malicious. Charles gave a faint smile. Esther had never heard the word 'arse' spoken before, and felt herself blushing, even as she gave a little high surprised laugh. Turning her head away, she said, 'It's a pretty putrid court. Mrs Sidney told me that we'll have to roll it and paint the white lines ourselves, if we want to use it.'

'Well, that puts *that* out of court,' said Charles.

'Oh, aren't you the witty one,' Brian said in a tone that suddenly reminded Esther of the way she sometimes spoke to Daddy when they were alone. A sort of teasing way.

'We could walk to the wood,' she said. 'That's more interesting than the other way, where the garden just goes on beside the drive.'

They moved to the left, across the terrace. Brian positively skipped ahead. 'To the wood, to the wood,' he carolled. Suddenly he reminded Esther of Jeremy, who was an old friend of her mother's. Jeremy spent all his time drifting around the Mediterranean on a little yacht, with a blond handsome Swedish boy as crew. Her mother was fonder of Jeremy than Daddy was – Esther had once heard Daddy describe Jeremy as 'decadent'. 'What does that mean?' she had asked. 'Hugo, you're just being stuffy,' her mother had said, but not crossly – she never sounded cross with him except, very rarely, in relation to Esther – and Daddy had smiled and said, 'Oh well, I know you practically grew up together, so I suppose I must be tolerant.' Esther's question had not been answered, and, afterwards, she had looked up 'decadent' in the dictionary. 'Falling away, declining, deteriorating,' the dictionary had said, and she had felt no wiser. But Brian really was very like Jeremy. Perhaps Brian was decadent, too.

On the east side, the terrace led straight onto a small stretch of lawn. From there, the ground sloped down steeply to a gravel path and, beyond that, a very large expanse of grass which needed mowing, though it was still a lawn, rather than a field. There were eleven stone steps – Esther had counted them on one of her boring solitary strolls, the previous week – with a funny sort of stone bear on each side, at the top. They went down the steps, and crossed the gravel path, and started to walk across the grass towards the wood. 'Something's moving in that wood,' Brian said. 'Something black. Do you think it could be wolves?' 'Highly unlikely,' Charles said, but Brian was running ahead, and Geoff was following him with clumsy leaps. 'They're sheep,' Esther said. 'Yes, most people are,' Charles answered. 'No, I meant they're sheep in the wood,' Esther said, and then realized how *unsophisticated* she was being. 'But I do *so* agree with you,' she added hastily – it was an expression of her mother's. Charles smiled quite kindly at her, but she felt that he had not been deceived.

Brian and Geoff had reached the iron railing that separated the grass from the little wood. It was a very small wood – an enormous clump of lilac bushes on their right was almost the same size.

'Black sheep!' Brian was exclaiming as Charles and Esther arrived at the railing. 'Hail to thee, my brothers. My father,' he went on, 'thinks that I am the black sheep of our family.'

'Really?' Charles's tone expressed a certain mild interest.

'Now why does he think that?' But Brian had climbed the railing, and was pursuing the sheep. 'Little black brothers,' he called, as they turned tail and trotted farther into the shelter of the trees. 'Come to Brian,' he pleaded, and the sheep's trot became more rapid, developed into a minor stampede. Geoff leaned against the railing, laughing. 'Oh, I say, Brian,' he gasped.

'Idiots!' Charles exclaimed. 'Silly, aren't they?' she agreed. And yet she had felt a great spring of – *very childish*, she told herself – laughter bubbling up inside her as she watched Brian chasing those sheep.

Now Brian sank down under a tree. The sheep were huddled together in a group, watching him suspiciously. Geoff still leaned against the railing, weak with laughter.

Charles turned towards Esther. 'Let's investigate that mysterious ring of lilacs,' he said. 'Have you been inside it?'

'Inside it?' she said. 'No, I thought it was just a mass of bushes.'

'I don't think so,' said Charles. He was looking at the tops of the lilacs. 'I have a feeling that there's a space in the middle.'

Together, they approached the circle. Charles pushed at the stems of the lilac bushes, tried to part them with his hands, moved on. Proceeding in this way, they arrived at the side which was farthest away from the house.

'Ah!' said Charles.

His hands had separated two of the thickly leafed bushes. He pushed between them, held them apart for Esther to follow. 'Yes,' he said, 'it's a little path.' And, though overgrown, so it was. Leaves brushed against her face as she made her way after him. How closely the bushes on either side were planted!

'Here we are,' he said.

They stood at the edge of quite a large clearing. It took Charles seven or eight steps to cross to a small, tumbledown, log summer-house with a completely collapsed thatched roof. 'Someone's hide-out a long time ago,' he said. 'All the same,' he went on, 'somebody has obviously been here recently.' And he pointed to where, right in the centre of the clearing, a great swathe of grass had been flattened. 'Animals of some kind, do you think?' Esther asked doubtfully. Charles laughed. He said, 'No. I should think quite definitely people.' 'But what could they have been doing?'

'Charles! Esther! Where are you?' From the lawn, Brian was calling. Charles put a finger to his lips. 'Charles! Esther!' For a moment, Esther enjoyed a delightful feeling of conspiracy. Then Charles shrugged. He pushed his way back along the little path. 'Brian!' he called. And then Esther heard him say, 'I permit you to enter.'

'What a s-s-super place!' Geoff exclaimed.

'Mysterious,' Brian said. 'Like Stonehenge.'

'Mmm,' Charles said. 'It would be a good place to have secret meetings.'

'Meetings?' Esther said.

'Yes. If one had some kind of club. Of course,' he added, 'one would be careful about who one allowed to join.'

Esther's and Brian's eyes met briefly. Brian raised his eyebrows, but Esther refused to become his ally against Charles, and glanced away. Charles really looked smashing, leaning against the one remaining corner-post of the summer-house so nonchalantly – a recently acquired word, and one which she wasn't quite sure how to pronounce. He looked like a picture of Lord Byron she'd seen in a book, only tidier.

'I think,' said Charles, 'that people would have to pass some kind of test, before they could become members.' He looked at his watch. 'Tea-time!' he said. 'We'll come here, and talk about it tomorrow.'

'Marvellous,' Brian said. 'Meetings in our own secret ring!'

From that moment, the clearing in the lilacs became the Ring.

They sat on the flattened grass in the centre of the Ring. It was a still hot afternoon with hardly a rustle among the leaves.

'It is called Trial by Ordeal,' Charles said. 'All the really important secret societies go in for it. A person has to prove that he is worthy to join. It's not just a test,' he went on, 'it's a kind of purifying, too.'

They all nodded their heads. Esther wasn't exactly sure what he meant, but all the same, she was fascinated.

'To become a member,' Charles continued, 'a person has to do his very worst thing.'

110

'Worst?' asked Esther.

'Yes,' said Charles. 'The thing that is worst for him.'

'Or her,' Esther broke in again. 'But how,' she asked, 'does one find out what that is?'

'To do that,' Charles said, 'one has to play the Truth Game.'

There was a pause. Then, 'What's the Truth Game?' Esther said.

'There's no need to ask so many questions,' Charles said. 'I shall explain the whole thing to you in a moment.'

She blushed, and was silent.

'We take it in turn,' Charles continued. 'We draw lots. And then the person who is picked has to answer every question we ask them. If they won't answer, or if they tell a lie – I shall know if they tell a lie– they're thrown out and they can never become a member. But if they do answer all the questions properly, then they have to pass an initiation test.'

Esther wondered if Brian and Geoff knew what 'initiation' meant; she didn't but she wasn't going to ask. She decided she'd look it up later.

'So,' Charles said, 'shall we draw the first lots now?'

'Yes,' said Brian. 'Yes,' said Esther. 'Yes,' said Geoff.

Charles felt in the pocket of his khaki shorts, and pulled out a small brown paper bag, which he opened. 'In here,' he said, 'I have three buttons.' He poured them into his hand. 'As you see,' he went on, 'they're all the same size, but two of them are white and one is black. Now I shall put them back into the bag, and shake it. Whoever draws the black one will be the first to do the test.'

'But why *three* buttons?' Esther said. 'Shouldn't there be four?'

'Esther', Charles said. 'I am *in charge* of the tests. I know how to run them, which none of you do. I'm perfectly willing to do the test myself. In fact I want to. But I shall do it last. That's worst, you know. You others will have got yours over when I do mine. Any objections?'

Brian and Geoff shook their heads. 'Esther?' Charles asked. And suddenly he gave her the nicest, the friendliest smile. She couldn't help smiling back. Something in her still wanted to resist him, but there was something else that didn't, and that won. 'No objections,' she said.

'Right then.' He was shaking the bag. 'You'll have to take

it in turns,' he said. 'Esther shall go first because she's a girl.' He smiled again, and held out the bag towards her. 'Shut your eyes,' he said. She shut her eyes, and put out her hand. She touched the bag. She felt for its crinkly paper top. She dipped down inside it, and her fingers closed on two of the buttons. She rubbed them between her thumb and forefinger, but they felt exactly the same, of course. She let one go, and pulled out the other. As she opened her eyes, 'White!' Charles said. 'So it's not you, Esther.' She wasn't sure if she were pleased or sorry.

'Who's next?' Charles asked. 'Me!' said Brian at once. His eyes were sparkling. 'Right,' Charles said. 'Now the chances are fifty-fifty.' He held out the bag. Brian closed his eyes, and felt inside it; with a quick gesture he pulled out the black button.

'So it's Brian,' Charles said. And 'Good old Brian!' Geoff exclaimed heartily. Brian blinked his eyelids rapidly. 'Well,' he said, 'do we start now?'

'No,' Charles said. 'We need plenty of time, and there's only an hour before tea. Let's make it nine o'clock tomorrow morning. Then we'll be free till lunch. We'll tell the old cow that we're going for a nice long walk. She's sure to think that's "jolly super, chaps!".'

Mrs Sidney made exactly this comment, and Brian was unable to suppress a giggle. 'You're a cheerful little chappie, aren't you Brian?' she said. Brian, Esther decided, was Mrs Sidney's favourite among them.

ten

It was fine again, next day, but there was a little breeze, and the leaves of the lilacs shook and whispered.

'Well,' Charles said, 'shall I begin? Esther and Geoff can ask questions too, of course, once they get the idea.'

'Goodness!' Brian said. 'I really feel quite nervous.'

'Right,' Charles said briskly, 'we're off! What is your full name, Brian?'

'Brian Arthur Bennet.'

'What is your father's name?'

'Stanley Bennet.'

'What does he do?'

'He's a business man.'

'What kind of business?'

'He owns a factory.'

'What does the factory make?'

Brian hesitated for a moment. Then, 'Plumbing things,' he said.

'Loos, you mean? Look, he's *flushing*,' Charles said, and Esther and Geoff both laughed.

'And baths and basins, and so on,' Brian said, recovering, but it was true that his colour had deepened.

'And what did your father's father do?'

'He just worked.'

'He was a workman, you mean?'

'Yes,' Brian said, jerking up his head defiantly.

'Is your father a gentleman?' Charles asked.

Brian hesitated. Then he said, 'No, not really.'

'And are you a gentleman?'

'Yes,' Brian said.

'A first-generation gentleman?'

'That's right.'

Esther was embarrassed, but, at the same time, she was fascinated. She'd never known anyone whose grandfather had been a workman. Yet Brian really seemed just like anyone else. He didn't have a funny accent at all.

'What is your mother's name?' Charles asked now.

'My mother's dead.'

A big red brick house with deep heavy sofas and armchairs. On the walls, there were pictures of shaggy highland cattle and draped Roman matrons. Amongst them, his mother's paintings of vases of gladioli and chrysanthemums had, even when he was very small, given him a sense of jarring brightness. 'They – stick out,' he had once said, but she had taken it as a compliment, and had enfolded him in her warm, heavy, scented embrace, which was at once comforting and stifling, like being wrapped in a thick eiderdown. 'Brian is such an artistic boy,' she would tell her friends. 'He takes after me. Now young Stanley, of course, is the image of his father.'

Young Stanley was Brian's elder brother – the elder by seven years. He was dark and stocky, like his father, whereas Brian's mother was big and blonde, and must have been very handsome before she started eating chocolates all day. (Even in the war years, there had always been a big box of soft-centred chocolates at her elbow – neither of Brian's parents had had any scruples about dealing on the Black Market.) But the time came when her small features, her round blue eyes ('Brian has my eyes') were almost buried in spreading flesh. She didn't do much painting any more ('It tires me, you know'), though she still called a big room on the top floor of the house her 'studio', and would still quite often say, 'My Art is such a comfort to me.' But, on the whole, she now expressed her artistic impulses only in her flower arrangements – tall, painted china vases of salmon-coloured gladioli, heavy silver bowls of pink and yellow roses.

'If you talk about "Young Stanley", why don't you call Father "Old Stanley"?' Brian had once mischievously asked his mother. And she had giggled, and said, 'You are a wicked boy,' and had hugged him. There had always been that con-spiracy between them: the conspiracy against the person she always referred to as 'Your Father'.

Brian's father had the habit of calling Young Stanley 'Stan'. His mother hated that; she said it was 'so unrefined'. And on his father's face would appear the heavy sullen sneer which, as Brian grew older, would often be directed at him. Young Stanley learned the sneer early on; he modelled himself on his father.

His mother often told Brian how much she had hoped, before he was born, that he would be a girl. 'But you're just as good as a girl, really, Briony,' she would add. 'Briony' was her secret pet-name for him, which she only used when they were alone. When they were alone, they played such wonder-ful games together. They would go into her bedroom, and Brian would dress up in her scarves and shawls, and put on all her jewellery, and she would paint his face with her make-up, till he looked, as she said, 'just like a beautiful little doll'.

For Young Stanley, the grammar school had been quite good enough, and as far as his father was concerned, it would have been good enough for Brian. But his mother had other ideas. Brian was to go to a public school; Brian was to become 'a real little gentleman'. In order to go to a public school, she learned, you usually went to a prep school. But she could not bear to part with 'Briony' so young. A tutor was engaged through a scholastic agency.

David Harbury-Williams was 'such a nice boy', according to Brian's mother — and 'a right nothing', according to Brian's father. He had a twisted foot which had kept him out of the army — it was just before the end of the war that he came to the Bennets. He was quiet and polite — except when he was alone with Brian, when he would exercise his stinging tongue on his pupil, and his pupil's home, and his pupil's father. He carefully avoided making Brian's mother the subject of his barbed remarks, but Brian observed the cold expression he wore sometimes, as he watched her eating her chocolates and reading the romantic novels which a Birmingham bookshop delivered in a weekly batch of six. They were the only books in the house, apart from Brian's.

Brian was a quick learner, but superficial — 'a real little grasshopper', David would say. Brian tended to forget things easily — except the things David told him about furniture and pictures and clothes, and about what words to use, and how to pronounce them, and which ones were 'not on'.

He longed to hero-worship David. But that was impossible. For one thing — he couldn't help it — David's foot put him off. And then there was David's chill — it froze him. So his mother remained the focus of his feelings. For his father and Young Stanley, he felt a mixture of disgust and fascination. Their maleness was so alien and so extraordinary.

Oh, the look, the smell of Young Stanley's room, with its discarded socks and sweaters, its muddle of Meccano. Stanley and his father were so ... coarse. 'Men are such dirty creatures,' his mother would say. And then, 'But I know you're different, Briony, I know you are.' Or: 'I can't tell you what a terrible time I used to have with your father. But *that's* all over now, I'm glad to say.' (What was *that*? All he could

115

guess was that it was something horrible that men did to women.) And she would take another chocolate from the box beside her. She had a way of nibbling a little of the milk-chocolate coating off, with her front teeth, to see what colour the cream filling was, inside. If it were coffee or marzipan, she would put it aside for the maid. She liked strawberry best, and violet – but she didn't have to test the violet ones, because they were identified by a little piece of crystallized violet, on top.

When he was twelve, his mother said, 'I suppose we really ought to stop our games now. Now that you're such a big boy.' But they didn't. Though, now, when they dressed up, she was careful to lock the door of her room. 'You're still as pretty as a girl, Briony,' his mother would say. He made himself up now – he did it better than his mother could. And as he spread blue shadow on his lids, and rouged his cheeks, the mirror confirmed his mother's words. Yes, he was as pretty as a girl. And he wasn't as silly as girls were. When he met them, he could never think of anything to say to them. If he talked about art, or about their clothes – which always interested him – they looked at him in such a funny way.

He passed the entrance exam to his public school. At the interview, his mother was quiet, awed by the atmosphere of tweed and pipe smoke and books, in the headmaster's panelled study. Brian sat with his hands folded in his lap, nodding and saying, 'Yes' or 'No' when it was expected of him. 'For heaven's sake,' David had said, 'don't giggle, and don't wave your hands about. School life is going to be quite tough enough for you without that,' he had added with grim relish.

How right David had been! The beginning of his first term was a nightmare of jeers and coldness and discomfort. Then, two things saved him. It was discovered that he was a very fast runner over short distances. And Sturgis, the Captain of Athletics, took him under his protection. Sturgis, like Brian's father and brother, was dark and stocky, but, unlike them, was wonderful, was a hero, with his prowess at games and his handsome, acne-pitted face. Brian became Sturgis's fag. And then, one afternoon, after running, when Brian had just started toasting the crumpets for tea, Sturgis suddenly took him to bed. After that, it happened often. Though always, when it was over, Sturgis behaved as if nothing had occurred.

116

Brian was in love. When he came home for the holidays, he could talk about nothing but Sturgis. 'Really,' his mother said, 'I'm getting quite sick of that Sturgis's name. What's so wonderful about him? That's what I'd like to know.' But that was what he couldn't tell her.

During those holidays, it became clear that dressing-up, as he had known it, was over. He and his mother never mentioned it. He missed it – but he knew that he didn't want to do it with her any more. However, once, when he knew that she was out for the whole afternoon, he slipped into her room, and locked the door, and dressed himself in the shawls and scarves – he longed to put on the jewellery, but it was locked up in the dressing-table drawer. He painted himself in front of the dressing-table mirror, and dreamed of Sturgis. If Sturgis could see him now, surely he would think him prettier than any girl?

His mother died, quite suddenly, at the end of his third term at school. It was the summer term – and Sturgis's last term. (How, he had often wondered, would he be able to bear life after Sturgis left?) He was called to the headmaster's study. He went there, shaking with fear. Could they have found out about Sturgis and him? When he saw his father sitting, ill at ease, with the headmaster, he felt almost faint with terror. When he heard what he had been summoned to learn, he felt, yes, an instant's relief: so it wasn't *that*. But then a wave of desolation swept over him. As it receded, he became aware of shame: for his father's accent, his father's loud check suit. He hoped that none of the other boys would see his father.

He was lucky. They were all in their classrooms when he and his father drove away. Because it was only a week before the end of term, the headmaster said that Brian need not return after the funeral. 'Oh, but I'd like to,' he said. But the headmaster patted him kindly on the shoulder: 'No, no, Bennet – quite unnecessary.' All that Brian could think of was that he wouldn't be able to say goodbye to Sturgis. He had lost his mother and Sturgis on the same day.

Almost worse than the horror of the funeral was the steady gloom of life at home: the dark house, the heavy furnishings, the hideous pictures – he could see now that his mother's paintings were particularly nasty – the garden with its dank laurels, its crazy paving, its flowerbeds which were just like those outside the town hall. It was a grey, damp Midlands summer. His father and his brother – whom his father was already calling 'Stan' with happy freedom – quickly took up the normal rhythm of their lives. As far as they were concerned, Brian thought, his mother might never have existed.

Stan was working in the factory now – 'working his way up from the bottom, just like any of the other lads', his father would say proudly. Though of course, Brian thought scornfully, it wasn't like that really. Stan was only spending three months in each department. It was obvious that he was destined for higher things than 'the other lads', but Stan was happy to fall in with his father's pseudo-democratic pretence. In the evenings, Stan was always out with his friends, or taking out girls. His father had given him a small car, a Morris – 'nothing showy'. Why didn't he give Stan a nice flashy sports car? Brian wondered. He could afford to. How boring he found his father's whole attitude to life.

Brian's father spent most of his evenings at the City Club, as he had always done. The last thing Brian wanted was his father's company. But how lonely the house was in the evenings. How dark and dreary it was without his mother. He read a little. He sketched. He went to films sometimes, and pretended that Sturgis was the hero and he the heroine. He had written Sturgis one stiff letter saying he was sorry not to have been able to say goodbye to him. He'd hoped Sturgis might have written back, even if only to say he was sorry to hear about Brian's mother, but he didn't. Perhaps Sturgis had never received the letter. He told himself that that was what had happened, but he didn't really believe it, and every morning he still hurried to look at the post as soon as it arrived.

He began to go up to his mother's room each afternoon. No one else ever went in there. The curtains were drawn. Her things were untouched – her make-up still in the dressing-table drawer, her clothes still in the wardrobe. He would put on her fur coat, and paint his face at the Dolly Varden dressing-table, and pose in front of the long mirror in the wardrobe door. He had found an old fan in a drawer, and he would unfurl it, and bat it to and fro, gazing at the reflection of his painted eyes, over the top of it. 'Poor little Briony,' he murmured behind the fan. That was what he was doing on the day when his father flung open the door, which Brian had forgotten to lock.

He would never forget the expression of horror and disgust on his father's face as he stepped forward. Brian shrank away. 'Did you think I was going to hit you?' his father said contemptuously. 'Ugh, I wouldn't touch you with a barge-pole you horrible . . . thing.' He went over to the window, pulled back the heavy curtains, flung the window open. 'Needs a breath of fresh air in here,' he said, and then, 'more than a breath. Now go on, take off all that stuff.'

Thank heavens, his father stood with his back to him as Brian hurriedly took off the clothes. He couldn't have borne him to see that, under the fur coat, he was wearing one of his mother's satin nightdresses, which hung around him like a shiny pink tent. Quickly he put on his own clothes, and bundled the other things into the wardrobe. His father confronted him. 'Now get out of here, and wash all that muck off your face,' he said. He was staring round the room. 'I must get all this junk cleared out of here, it's overdue for a clean-out.' 'No, please no,' Brian begged. '*Yes.*' His father turned on him. 'I'm not going to have this happening again. Now go on – off!'

As he ran down the corridor, tears welling from his eyes, Brian could hear his father shutting the door of the room, turning the key in the lock. One thing he was sure of: his father would never tell anyone what had happened; he would be too ashamed of his son.

His father avoided him, hardly spoke to him for the next three days. And then, on the fourth day, after breakfast, when Stan had left for work – Stan always went to the factory half an hour earlier than his father – he said to Brian, abruptly, putting down his *Daily Express*, 'I've been thinking, and I've decided that it's no good for you, hanging about here. And, anyway, to be frank, at the moment I just can't stand the sight of you. I've been making inquiries, and I've heard about a hotel in Wales. Just over the border,' he added, as if the nearness of the place would absolve him of any trace of guilt he might feel for sending Brian away. 'A man at the Club told me about it. It's for young people. Wholesome food and plenty of fresh air, and swimming, and so on. I've arranged for you to go there tomorrow, and you can stay until it's time for you to go back to school. Though I never agreed with your mother that it was right for you to go to that fancy place.' Brian's heart was pounding. 'However,' his father added, 'what's done's done. And,' he went on heavily, bitterly, 'it's not likely that you'd fit in with the lads at the Grammar, now.' His father was standing up, was giving him a curt nod. 'The train's at half past eleven tomorrow morning. You can get a taxi to the station. I shan't be in this evening, but I'll see you in the morning, to say goodbye.'

'So you were sent here because you dressed up in your mother's clothes?' Charles said. 'A very funny thing to do, I must say.' But his tone was quite friendly, and Brian heaved a great sigh of thankfulness. It was odd. He really felt quite glad he'd told them. Though he'd managed to leave out everything about Sturgis, and he hadn't told them how much the dressing-up meant to him, saying that it was just a game. 'Like charades,' Esther had said helpfully, and he had nodded eagerly.

'Well,' Charles said, 'the next thing will be to work out your test. But that will take a little time.' Now Charles was standing up. 'Who's for a swim before lunch?' he asked. For that morning he had cornered Mrs Sidney into agreeing – yes, Esther thought, Mrs Sidney was definitely a little in awe of Charles – that they should be allowed to swim on their own. 'I'll be responsible for them,' he had said with one of his rare charming smiles. And she had assented without any more talk of 'discussing it with the Major'.

There were great flat stones in the river, round which the water swirled and eddied. Geoff lingered in the shallows. Brian extended himself on a rock. Side by side, Charles and Esther swam across to the opposite bank. Esther loved swimming – she had done so much in Spain. She outstripped Charles, reaching the bank before he did and, laughing, turned and swam back. She pulled herself up on to the rock where Brian was lying, shaking water over him. 'Don't be so *hearty*, Esther,' he exclaimed petulantly. Charles glided towards them, hardly stirring the water. Drying her hair, she watched him. She found that she was spending more and more time watching Charles.

Silently Charles swam up behind Geoff. He pulled him

backwards into the deeper water, and ducked him. Geoff struggled, as Charles held him under. Geoff's flailing arms had a desperate look, Esther thought. 'Charles,' she called, 'stop!' Charles turned, releasing his grip on Geoff's shoulders. Struggling to his feet, Geoff was pale. He gulped, and fought to smile. 'Poor old Geoff,' Esther said, and then, 'Charles, you're horrid.' 'What an interfering girl you are, Esther,' Charles said. He slid towards her through the water. He grasped her feet and pulled her in. Scraping her leg on the rock, she called, 'Ow!' Now he was pushing her down under the water, but with a twist of her body she slid from his grasp, and struck out into the pool. Now she was laughing, but what she was thinking about was the feeling of Charles's hands on her shoulders, and the sudden closeness of his pale eyes.

She wrote to Mummy and Daddy that afternoon. 'The hotel,' she wrote, 'is not as bad as I thought it was going to be, as there are some quite nice people here now.'

When she came downstairs to tea, carrying the letter, Charles was standing in the hall. He took the letter from her hand, and studied the envelope. 'What cheek!' she said, trying to snatch it from him, but he held it out of her reach. 'Sir Hugo and Lady Severn,' he said. 'What a very strange person for you to be writing to, Esther – Sir Hugo Severn.' 'What do you mean?' she said coldly, and then added, 'He's my stepfather.' 'Is he indeed?' Charles said. 'Well, well.'

'What's so strange about that?' she asked. Her mother had explained that some people in England still had silly views about Daddy, of which she must take no notice, but she hadn't paid very much attention. And now here was Charles giving her this peculiar look.

Charles shrugged. 'It's just that he's very famous,' he said. She smiled, and then he added, 'Famous as a traitor.'

She felt herself going red with anger. 'How dare you say that!'

He shrugged again. 'Well, if it isn't true, why did they put him in prison? And your mother was put in prison too, wasn't she? My cousin Violet says they should have shot them both. They were great friends of Hitler's, weren't they?'

'Who cares what your stupid cousin Violet says?' Esther retorted. And she added, 'Daddy – my stepfather – says that the Führer was a much misunderstood man.'

'Oh, so you call him the Führer, do you? Are you a traitor too, Esther?'

'I simply don't know what you mean,' Esther said. 'Anyway, the war's over, isn't it?'

'Not for my cousin Violet, it isn't.' And Charles gave her one of those wonderful smiles. 'Cool down,' he said. 'I didn't mean to get you so worked up. I was just stating facts. I don't care a damn about them.'

'But they aren't facts,' she said.

'All right, all right.' He put his hand on her arm. 'Let's go and have tea.'

'We'll talk about it another time,' she said.

'If you like.' He put her letter down on the hall table, where the Major picked up the post when he drove into Crickhowell, and they went on to the terrace where, every day when it was fine, the whole household gathered for tea.

Next day, they went for a bicycle ride. 'Bicycles are an extra,' Mrs Sidney told them, and she added, 'Charles's and Brian's and Esther's parents all agreed to reasonable extras, but I'm afraid Geoff's parents didn't.' 'I'll pay for Geoff's bike,' Brian said quickly. 'Are you sure, Brian?' Mrs Sidney said eagerly. 'Yes, quite sure. My father gave me a fiver, when I left.' Five pounds! – Esther was awed by the vastness of the sum.

'Geoff, isn't that nice of Brian?' Mrs Sidney said brightly.

'S-s-super,' Geoff said.

'Brian, what a kind little fellow you are. It's a pity that the bicycles have to be an extra, but in the past guesties have damaged them, and then of course the Major has to pay for the repairs. That's why he decided that we should have to charge.'

'Brian, what a kind little fellow you are,' Charles mimicked, as soon as they were out of earshot. 'Such a dear little guestie!'

'Oh shut up, Charles,' Brian said, but he smiled and looked up at Charles from under his eyelashes. Brian looked at Charles almost as much as she did, Esther had noticed, whereas Geoff always had his eyes fixed on her. Charles had started to tease Geoff about his devotion to Esther, and whenever he did so, Geoff would turn bright red. Charles wasn't nice to Geoff. He treated him with a contempt which he never showed for Esther or Brian. Poor old Geoff – but she did find him rather irritating. He was so slow and clumsy, and his stammer was maddening. There it was again now: 'It's awfully k-k-k-kind of you, Brian,' he was saying.

'Oh nonsense,' Brian said. 'We couldn't all go off and leave you behind.'

Esther glanced at Charles. From the expression on his face, it was clear to her that he would have been quite happy to leave Geoff behind.

In a line of four, they bicycled down the narrow road to Crickhowell, where they were going to look at the old castle: first Charles, then Brian, then Esther, and last of all, Geoff. Brian, being the smallest, had taken the smallest bike – which was too small. He clowned, sticking out his knees at an absurd angle.

It was when they were back at Glan-yr-Afon, and were putting the bicycles away in the shed, that Charles said, 'I think that Brian should do his test tomorrow. But first, Esther and I – and Geoff,' he added perfunctorily – 'will have to have a meeting. Shall we go off now, before tea?'

'All going off to talk about little me!' Brian exclaimed. 'To decide what dreadful fate lies in store for me!'

'What I think,' said Charles, 'is that he should have to dress up as a girl, and walk across the terrace at tea-time, when everybody's there.'

'But mighn't that remind him,' Esther asked, 'of that awful time when his father found him dressing up in his mother's clothes?'

'That's the whole point,' Charles said impatiently. 'He has to do his worst thing. We all agreed that.'

Esther was silenced. Then, 'I suppose so,' she said after a moment.

The three of them went together to tell Brian. When he heard, he said, looking at Charles, 'I *see*.' Then he giggled.

Charles frowned. He said, 'You're not being very serious about this, Brian. It's a serious matter, you know.'

'Oh yes,' said Brian, 'I know.'

Tea on the terrace. The children sat in their low chairs at their little tables. Esther, Charles and Geoff were on their usual bench. Mrs Sidney, behind a trestle table, poured out milk and weak tea. Gwyneth, the harassed maid of all work, and the two horsy girls whom Mrs Sidney called her 'lady helpers' dispensed bread and margarine and what Esther thought of as 'Glan-yr-Afon cake': heavy and yellowish, two squat layers sandwiching a thin scraping of pink, unidentifiable jam. Suddenly, everything came to a halt, the children's chatter died away, the clatter of crockery was stilled.

Brian had appeared on the far left of the terrace. He was wearing Esther's white party dress – lawn, with a toby frill around the neck. On his legs were Esther's long white socks, and on his feet were her red shoes that fastened across the instep with a strap and a button. But she wondered where he had found the white straw hat, decked with two dark red roses, from beneath the brim of which his face appeared, looking tiny, pale against the red cupid's bow he had painted on his lips.

They had told him he must walk across the terrace, but he did more – he pirouetted, pausing to point his toes in the five ballet positions, then extending his arms in an arabesque. Then he began to circle, on tiptoe, faster and faster, whirling across the terrace. Bemused, his audience gazed, following his progress. The children's mouths, bordered with milk and crumbs, were open. Mrs Sidney stood, teapot poised in mid-air; Gwyneth and the 'lady helpers' had paused, frozen in their tracks.

He reached the far end of the terrace. Facing his audience, he raised himself onto the very tips of his toes. From his lips, with his fingertips, he scattered a shower of little kisses as, still on tiptoe, he moved a few steps backwards. Then, with a final pirouette, a final wave, he was gone.

Shattering the silence, the children burst into a great roar. Then, in unison, they began to clap their hands. Gwyneth and the two 'lady helpers' looked around them, as though waking from a trance. Then, simultaneously, they turned their eyes towards Mrs Sidney.

She, behind the trestle table, was convulsed. Tears in her eyes, she gasped, 'Oh, that naughty boy!' Then, once more, she was possessed by laughter.

Brian had certainly come through his test with flying colours, Esther decided. It had been almost as though he had *enjoyed* it. She exchanged a happy, startled glance with Geoff. Then she turned to Charles. But Charles's expression was cold, remote. Charles did not look pleased, and Esther could not understand why.

'Well,' Charles said grudgingly when, half an hour later, the four of them met, as had been arranged, in the Ring, 'you brought it off, Brian.'

Brian giggled. 'Yes,' he said, 'I did, didn't I?'

Then, seeing Charles's frown, Esther understood. Charles had not really wanted Brian to pass his test.

eleven

They bicycled, they swam, they stole fruit from the walled garden – as much because it was forbidden as because they were hungry. They all hated Mrs Sidney – she was so stingy. Although the fruit grew in profusion – peaches, plums, gooseberries – it was doled out to the children very meagrely.

There was a seven-year-old girl called Mary, whose parents hadn't paid their bill – Mrs Sidney was always talking about it, so everybody knew. Poor little Mary didn't get any fruit at all. 'Fruit is really an extra,' Esther had heard Mrs Sidney say, 'even though the Major is so generous that he doesn't charge for it. But no fruit for Mary till her parents meet their obligations, I'm afraid.' Mary always seemed to be on her own. Inevitably, the other children were affected by the outcast role which Mrs Sidney had ordained for her, and they shunned her.

Esther said, 'I think we should do something about that wretched child. The way Mrs Sidney treats her is really cruel.'

Charles raised his eyebrows. 'Do you think so,' he said. And then, 'Yes, it would be rather a tease, wouldn't it, for Mrs Sidney?' From that moment, the four of them made Mary a special pet. Peeling her own peach for Mary, cutting it up for her – she would steal any fruit she wanted for herself, later – Esther would be aware of Mrs Sidney, *seething*. 'Seething is the word for it,' Brian had said gleefully. And little Mary repaid the attention paid her by developing a dog-like devotion to Esther – so now, Esther thought, she had two doggy followers, Mary and Geoff. Mary trotting after her could have become quite boring. But the four were out so much, swimming and bicycling, that, really, it wasn't too bad. 'Perhaps we should drop little Mary,' Charles said one morning when she was hanging round them. 'But think how pleased Mrs Sidney would be if we did,' Esther said, and that clinched it.

It was nearly a week after Brian's test that Charles said, 'I think it's time we drew lots for the second test.'

Again they gathered in the Ring. It was a grey day, with promise of rain. 'There are two buttons in the bag, this time; one white, one black,' Charles said. 'So only one person needs to draw. Come on, Esther.'

'But why me, not Geoff?' Esther asked.

'Ladies first,' said Charles.

'I think that's silly,' Esther answered.

'Do as you're told,' Charles said, and something inside her weakened. She shut her eyes; she stretched out her hand to the bag; she pulled out a button. She opened her eyes, and the button was black.

'So it's Esther's turn,' Charles said. Geoff, she saw, was looking relieved. She picked up the paper bag, to put her button back inside it. She opened it – and saw the other button, as she dropped hers in. Her eyes and Charles's met in a stare.

'Tomorrow,' Charles said. 'We'll meet here tomorrow, after breakfast, and Esther shall play the Truth Game.' He stood up, and so did the others. He motioned Brian and Geoff to go ahead along the little path.

As soon as they had gone, she held up the bag, pulled out the two black buttons: 'You cheated, Charles. You cheated!' she exclaimed. He stepped forward, grabbed the bag, the buttons. How close to her he was. Then he burst out laughing. 'You can't blame me,' he said, 'for putting off Geoff's test? I mean it's going to be so boring.'

'But you don't think *my* test's going to be boring?' she asked. She could feel a flush on her face, and a sort of hotness spreading all over her body. Suddenly she was aware of her nipples swelling under her green aertex shirt. Confused, she swung away from him.

'No, Esther,' he said, 'I'm quite sure it isn't going to be boring.'

In bed that night, she wondered what her *worst thing* was. She realized that she hadn't any idea. What Charles had thought was Brian's worst thing hadn't turned out to be so bad in the end. *Could*, she suddenly wondered, *one's worst thing be, in a way, one's best thing*? But that sounded like absolute nonsense. Anyway, perhaps she would find out what her worst thing was tomorrow when she played the Truth Game?

'What is your full name?
'Esther Arabella Farringdon.'
'What is your father's name?'
'My father's dead.'

She could hardly remember her father at all. There was just one picture of him in her mind. He was standing at the bottom of a flight of stairs. 'Jump,' he had said, and she had jumped the last four steps, and had been caught up in his arms and swung high in the air – a wonderful feeling. Her father had been in uniform – he was a soldier – and he had a bristly moustache. In the picture, her mother was standing at her father's side in a long soft jersey and a smooth pearl necklace.

That was all she could remember; she couldn't remember the divorce – her father had let her mother divorce him, though it had been she who had left him, running away with Hugo Severn. Her father had been killed in the first year of the war. By then Esther's mother and stepfather were in prison with Sir Oswald Mosley and other British Fascists. Mosley was the head of the Fascist Party, but Esther's mother always said that Hugo had been 'the coming man', that he might have been Prime Minister, if it hadn't been for that quite unnecessary war, and that stupid obstinate Winston handing half the world over to the Reds.

She remembered being taken by Nanny to see her mother in prison. There were clanging gates and women in uniform. Esther and Nanny had been shown into a little room where her mother sat on one side of a table and they sat on the other. Esther had cried when they had to go and Nanny had had to carry her out, kicking and screaming. She didn't visit her mother again – it had been decided that it was too upsetting for her.

She and Nanny had stayed with her stepfather's aunt in the Dower House at Mortmere. They went for walks in the park. She remembered a winter when the branches of the trees had clinked like the lustres of the chandeliers when the maid cleaned them. They never went to the house itself, which was full of soldiers. Whenever Esther passed one of the soldiers, she turned her head away; she thought of them as the people who had put her mother in prison for two years, and her stepfather for three. When her mother was released, they had moved to a house in a village near Stratford-upon-Avon, an old red-brick rectory – the village church was in their garden. Esther and her mother and Nanny went to the church on Sundays, but no one spoke to them afterwards except the vicar. When, after a year, Esther's step-father joined them, some people got up a petition to stop them living there, but nothing ever came of it.

At that time, her stepfather had been always pacing, pacing the dark rooms of the rectory, pacing the country lanes with Esther at his side. He had spent a lot of time with Esther. It was at the rectory that she had come to love him so much, and had started to call him Daddy.

Sometimes when he talked to her, she felt that he was really talking to himself. She didn't understand a lot of things he talked about, but she picked up bits and pieces, here and there. 'I'm not against England, Esther,' he would say. 'You must never think that. All I wanted was a better England, a stronger, prouder England. The Führer never wanted war with England, Esther. He often told me how much he admired the English nation. It was all the fault of the bankers, of the international Zionist conspiracy. But there, Esther,' he would say, breaking off, 'you don't understand what I'm talking about. But you will, Esther, you will when you're older, when you're grown up. Though heaven knows what kind of world we shall be living in then.'

Daddy and Mummy gave Esther lessons. Daddy taught her Arithmetic and Geography and History, and Mummy taught her English and French. She remembered some kind of school inspector coming to the house and asking her a lot of questions. Apparently the answers were satisfactory, for Daddy and Mummy continued to teach her. But when the man had gone, how angry Daddy had been. 'The days when an Englishman's house was his castle have certainly gone for good,' he had said. 'Now any little jumped-up busybody can just walk in.' And, as always when his colour mounted, and his hands began to shake, Mummy had calmed him down. 'Don't get upset, darling. It simply isn't worth it.' How often Esther had heard her mother speak those words.

At last, the war had ended, and a few months later, they had moved to Spain. Daddy owned property in Spain and in Argentina, as well as Mortmere. Esther had always known that they were very rich. When they moved to Spain, Nanny stayed in England, pensioned off, and Esther had a Swiss governess. The governess stayed for nearly four years. But then, just when Daddy and Mummy were going to Argentina for six weeks, her mother in Zurich became ill, and she had to go home. Otherwise, Esther would probably have stayed with her in Spain, at the villa, and would never have come to Glan-yr-Afon, to the children's hotel.

'What do you feel about your stepfather being a traitor?' Charles asked.

'He isn't,' she said fiercely.

'He was on the side of the enemy,' Charles said, and Esther answered, 'The Führer never wanted to go to war with England.'

Now it was Brian who spoke. 'But what about all the awful things Hitler did? Like killing the Jews, and putting them into concentration camps.'

'I've never heard that he did that,' Esther said. 'I'm sure it can't be true. What's a concentration camp, anyway?'

'Hitler herded all the Jews into dreadful prison camps – that's what they were – and tortured them, and killed them in gas ovens.'

'He didn't, Brian,' Esther said. 'It's a lie. Daddy wouldn't have believed in him if he'd known that he'd done that.'

'But everybody knows that's what went on.'

'Why didn't I know then?' Esther asked defiantly.

'Well, you were away in Spain, weren't you? And of course your stepfather wouldn't have told you,' Charles said. 'But every grown-up person knew.'

If everybody had known, then Daddy would have been sure to. He knew so much about everything.

'I don't believe any of it,' Esther said.

'Well, we shall have to prove it to you,' Charles said. 'If I showed it to you in a book, would you believe it then?'

'I don't know,' she said. And then, 'I don't believe there is such a book.'

'If there were,' Charles taunted, 'you wouldn't read it. You'd be too frightened.'

'I would read it,' she said hotly. 'I'm not afraid to read anything.' She remembered a terrible book called *Ghost Stories of an Antiquary*. There had been a shapeless thing that climbed out of a tree at night, to steal children. She could hardly bear to read the stories, even during the day, because they frightened her so much. She had kept her bedside light on all night, for nearly a week. But she had finished the book. Charles's book, if it existed, couldn't possibly be as bad as that.

Charles was standing up. 'You swear you'd read it?' he said.

'Yes, I swear,' she said, tossing her plait back over her shoulder.

Two days later, they bicycled to Llangynidr, a village which they reached by taking the winding climbing lane on the left of the drive. They bicycled between high hedges, then freewheeled down a steep hill to a long, ancient stone bridge over the Usk. In the village on the other side of the bridge, they bought sweets at a little shop – for Brian had brought his sweet coupons. Leaning on the parapet of the bridge, they ate all the sweets, and then started back to Glan-yr-Afon. They were nearly back at the gates, when Charles said, 'Look!' He got off his bicycle, and Esther, Brian and Geoff did the same. Through a gap in the hedge on their right, they could see, far below, a stretch of the gravel in front of the hotel.

Charles looked up to where, on the other side of the road, a tall field rose above the hedge. 'If we climbed to the top of that field,' he said, 'we would be able to see the whole of Glan-yr-Afon.'

They parked their bicycles just inside the gate to the field. They climbed to the top of the steep slope, and looked down. Below them were spread the hotel and its gardens, reminding Esther of a toy farm she had been given when she was little.

There was no one to be seen – the children rested on their beds in the afternoon. Faintly, she heard the clock on the west tower chime three times, breaking the glass dome of silence in which the house seemed held.

She could see two of the black sheep at the end of the wood; they were little toy animals. The thick bushes around the Ring were a clump of toy trees. And then she saw the Major, curiously furtive, moving towards it.

It was at the back of the Ring, by their entrance, that he paused. He turned and looked quickly all round him. Then he pushed in, where the little path was, and the bushes concealed him. 'How very, very strange,' Charles said.

'Look!' Brian exclaimed. From the old stables, next to the walled garden, a fat little figure was creeping. 'Gwyneth,' said Esther, for it was the little maid of all work, with the bow legs that so many of the peasants in Spain had. 'Rickets in childhood,' Daddy had explained. 'They're stupid – they don't feed their children properly.'

Gwyneth, like the Major, was looking to left and right, as she sidled along by the garden wall. Then she hurried over the grass, and she too vanished into the bushes at the back of the Ring.

'The Major and Gwyneth! What c-c-c-can they be doing?' Geoff said.

'What do you think they're doing, you fool?' Charles said. For a moment Esther didn't understand, and then a burning blush covered her face. The Major and Gwyneth – oh surely not!

Though Gwyneth was ugly, with her bow legs and greasy hair and blackened teeth, she was quite young. And the Major was so old. Esther imagined his short grey hair and his pouchy eyes and the purple veins on his nose which Charles said came from drink. Sometimes, in the evening, when the four of them had cold supper with the Sidneys, after the children had gone to bed, he talked in a funny slurred voice, and stumbled when he walked, while Mrs Sidney looked daggers. Silly old Major! Though he wasn't as awful as Mrs Sidney.

'Well,' Charles was saying, 'I vote we investigate this further. Not this afternoon – we probably wouldn't be back in time. But on other days we could keep watch – in the bushes perhaps. Or we could hide behind the old summer-house.'

As they parked their bicycles in the stables, Charles said, 'Just think if Mrs Sidney found out about the Major and Gwyneth.' Esther didn't really want to think about that. There was something about Mrs Sidney, though she was always so polite to the four of them, that rather frightened Esther. Sometimes she had such a horrible look on her face when she talked to little Mary – the same look she gave the Major when he stumbled about in the evenings. Esther had had a dream a few nights before in which Mrs Sidney turned out to be a witch – she hadn't told the others because it was so babyish to dream about witches.

'If we keep watch, and find something out, what would we do?' she said to Charles.

He shrugged. 'I haven't thought about that yet,' he said. 'It's the tracking that interests me at the moment.'

Next morning, after breakfast, Charles disappeared. Esther wondered where he had gone. She went to the stables, and found that his bicycle was missing.

It was a warm grey day which gave her skin a clammy feeling. Suddenly she didn't want to spend the morning with Brian and Geoff. She went up to her room, and fetched *Jane Eyre*, which she was reading for the first time. She put it in her bicycle basket, and pedalled off down the drive. She went to the tall field where they'd been the day before. She sat with her arms round her knees, looking down at the hotel. It gave her a powerful feeling to be up there, watching but unseen. The Major was setting off down the drive with his rake and wheelbarrow. *The Major and Gwyneth*, she thought – *could Charles possibly be right*? She opened *Jane Eyre*, and began to read. She thought Mr Rochester was super. He was mysterious – rather like Charles, in a way.

She became completely absorbed in the book. At last she looked up, and glanced at the little watch that Daddy had given her on her thirteenth birthday. Half past twelve. How quickly the morning had passed. It was time to go back for lunch. She stood up and stretched, and looked down at the hotel. Charles was getting off his bicycle outside the stable. He took it inside, and came out carrying something – a little parcel. And suddenly she knew what it was. It was *the book*, the book that she had sworn to read.

She was right. After lunch, it started to rain, and she wanted to get back to *Jane Eyre*. 'I'm going up to my room to read,' she told the others.

Her room was on the attic floor. It was small, but quite comfortable. Charles, Brian and Geoff shared a much larger one – almost a dormitory – on the floor below. She had just become immersed in *Jane Eyre* again, when there was a knock on the door. 'Come in,' she called. It was Charles. He came in, and went over to the window, where he leaned against the sill. His eyes lighted on the two big leather-framed photographs of Mummy and Daddy, which were on the dressing-table with her Mason-Pearson hairbrush, her comb, a bottle of Yardley's Lavender Water, and the jar of hand lotion her mother had given her, which she never remembered to use. 'Your mother and your stepfather?' he asked. She nodded. 'They're both very good-looking,' he said.

He had been holding his right hand behind his back. Now he brought it forward. In it was the book. He came over to the bed and handed it to her. 'Here you are, Esther,' he said. 'I bought it in Abergavenny this morning. Now, are you going to keep your promise?'

'Of course I am.'

'Right then,' he said. 'I'll leave you to it,' and went out of the room, closing the door quietly behind him.

She just looked at the cover of the book for a minute or two. The cover was yellow with a scarlet swastika on it. The book was called *The Crooked Cross*. Really, she didn't want to open it at all, she realized. How she wished she could return to *Jane Eyre* instead. But she had sworn. And wouldn't it be better to get it over as quickly as possible?

Across Europe marched an iron column of iron men. And wherever they marched, they brought torture and death. The words were bad enough – there were moments when she squeezed her eyes tight shut, as if to try to blot their meaning from her mind with darkness. But she read on. Then she came to the section of illustrations. Those, she knew, she would never be able to blot out. Those skeletons in their striped rags. with their great eyes, made her draw in her breath. But somehow the worst picture of all was one of a little boy in a peaked cap, with his hands above his head, who was being driven along by a heavy, helmeted figure.

It would have been impossible not to believe those pictures. *She believed it all.* So this was why Daddy (ugh; it seemed disgusting to call him Daddy now) wasn't popular in England; because this was what he had believed in. This was the reason why he had been put in prison; this was the reason why they had moved to Spain. Everything he had ever told her was a lie, and, behind all the lies, were the living skeletons with their branded arms, was the smoke coming from the chimneys of the gas ovens, was the little boy in the peaked cap. Skimming over the political bits, she finished the book. She closed it, but her fingers fumbled it open again, to turn the pages of photographs once more.

Everything was different now. Somehow, everything was shades darker: the room around her, the thoughts inside her head. She put the book into one of the dressing-table drawers, under a pile of clothes, and shut the drawer. She'd done that with *Ghost Stories of an Antiquary,* and it had seemed to help to distance her fear. But it didn't help this time. This was real, and *Ghost Stories of an Antiquary* suddenly seemed silly.

She stood by the dressing-table, staring at the photograph of her stepfather. (After all, he wasn't her real father; he wasn't truly Daddy; her Daddy was dead.) From his dazzlingly white collar and beautifully knotted tie rose his head. His thick moustache, his bright eyes, his handsome aquiline nose – all the features of his face looked different to her now. And her mother's neatly perfect features, slightly misted by the photographer, looked different too. How could her mother have left Esther's *real father* for *him*, for the man who approved of the skeletons, the ovens? *In one of the concentration camps, a wardress had made lampshades out of human skin.*

There was a tap on her door. Automatically she said, 'Come in.' The door opened and Geoff looked round the edge of it. 'Are you all r-r-r-r-right, Esther?' he asked. 'You're late for tea.'

'I'm quite all right,' she said.

'Are you sure?' Geoff persisted, coming farther into the room. And suddenly she broke. She flung herself on to the bed; she was sobbing; she was burying her face in the pillow. After a moment, she felt Geoff's nervous hand on her shoulder, giving it little pats, and she heaved her shoulders to shake his hand off, but he went on patting, and she didn't try to stop him again. He was saying, 'Cheer up, Esther. P-p-please cheer up.' She went on crying till, at last, her eyes felt hot and dry.

She shook her head. She got up, and went over to the jug and basin that stood on a washstand in the corner of the room. She dipped her flannel in the jug, and wiped her face until it felt cooler. Then she dried it, and looked at herself in the dressing-table mirror. She didn't look quite as bad as she'd expected, though her eyes were red. She pinched her cheeks to make them pinker, so that her eyes wouldn't be so conspicuous. She turned to Geoff. 'You mustn't tell anyone,' she said fiercely. 'You mustn't tell Charles or Brian.'

'T-tell them what?' he asked.

How stupid he was! 'That I was crying, of course,' she said scornfully. 'Swear that you won't.'

'Of course I won't if you der-der-don't want me to,' Geoff said. He had that doggy look on his face.

'Swear,' she said.'

'I swear.'

'All right then.' Her hair was looking very untidy, she saw in the mirror. Briskly she unplaited it, aware of Geoff watching as it tumbled down, so thick and brown. Briskly she brushed it, and started to plait it again.

'You've got super hair,' Geoff said.

'It gets in the way,' she said. 'I shall cut it all off soon.'

Her mother had suggested that Esther should have her hair cut, but Daddy – *her stepfather* – always said that he liked it long. 'I shall cut it off *now*,' she said.

'Oh Esther, don't do that,' Geoff pleaded.

She opened the top drawer of her dressing-table, and took out her nail scissors. She pulled the long thick plait forward over her shoulder, and started to hack at it with the curved blades.

'Oh please, Esther, der-der-don't,' Geoff was bleating. She increased her attack on the plait, driving the scissors through it. It was heavy going, but, at last, with a final jab of the scissors, the long snake of hair came off in her hand. It felt so thick and solid and warm – almost as though it were alive. *A part of her.* She dropped it into the wicker wastepaper basket by the dressing-table. 'That's better,' she said, shaking her head, and then running her hands over it. Her hair had a ragged lopsided look. She brushed at it angrily. 'Let's go downstairs now,' she said, 'and see what the others are doing.'

When she woke next morning, the sun was shining brightly. *Super,* she thought – *we'll be able to swim.* She sat up, and as she did so, remembered everything. She lay down again, and pulled the bedclothes up around her neck. She shut her eyes tightly, but she knew it would be no use; she would never be able to get back to sleep. After a minute or two, she opened her eyes again, and sat up. Her hand went up to her head, and she felt the uneven straggle of hair round her neck.

'Oh Esther, your pretty hair!' Mrs Sidney had exclaimed when, followed by Geoff, she had slouched defiantly on to the terrace where everyone was finishing tea – it must have stopped raining long before; she hadn't noticed.

'Thought I'd cut it,' she said. 'It got in the way, and it made me feel hot.'

'Oh Esther,' said Mrs Sidney, 'I do hope your parents won't be annoyed.'

'My mother won't mind,' Esther said. 'She's often said I should have it cut. And it's nothing to do with my stepfather.'

Her eyes suddenly met Charles's, and quickly she looked away.

'It's a *leetle* bit untidy,' Mrs Sidney said with heavy tact. 'Would you like me to trim round the edges for you?'

'No thanks. I think it's all right,' Esther said stubbornly.

Mrs Sidney closed her eyes for a moment, with a martyred look. She sighed. 'Dear me, you young people are so headstrong,' she said. And then – *putting on her cloak of heartiness again,* Esther thought – 'Oh well, boys will be boys – and girls will be girls, eh, Esther?'

'Well, well,' Charles said, when the four of them had left the terrace, 'now I shan't be able to pull your hair, Esther.'

'Perhaps that's why I cut it off,' she said, tossing her head. It was strange not to feel the heavy plait swing in response.

'Goodness,' Brian said, 'if I had hair like that, I couldn't chop it off, I can tell you.' And they all laughed at the idea of Brian with a plait. 'What did you do with the part you cut off?' he asked.

'Threw it in the wastepaper basket,' Esther said briskly. 'Why? Do you want it, Brian?'

'Just what he needs for *dressing up as a girl*,' Charles said, and they all laughed, but Brian was blushing.

'You can have it if you like,' Esther said.

Brian shook his head. 'What nonsense,' he said. 'Of course I don't want it.' But when Esther went to bed that night, she noticed that the plait had gone.

'Meeting in the Ring at ten,' Charles said softly at breakfast, when she sat down next to him. In the dining-room, they always sat at the end of the long table that was farthest from Mrs Sidney. The Major never came to breakfast – 'His hangover's probably too bad,' Charles had commented knowingly, one morning.

'Well,' he said, when they were all seated in the Ring, 'there are two things we ought to deal with this morning. The first is Esther's test. We can get that done right away. And then we'll move on to the question of the Major and Gwyneth.'

We can get that done right away. 'But haven't I done my test?' she said.

'Reading the book?' said Charles. 'No, that was only half of it. But you did read the book, didn't you?'

'Yes,' she said.

'And did you believe it?' he asked.

'Yes,' she said, very quietly.

'So what I told you about your stepfather is true?'

'Yes,' she repeated.

'Well, Esther,' Charles said, 'then I think you ought to prove that you don't like him any more. Esther, I think you ought to burn that big photograph of him that's in your room – burn it here in front of us.' And he took a box of matches from his pocket, and dropped it on the grass.

'Oh I s-s-say,' Geoff protested, and Brian said, 'Oh Charles! After all he is her father – well, almost.'

'No, he's not,' Esther broke in. She turned to Charles. 'Yes, I'll do that,' she said. 'I don't mind at all.' He lowered his eyes. She'd known he wouldn't like that, wouldn't like her *not minding*. Because he hadn't liked that with Brian. How hard and strong she felt! She stood up. 'I'll go and fetch it now,' she said.

Once outside the Ring, she started to run. She ran up the slope, up the steps onto the terrace; it was quicker that way.

Mrs Sidney was sitting on the terrace in a circle of children. She was reading them a story. Little Mary was standing at some distance from the others – had Mrs Sidney told her she couldn't listen? Esther wondered. 'Goodness, you *are* in a hurry, Esther,' Mrs Sidney broke off to exclaim. 'Esther, can I come and play with you?' Mary asked. She started to jump up and down.

'No, not now, Mary. I'm busy,' Esther said sharply. She saw the pleased expression on Mrs Sidney's face – and she saw how Mary's face fell. But she didn't care if Mrs Sidney were pleased; she didn't care if little Mary were unhappy. Suddenly, she didn't feel that she'd ever care much about anything, ever again.

She hurried in through the terrace door. Mary was setting up a wail, and Mrs Sidney's voice rose harshly. Up the stairs Esther ran, two steps at a time. She flung open the door of her room.

At the dressing-table, impatiently, she fiddled with the catch on the back of her stepfather's photograph, pulled out a sheet of cardboard, and then the photograph itself. For a moment, she hesitated, and then, quickly, she took her mother's picture out of the other frame. She bundled the two frames into the dressing-table drawer that had *the book* in it. Then, with the two photographs, face to face, in her hand, she left the room, slamming the door behind her. She'd better go out of the front door, she decided, in order to avoid Mrs Sidney and little Mary.

As she pushed through the bushes, Charles said, 'That was quick.' She heard her own breathless laugh. 'Yes, it was,' she said, 'wasn't it?' She bent down and placed the two photographs, face upwards, side by side, in the very centre of the Ring. Now they were all looking at her with surprise – even Charles. Brian exclaimed, 'Oh Esther, not your mother's picture too! You don't have to do that.' After an instant's pause, Charles said, 'You were only told to burn your stepfather's photograph.'

'They must burn together,' she said, and no one else said anything. She moved the photographs closer to each other, so that their inside edges were touching. Then she picked up the box of matches that Charles had dropped on the ground. *Like a gauntlet*, she thought – well, she had accepted the challenge.

She struck a match. Its flame was pale in the bright air. Carefully she stooped, and held it to first one, then the other outside corner of her stepfather's photograph. Both caught light. The match went out. She struck another, and lit the corners of her mother's picture. 'Your hand's shaking,' Charles said. 'That's because I've been running,' she replied. Again, when she looked straight at him, he lowered his eyes. She remembered reading, in *The Jungle Book*, that if a person looked into the eyes of a wild animal, it would always be the first to look away. That was what she was doing with Charles, she thought, and she laughed again.

The flames were growing, were spreading towards the centres of the pictures. The edges went curling up, and then crumbling. The left side of her stepfather's face was gone now. The flame was eating away her mother's cheek. Now the flames were rising higher, and moving faster. At last they met in the centre; they rose, and then died. She stood up, and she stamped on the crumbling blackened paper, crushing it into ashes beneath her heel. 'There,' she said. 'There.'

There was a silence. Then Geoff said – there was doubt in his voice – 'You did jolly well, Esther.' Charles gave a little, non-committal nod. Brian, Esther realized, with sudden exhilaration, was shocked. He said nothing. He was looking down at the ground. Oh how strong she felt!

'Well,' Charles said, 'we come to the subject of the Major and Gwyneth.'

twelve

It was the third afternoon on which they'd set the trap. Charles, Esther and Brian lay, side by side, on their stomachs, propped on their elbows, their palms cupping their chins. They were screened by the logs of the summer-house, but through the gaps between the logs, they had an excellent view of the centre of the Ring.

The string was wound tightly round Charles's fingers. The string was a long length of green cotton. The other end of it was held by Geoff, who was crouched in the little wood, behind a tree. The signal they had arranged was that, if he saw any-one approaching the Ring, he would tug violently at the string, and then release it. Geoff had not protested at being given this distant role, but he had looked a little downcast. 'It's the most responsible part of the operation,' Charles had told him, and Esther had nodded vigorously.

Esther lay between Charles and Brian. She was conscious of Charles's arm touching hers. Brian's hair smelled of sham-poo. 'Don't *breathe* on me, Esther,' Brian said peevishly, giving a little wriggle of his body. 'I have to breathe, you know, to keep alive,' she whispered crossly. At that moment Charles's arm stiffened. Esther saw the string jerk, and then go loose. They were all suddenly and absolutely still.

A minute passed. Then they heard a rustle of branches from the direction of the little path.

It was Gwyneth who appeared in the Ring. She was wear-ing her blue uniform overall, but not her apron. Her dank hair straggled round her neck. She raised a hand to scratch her head, and Esther saw a dark patch of sweat under her arm. She sank down on the ground in the centre of the clear-ing, and kicked her shoes off. Esther noticed how dirty her feet were.

Again a rustle came from the pathway. Charles gave a tiny inhalation of breath as the Major shambled into the Ring, in his baggy grey flannels and old Viyella shirt.

Gwyneth giggled. And then the Major was down on the grass beside her. His hand fumbled with the buttons of her

140

overall. From the front of it, he pulled out a big white breast. He squeezed it.

At one point, as the Major and Gwyneth rolled and grunted in the Ring, Esther closed her eyes. When she opened them again, Gwyneth's bow legs were waving ridiculously in the air. At that moment, Brian gulped. She glanced sideways at him. He had both hands pressed over his mouth, but vomit was oozing between his fingers. Hastily she looked away.

She felt as if it were going on for ever. But really, she supposed, when it ended, it hadn't lasted all that long. The Major rolled off Gwyneth's body, and then both of them began to fasten their clothes. Neither of them, Esther realized, had spoken a single word.

It was the Major who left first. He moved towards the little path. Gwyneth called, 'Hey!' She was sitting up. There was a sullen look on her face. The Major stopped, and turned round. He felt in his pocket, and pulled out a crumpled banknote – Esther couldn't see if it were a pound or ten shillings. Slowly, he came back, and slipped it into Gwyneth's outstretched hand.

After he had gone, Gwyneth stayed sitting in the Ring for a few minutes. Then she yawned, she stretched. She stood up, and scratched under her skirt before making her way towards the path.

When the sounds of her going had died away, Esther, Charles and Brian on a shared impulse, moved apart. Brian rolled over. He wiped his hands on leaves. Then he got up, and without looking at Esther or Charles, groped blindly round the summer-house. They heard him stumbling along the path. Charles was sitting up now, his elbows on his knees, his hands clasped on top of his head – *as if he were holding his brains in,* Esther thought suddenly. 'Beasts. Filthy beasts,' he said. 'That's what people are.' Then he stood up. He shook his head violently. He said, 'Well, now we have the Major in our power.'

'In our power? How do you mean?' said Esther.

'We could make him do anything we wanted, if we said that otherwise we'd tell Mrs Sidney.'

'What sort of thing?' Esther said.

'I don't know. I shall have to think about it.' He shrugged.

'Meanwhile, I suppose it's about time that Geoff played the Truth Game.' He paused. 'Do you think the Major and Gwyneth *enjoyed* that?' he said.

'I don't want to talk about it,' said Esther.

'Oh, so Esther's on her high horse, is she? One of these days someone will take you down a peg or two.'

'Well, it won't be you,' she said. Suddenly she was feeling better.

'Don't be too sure,' he said.

'Oh, but I'm perfectly sure,' she answered, tossing her head, and missing the swing of her plait. She turned. She moved towards the Ring. Then she felt his hands on her shoulders, and then, lightly, he closed them round her neck, his thumbs touching in the hollow of her throat.

She had that funny feeling again. 'Let go, Charles,' she said, but at the same time, she leaned back. She could feel his warm breath on her neck. 'Esther,' Geoff was calling. She could hear him on the path. She broke free. She bent down and pulled up a handful of grass from the edge of the Ring. She threw it at Charles. 'Can't catch me,' she said, and ran.

But he didn't try to.

The next three days were rainy, but on the fourth it was fine again, and after breakfast they gathered in the Ring.

'What is your full name?'

'Geoffrey Arnold West.'

'What is your father's name?'

'D-d-d-david West.'

'What does he do?'

'He's a schoolmaster.'

'What kind of schoolmaster?'

'Head of a p-p-p-p-prep school.'

He wasn't the youngest of the family, though, for a long time, he had been; for six years, in fact, until his sister was born. After she was born, everything changed. Before that he'd been the family pet, a clumsy puppy. They'd laughed fondly at his clumsiness, even though none of them was clumsy. His mother and father were the best mixed doubles team at the local tennis club, and the twins – five years older than Geoff – were natural athletes. The high standard of sport at the prep school was one of the reasons why it was doing so well.

Of course, when he'd started the school, Geoff's father had just come from a very successful housemastership at Harrow. And he and Geoff's mother were such a charming couple – everyone said so. They were both so good-looking. Geoff's father looked so splendid in his gown, preaching his simple but inspiring sermons in chapel. And his mother was so tall and queenly. 'Just as one imagines a Greek goddess,' he'd heard a visiting mother say – hastily adding, 'but of course absolutely a lady.'

Yes, he had been the pet, the clumsy tumbling puppy, but then when Sally was born, she had taken his place as pet – though *she* was more like a graceful kitten. It was after Sally was born that he had started to stammer – and no one had been sympathetic. 'He's just trying to draw attention to himself,' his mother had said. 'If we ignore it, he will probably grow out of it.' But he hadn't.

Then the terrible things had started to happen. They'd put him on a pony, and he had screamed, 'Will I fall? Will I fall?' He'd hoped that if he made it into a question it wouldn't happen. But his mother had hit the pony's rump, and it had started to trot, and he had fallen off. *The fear of falling was worse than the fall,* he had realized then, but realizing didn't seem to help. Then there was the horror of swimming, where you had to jump off the diving board (little Sally was jumping off the board, laughing, at the age of four). Even walking along the top of an upturned form at gym made him feel giddy, and, over the stream at the bottom of the school garden, there was a bridge made of widely separated timbers, and with a wire handrail on one side, which he just couldn't bring himself to cross.

Once, in the hols, the whole family went for a picnic in a field on the other side of the stream. To get to it, you had to cross the bridge, unless, of course, you went round by the road. That was what Sally had suggested – Sally was jolly sweet, really – when Geoff hadn't been able to walk across the bridge. 'Geoff could come round by the road,' she had said. But his father had been firm: 'If Geoff can't cross the bridge, then he can't come to the picnic, dear. Geoff has got to learn to be a man.'

From the other side of the bridge, he could hear them all

talking and laughing. He stood there for a long time, listening. He took one step on to the bridge. He clutched the wire, and it quivered under his hand. He looked down and saw the water moving under the timbers. He snatched his foot back, and sank down on the grass, feeling dizzy. After a time, he got up, and walked slowly back to the school, which, anyway, always seemed rather desolate in the holidays, with all the empty, echoing dormitories and classrooms. He sat down at a desk in one of the classrooms. How he wished there were just one thing that he liked, and that he was really good at. He didn't even like reading – if he'd been bright, he felt his father might have forgiven him for being so bad at games. But he was slow at lessons, and he only enjoyed reading comics, which weren't allowed.

Worst of all was climbing. His father had been a mountaineer at university, before he went into the Church and became a schoolmaster. His mother liked climbing too, and so did Simon and Peter, his older brothers. And Sally had made a good start when they all went to Wales the year before. But Geoff couldn't bring himself to go up anywhere that was steep at all. So that was why, this summer, when they'd planned their walking party in the Alps – it was going to be the family's first trip abroad together – they had sent him to the children's hotel.

'Though I'm j-j-jolly glad now that I came,' he said now. 'It's been super.' And he fixed his dogged gaze on Esther.

It was nearly a week later that, at Charles's suggestion, they went onto the roof. They climbed the little staircase that led up to it from the attics. The roof was flat, with the towers rising on the east and west sides. All round the edge of it was a raised parapet, which was about four feet high, and about nine inches wide. It was this that Charles inspected. Then he said, 'My idea is that Geoff's test should be to walk round the edge.'

They all looked at Geoff. 'Oh I s-s-say,' he exclaimed. He sounded horrified. He looked imploringly at Esther.

'It's not difficult,' Charles said. 'It's not as if it were narrow. Why it must be about a foot wide.' He got up onto the parapet, ran quickly along one side, and jumped down again onto the roof. 'You see,' he said, 'it's easy.'

'Don't you think it might be dangerous? I mean ... seeing that Geoff is afraid of heights?' Brian asked hesitantly.

'Nonsense,' Charles said. 'It isn't dangerous at all. Geoff can always jump back onto the roof if he feels wobbly. I know he's afraid of heights. But that's the whole point of the test. It has to be your worst thing.'

'But the things Esther and I had to do weren't *dangerous*,' Brian persisted.

'Isn't little Brian being wet?' Charles said to Esther. 'You'd think we were asking him to do it, not Geoff. I'm sure Geoff's much braver than Brian seems to think – aren't you, Geoff?'

'I der-der-don't know,' Geoff said. 'How far round would I have to go?'

'Oh, right round the roof, I thought,' Charles said easily.

Brian was shaking his head vigorously, and Esther said, 'Oh no, Charles. I think that's too far. Just along one side would be quite enough, I think.'

Charles shrugged. 'Oh well ... if that's what everybody feels, I agree. OK by you, Geoff?'

Geoff shut his eyes, screwing up his face, for a moment. Then he looked at Esther. There was a plea in his eyes, but she ignored it. After all, she'd done her bit for him. Then 'All right,' Geoff said. 'Do you want me to do it n-n-now?'

'Oh no, not now,' Charles said. 'Too many people about. Someone might see you and make a fuss.' Looking over the edge of the parapet, Esther saw a group of children playing hopscotch on the gravel with one of the 'lady helpers'. 'After lunch tomorrow, I thought,' Charles went on. 'When everyone's out of the way.'

Geoff was peering over the edge of the parapet, one hand gripping the edge of it. There was a look of horrified fascination on his face. Now he stepped back. He said, looking at Esther, 'All right then. T-t-tomorrow afternoon.'

That night, Esther woke suddenly, startled by a noise. She had been dreaming. The little boy in the peaked cap had been in her dream. Waking, she saw a shape by the window. There was someone in her room. She sat up in bed, her heart pounding violently. 'Who is it?' she said in a loud voice.

'Sssh!' Geoff moved into a bright patch of moonlight. 'It's m-m-me,' he said.

'What on earth do you want. What's the time?' she asked.

'It's half past twelve,' he said. 'I couldn't sleep.' He sat down on the foot of her bed.

'That doesn't mean you have to wake *me* up,' she said.

'I'm s-s-s-sorry.' He was silent for a moment. Then he said, 'I don't know if I c-c-c-c-can do it tomorrow.'

Her dream was ebbing away now, but it still lapped darkly at the edges of her mind. She said, 'Oh Geoff, don't be silly. Of course you can do it. You want to become a member of the club, don't you?'

'Of course I do,' he said. 'But I just der-der-don't know if I can.'

'Of course you can.' She tried to speak kindly. 'As Charles said, you can always jump back if you feel dizzy.'

'Yes,' he said, 'but then that wouldn't count, would it?'

'I'm sure we'd let you try again,' she said.

He shivered. 'Yes,' he said, 'but it would be w-w-worse the second time.'

'You shouldn't think about it so much,' she said. 'Just forget about it till it happens. Why don't you go back to bed now? If you have a nice sleep, I'm sure you'll feel better in the morning.' Firmly she snuggled down in the bed, pulled the sheet up under her chin. She turned over on to her side, facing the wall. '*I* want to go to sleep now, anyway,' she said.

'Yes,' he said, and then, 'I'm sorry.'

'It's all right,' she said. 'Good night.'

She felt him get up. 'Esther,' he said.

'Yes. What is it?' she asked rather crossly.

'You won't tell Charles, will you? That I c-c-came and talked to you.'

'No, of course I won't,' she said. 'You didn't tell about me, that time.'

'N-n-no. Of course I didn't.'

'Well then,' she said. 'Good night, Geoff.'

'Good night, Esther.' She heard him moving across the room, and the door opening and closing.

With a sigh of relief, she burrowed down farther into the bed. How silly he was being. The parapet, as Charles had said, must be nearly a foot wide. She and Brian hadn't made all that fuss about *their* tests. She dismissed Geoff from her mind. She would think about Charles, she decided. She closed her eyes. *His hands meeting round her neck. 'One of these days, someone will take you down a peg or two.' 'Well, it won't be you.' 'Don't be too sure.'* She smiled.

She'd never seen anyone look as pale as Geoff. More than pale: his skin was nearer green than white; against it his freckles seemed almost red, like his hair. Geoff was very ugly, her mind registered, as she watched his infinitely slow progress along the parapet.

His eyes were fixed ahead. His arms were outstretched, and with every step he took, his body swayed a little. But he was doing very well. Geoff, she had to admit, was being braver than she or Brian had had to be. Geoff, she understood now, was being very brave indeed. Suddenly she became aware of a rhythmic sound on her right. She looked round.

Charles was standing about a yard away from her. He had taken a tennis ball from his pocket, and was bouncing it up and down, with his palm, on the flat roof. *That wasn't fair.* It might distract Geoff's attention. 'Charles,' she whispered angrily. Continuing to bounce the ball, he glanced towards her. She frowned and shook her head vigorously. He frowned back, and gave the ball a vicious slap. It bounced off at an angle. It struck the parapet just in front of Geoff, and disappeared over the edge. Geoff's outstretched, balancing arms convulsed. The spread fingers of his hands tensed into claws. His right foot rose and wavered in the air. That was when he looked down, over the edge of the parapet. 'Come down,' Esther shouted. 'Jump this way.' His eyes swivelled back, met hers, but then, apparently irresistibly, were drawn back once more to the edge. For an instant, he was absolutely still. Then he toppled, he vanished, leaving a faint wailing cry behind him in the air. There they were – Esther, Charles, Brian – stranded in a sudden echoing space.

For a moment they all stood frozen. Then they rushed to the edge. Looking down, Esther saw Geoff's body lying in a strange twisted position on the gravel. She raised her eyes and, at her indrawn breath, so did Charles and Brian. On the far side of the gravel, by the beginning of the drive, stood the Major staring from Geoff's body to them, and back again.

'Quick!' It was Charles. They all stepped back from the parapet. 'You two,' he said, 'down to the Ring – fast. Quietly,

147

by the back stairs. I'll join you there. Wait for me. I'm going to talk to the Major.'

He was off, ahead of them, through the trap door, and scrambling down the steps.

In the centre of the Ring, Esther and Brian huddled together, their arms around each other. Brian was shivering and crying, and Esther, who was crying herself, repeated over and over again, 'Don't cry, Brian. Don't cry.'

'Poor Geoff,' Brian sobbed, 'poor old Geoff. We should never have made him do it.'

'No,' Esther said, and then again, 'Brian, don't cry.'

When was Charles going to come? she wondered. In a way, she didn't want him to, because then they'd have to go and face everyone. How brave it was of Charles to have gone on his own to tell the Major what had happened!

Here he was, at last, pushing through the bushes. He was breathless. What astonished her was the expression of triumph on his face. He crouched down in front of them, putting one hand on Esther's shoulder, one on Brian's. 'It's all right,' he said. 'Everything's all right.'

'All right?' Esther said. 'What do you mean, Charles?' Brian just stared.

'The Major,' Charles said, 'I've fixed it. He won't let anyone know we were there. I told him that, if he did, I'd tell Mrs Sidney about him and Gwyneth.'

'But—' Esther said.

'There's no "but" about it,' Charles interrupted. Looking from one to the other of them, he went on, 'It wouldn't do any good to Geoff – poor Geoff,' he added – 'if we told. He was a decent chap. He wouldn't have wanted us to get into trouble. Of course, Esther, you shouldn't have shouted at him like that—'

'It was you,' she broke in, 'bouncing that tennis ball.'

'You see,' Charles said quickly, 'what a horrible muddle it would be. As it is, all we've got to do is to say that we were here all the time. No one will ever know. The Major won't tell. And none of us will.'

Esther and Brian were silent. 'None of us will,' Charles repeated. 'I won't, and you won't. We must swear that we will never tell. We must take an oath.'

He was feeling in his pocket. He was pulling out his penknife. 'We shall swear on our blood,' he said. 'We shall mix our blood, and then there will always be a blood bond between us.'

With the penknife, he made neat little cuts in their wrists, between the veins. Then, in turn, they pressed their wrists together, and, in turn, as the blood merged, stinging, they swore that they would never, never tell.

However many questions they were asked – by Mrs Sidney first, and then by the police – they never wavered. They only repeated, again and again, that they had been down in the clearing in the lilacs – 'We often go there,' Charles said, glancing at the Major, who looked away. They said they hadn't known where Geoff was or what he was doing. They hadn't seen anything, they didn't know anything – they had been down in the clearing in the lilacs.

Repeating the story, Esther found that she was almost beginning to believe it herself.

The constable from Crickhowell went away. Later, two policemen in ordinary clothes turned up. They weren't so easily satisfied. They said that they would come back next day and question each of the three separately.

'I don't think those two believe us,' Charles said afterwards. 'Horrible oafs – I'm sure they'll try to bully us. I shall telephone my cousin Violet.' And he did so, from the telephone in the Major's office.

Geoff's parents arrived early next morning – they had flown back from Switzerland. 'I can't understand it,' Geoff's mother said. 'He was always so frightened of heights.' Geoff's father had patted her hand. 'I can understand it,' he said. 'Geoff turned up trumps in the end. He was determined to conquer his weakness, so he went through that lonely ordeal. He failed, but, in a sense, he triumphed. I'm proud of the boy.'

Lady Violet arrived shortly before the two policemen returned. She came in a chauffeur-driven Daimler, they in a small Morris.

From the first, she was on the attack, insisting on being present while the children were questioned, talking about having a question asked in the House of Commons about police intimidation of minors, threatening to write to *The Times*.

'She certainly swept the floor with those two,' Brian said afterwards, with a trace of his old high spirits. *Was Brian starting to believe the story, too?* Esther wondered.

Lady Violet's final announcement had been that she was taking Charles away immediately. 'I hardly feel that he's in very good hands here,' she had said, including the Sidneys and the policemen in the same cold, brilliantly blue stare. 'If you have any further questions, here is my address in London,' she said, producing an engraved card. One of the policemen muttered that he thought everything had been sorted out.

Down the stairs came Charles, carrying his suitcase. Esther and Brian followed him out to where the Daimler waited on the gravel. Lady Violet nodded to them from the back seat. 'Goodbye, you two,' was all Charles said. Esther was conscious of a dull ache in her chest as he got into the car beside Lady Violet. He turned once, and waved, as the car turned into the drive, and Esther and Brian waved back. Then Brian hurried into the house.

Esther stood on the gravel. *Another ten days*, she thought. How horrible! And then she would be going to horrible Spain, back to her horrible mother and stepfather. In fact, everything was horrible.

Mrs Sidney had told her that when the policemen went through Geoff's things, they'd found Esther's plait among them. 'So touching,' she said. 'I thought you'd want to know.' Esther had just stared at her coldly. She hated Mrs Sidney, and she hated the Major and Gwyneth: as Charles had said, people were filthy beasts. So she'd decided that when she left the hotel, she was going to leave a letter for Mrs Sidney, telling her about the Major and Gwyneth. It would serve them all right.

She imagined the Daimler gliding along the road to Crickhowell. Charles was gone. He had escaped; he had escaped without playing the Truth Game. He had escaped without having to do his test.

part four

1963

thirteen

The shadow moved; the face retreated. The figure outside the window drew back, and at once she recognized Charles. The relief from terror was so acute that she put her hand on a table, to steady herself.

Swiftly he moved from the window. A moment later, he was with her in the drawing-room. She took a step towards him, and then her face was pressed against his sleeve. She clung to him, shivering, murmuring, 'Charles, oh Charles.'

He was patting her shoulder, murmuring soothingly, 'There, there, Esther. There, there.' And when at last, she raised her head to look up into his face, he smiled at her very gently, and said, 'Poor Esther.'

'Poor Brian,' she said. 'Poor, poor Brian.'

She could feel the tension in his body. Though he looked so calm, she was sure that he was suffering too.

'What can have happened?' She gestured to the sofa behind her. She found that she couldn't bring herself to look round. In her ears was the low, continuous buzzing of the flies.

After a moment, Charles said, 'I think it's pretty obvious. From the way he's ... dressed, and so on. He must have had some pick-up here who turned violent. "Rough trade", I believe they call it.' His lips twitched with distaste.

'Yes,' she said. 'Yes, that must have been it. As a matter of fact, I know he had someone here yesterday. I heard a man's voice in the background when I telephoned.'

'Really.' Charles's tone was thoughtful. 'Then it probably happened yesterday. That would make sense.' He was looking past her now, frowning. Yes, she understood what he meant. *The flies. The smell.* She shuddered.

He took her hand. 'Let's get out of this room,' he said. 'Let's go into the garden.' He led her from the room. She sighed with relief as he closed the door behind them.

The garden looked completely unreal to her: its neat flower beds, its bright green lawn, the white-painted wrought-iron table and chairs on the tiny paved terrace. As they came through the door, the cat, Smoothie, streaked across the

153

grass, leaped on to the back wall, and disappeared. 'That cat has become completely unhinged,' Charles said.

They sat down on two of the wrought-iron chairs. 'Oh Charles,' she said, 'I'm so thankful that you're here.' Then she asked, 'How did that happen – that you were here, I mean?'

'It's a strange coincidence,' he said. Then he smiled slightly. 'Well, actually not entirely a coincidence. You see, I telephoned Brian yesterday, too, and he told me you were coming round this evening. I decided' – he paused – 'that it would be rather nice to see you.'

Even now, even here, with poor Brian inside on the sofa, her heart jumped. She said, coolly, 'That rather surprises me.'

'It shouldn't,' he said very quietly, and then, raising his voice to its normal pitch, 'I rang the bell, just as you did. It must have been about ten minutes before you arrived. And, like you, I tried the door when no one answered, and came in ... and found him. Then, when you rang the bell, I suppose that – well, perhaps I panicked. I thought it might be ... whoever had done it ... coming back. I was so startled that I never thought of it being you. I wish I had had more presence of mind. I could have saved you from seeing – that.'

'It's all right,' she said. His hand was resting on the table. She raised it, and rubbed it against her cheek, then put it down again. She said briskly, 'Well, what are we going to do? I suppose we should telephone the police right away, shouldn't we?'

Now it was he who took her hand, and held it between both his, massaging it gently. He leaned towards her. 'Esther,' he said, 'I don't think we should telephone now.'

'You don't?' she said, startled. 'But surely—'

Shaking his head, he interrupted her. 'No,' he said. His expression was very serious. 'The main reason being, Esther, that I just don't think I could face ... all that ... at this moment. So soon after that terrible business with Violet.' He shook his head again, and raised his eyebrows; he very faintly smiled, as he said, 'They might think it rather strange to encounter me again so soon, in connection with another violent death.'

'But that's absurd,' she said.

Very gently, he placed a finger on her lips. 'Do as I ask you,

Esther,' he said — and even here, even now, a ripple ran along her nerves. 'There's nothing,' he went on, 'that we can do for poor Brian, is there? Telephoning the police isn't going to help him.' (That reminded her of something, but she couldn't pin down what it was.) 'All we would be doing,' he said, 'would be involving ourselves in a hell of scandal and sordid publicity.'

'But,' she said, 'we can't just *leave* him here.'

'Esther,' said Charles, 'that thing in there isn't Brian.'

She gave a sudden little sob. The shadows in the garden were lengthening. Somewhere in the distance, a child was shouting. She said, 'Surely we ought to let them — the police I mean — know about the man who was here. He's dangerous.'

'Esther,' said Charles, 'what could we tell them about him? It will be just as obvious to them as it is to us what kind of crime this was. Anyway, we'll think about that. We'll talk about it. What I think we should do now is go back to your flat, your lovely peaceful flat, Esther, and be quiet for a little, together. Don't you agree?'

Weakness flooded her. For of course they ought to telephone the police. But she felt physically incapable of refusing him. Slowly she nodded her head. He gave a little sigh. He smiled.

'Couldn't you,' she said, 'cover him up?'

'That thing in there isn't Brian,' he said again. 'But yes, I'll do that. What *you* must do now is let yourself out of the house. Quietly. Look to make sure that no one is about. When you're sure, turn right, and go to the corner. Turn right again, and you'll see my car just down the road. Let yourself in. Here are the keys.' He took them out of his pocket, as he spoke, and handed them to her. He smiled. 'I must remember to collect *your* keys again, Esther.'

She looked at him. 'I thought you didn't want them any more,' she said.

He smiled again. 'That was my revenge. After all, you had behaved very badly. But you're forgiven now.'

'What a nerve you have,' she said.

He flicked his thumb and forefinger against her cheek. 'Now off you go. I'll do as you asked me, and I'll shut up the house, and then I'll join you in the car.'

'Don't be too long,' she said. 'I don't really feel like being alone.'

'I'll only be a minute or two,' he said. 'After that, I promise that you won't be alone again tonight.'

She closed her eyes for a moment. Then she stood up, and so did he. He stood behind her, and put his hands on her shoulders, and gently propelled her into the house. In the cool dimness of the hall, she leaned back, resting against him for a second. He pressed her shoulders lightly, and then released them. 'Esther,' he said, 'you are on your way.'

Down the hall, obediently, she went. As she turned the handle of the front door, she heard Charles going into the drawing-room, and shivered. Cautiously, she opened the door, suddenly feeling as guilty as if she had committed a crime. Which, of course, she had – for wasn't it a crime not to inform the police of a murder?

A boy in blue jeans was walking along the pavement opposite. He looked preoccupied. His eyes were fixed on the ground, and he certainly didn't notice her, peering from the doorway. She waited until he was out of sight, and then, after a swift glance to left and right, slipped out of the door, and pulled it shut behind her. Quickly she turned right, and started down the street to the corner, looking straight ahead of her, her footsteps sounding loud on the pavement.

She turned the corner, saw Charles's car a little way down the road. She passed a house where someone was playing Chopin. How was one always able to tell live music from a recording? she wondered. She longed to reach the car, but forced herself not to quicken her pace. Her hand with the keys clutched in it was sticky. When she arrived at the car, she had difficulty fitting the key into the lock. At last, the door was open. She slid into the driver's seat, and then over into the seat next to it.

It was hot in the car. The roof was closed. A fly was buzzing against the windscreen, and suddenly she felt sick. Quickly, she wound the window down. She breathed fresh air in deep gulps, and gradually her nausea subsided. Then, *Brian*, she thought, and vividly before her eyes appeared the battered head, the painted nails, the hairs curling in the V of the blood-soaked nightdress. The sickness came up again in a wave. But here was Charles, coming round the corner. She couldn't be sick in front of Charles.

She fixed her eyes on him. How light, almost springy, his

tread was. By the time he reached the car, she was starting to feel better. He got in, and she handed him the keys.

He pressed the button that made the roof roll back, and started the car. Within seconds, they were in the King's Road, heading towards Sloane Square.

How horrified all the people loitering indifferently in the summer evening would be if they knew what she knew. Suddenly, glancing sideways at Charles, she felt superior to them all. *She was in his hands.* In the windows of Peter Jones, the blank-faced dummies were wearing autumn outfits. How cool the air was on her skin.

Green Park was a pool of shadow, pin-pointed with the sun's last little darts of light. One of the trees there was haunted, she'd read in some book, and if you fell asleep beneath it you had terrible dreams. Tonight, if she had been alone, she would have been afraid of what she might dream. But Charles would be with her. *'I promise that you won't be alone again tonight.'*

She wondered what had happened to that silly art student, that Sue. She felt suddenly convinced that Charles had tired of her, had got rid of her somehow. *It's only me he wants,* she thought.

Standing on her doorstep, she felt in her bag for her keys. As she pulled them out, Charles took them from her, and opened the door.

Now, at last, they were in her room. He closed the door behind them, smiled, and put the keys in his pocket.

The room was cool and peaceful in the dusk. The floorboards, which she had polished yesterday – how far away yesterday seemed – gleamed palely.

Suddenly she was aware of an odd feeling of awkwardness. She dropped her bag on the bed. She went over to the window, and looked out. A street lamp came on, orange against the pearly sky.

'Esther,' he said behind her. She turned. He was sitting in the rocking-chair. Now, she thought, they would have to have their talk, would have to discuss everything: Brian, the police, what they were going to do. She felt her body droop at the idea. Then she straightened up, she raised her head, she came over to sit on the bed, facing him.

'Esther,' he said. 'Esther. Aloof one. What are you going

157

to wear for me tonight? What are you going to wear with that black velvet mask?'

fourteen

It was Tuesday morning. She sat in the rocking-chair, wearing her striped kaftan. When Charles came out of the bathroom, she would bathe and, for the first time since Saturday, put on everyday clothes, fasten her hair in its austere everyday knot. This morning, Charles had woken beside her, had stretched, had got up, had gone over to the window, and pulled back the curtains – which had been drawn since Saturday – letting in the harsh grey daylight.

They hadn't discussed Brian; they hadn't discussed anything. They had lived in the curtained dimness of their under-sea world – they had sunk down such fathoms deep together. Down to the ocean floor, where little gilded shoals drifted like transparent feathers, and sometimes there was a grin of teeth as a shark cruised past. She had lain on sand, shifted by the inexplicable ebb and flow of tides. Down, down, down; what was this desire of hers to drown so deep? He had it also. Oh yes, he too had drowned.

Occasionally, she had wandered into the kitchen to collect food and drink. She hadn't laid the table, just brought plates and glasses to the bed – plates and glasses which, now, scattered on the floor, looked squalid in this heavy grey morning light. She ought to tidy up, she supposed, but she didn't feel like moving.

Yesterday, she had telephoned the college, and had cancelled her lecture, saying that she was ill. And she knew that she would do the same this morning, whatever his plans were.

Would he go now, when he had shaved and showered and dressed? For by tomorrow she knew that everything would have to end. Except for Thursdays. But certainly not this particular Thursday. For tomorrow – Wednesday – was the day of Clare's return.

How, she wondered, would she be able to bear returning just to Thursdays after these three nights, two days? They had been different in kind, rather than in degree. *Down, down, down.*

She smiled, she closed her eyes, she leaned back in the chair, rocking gently. Charles had hung his coat over it. She could feel the collar behind her neck. She raised a slow hand, and stroked the coat's lapel. Then, as if of its own volition, as if independently curious, her hand crept down to his pocket, where it found, and rejected, her keys, his keys, and stirred a little jingle of coins. Her hand, she realized, was looking for paper. A letter perhaps. But from whom? She didn't know.

There was no paper in the pocket. But there was something soft, and the softness enfolded something hard. A handkerchief, she decided, with a hard spiky object wrapped in it.

She raised her head, she opened her eyes, she listened. She could hear water running in the bathroom. Carefully, she extracted the wrapped object, and examined it. One of the large creamy silk handkerchiefs that Charles always used had been wound tightly around whatever lay within. Swiftly, she unrolled it. A glitter dazzled her eyes. Then all she could do was stare at what she held in her hand, at what she recognized immediately as the emerald and diamond star that had blazed on Lady Violet's shoulder that first evening in Duke Street, the star that had so recently been described in the newspapers. What was it called? The Colgong Star. Yes, she was holding the Colgong Star.

There was a pounding sound in her ears, a dryness in her mouth. And her fingers twisted, twisted, re-fastening the handkerchief around the Star. Her hands were shaking so much – but she must get the parcel right, must get it back into his pocket. Doing that was part of the one thing that she was sure of: *he mustn't know she knew.*

She compelled her fingers to obey her will. Yes, now the little parcel looked as it had done. As she thrust it deep down into the pocket, amongst the keys and coins, she heard the bathroom door open. She stood up. She was over by the wardrobe, shifting hangers on the rail as if she were looking for something to wear, when she heard him in the room behind her.

'Esther,' he was saying, and she knew that she must turn, must face him. And she must look natural; she must face him with serenity. She took a hanger with a pair of jeans on it from the wardrobe. Holding its wooden frame with both hands – they might shake, if she didn't hold on to something – she turned.

How cool and clean and tidy he looked – freshly shaved, his hair combed smoothly – wearing his dark trousers, his white shirt, his precisely knotted tie. 'We must talk,' he said. 'We must get everything sorted out today.'

'Yes,' she said. 'Yes, of course we must, Charles.' Her voice seemed to her to sound quite normal.

'I've decided,' he said, 'that we must get out of here to do it.' He surveyed the tumbled bed, the unwashed plates and glasses, a tangled heap of discarded garments on the floor – the mask was coiled like a black snake on the rug. Registering his cold, censorious look, she found herself putting the jeans, still on their hanger, down on the table, going across the room, and stooping to pick up two plates from the floor.

'We'll get away from everything, Esther,' he said. 'We'll go for a drive, a long drive. We'll go to Glan-yr-Afon.'

She stood up, the plates in her hand. A fork slid off one of them, and clanged on the floor. 'To Glan-yr-Afon?' she said. 'But it's so far away.'

'If we leave in half an hour's time, we'll be there this afternoon,' he said. 'I have quite decided, Esther, so you must hurry up and get ready. It will be a kind of pilgrimage. In memory of Brian.'

Brian. Now Brian was rattling at the back of her mind, whistling like a thin wind through an empty keyhole. It wasn't just Lady Violet that she had to think about; she had to think about Brian as well. But she didn't seem able to think at all. When she was in her bath, she would try to think.

'Hurry up, Esther,' Charles was repeating. 'Just leave those things in the kitchen. You haven't time to wash them up now. Have your bath, get dressed, and we'll be on our way.' *How difficult it would be not to obey him, when obeying him was such a rooted habit.*

'I must telephone the college,' she said.

'Is that necessary? Surely they'll believe that you're still ill, if you don't turn up?'

'No, I really ought to,' she said. 'If I didn't they might telephone me, and there'd be no answer. What would they think then?'

'Oh all right,' he said impatiently, 'but be quick about it.' He looked at his watch. Then he took his coat from the back of the rocking-chair, and put it on. When he had done so, she saw his right hand automatically go down into his pocket. She imagined the little parcel nestling in his palm.

She took the plates and glasses into the kitchen, and piled them in the sink, as he had told her to. She came back, and quickly she made up the bed. She took the clothes from the floor beside it, and dumped them in the laundry basket in the bathroom. Then she telephoned the Head of her Department. As he expressed sympathy, hoped that she'd be better soon, told her not to hurry back to work – her reputation for conscientiousness was high – she felt a wild urge to interrupt him with a cry for help. But what could she possibly say, with Charles sitting there, in the rocking-chair, contemptuously flipping through Saturday's edition of the *Guardian*.

She collected clean clothes from the wardrobe, picked up the pair of jeans she had left on the table, and went through to the bathroom.

At last she was behind a locked door; she was safe, she could think. She turned on the taps, and sat on the edge of the bath. But her mind was blank except for shifting images: the Colgong Star, Brian's blood-red nails, the cat, Smoothie. After a moment, she stood up, and went over to the open window. Too small a window to climb out of, and anyway there was a sheer drop down to the yard below, where two men were leaning against the side of a van, lighting cigarettes. One of them looked up, and waved at her, and immediately she stepped back, out of sight.

She turned off the taps. She took off her kaftan. She slid down into the water, rested her head against the back of the bath. She closed her eyes, and waited for clarity. The Colgong Star glittered, Brian weltered in his blood. *Battered to death*. Charles's shadow darkened the garden window. Then down, down, down, she and Charles sank to the ocean floor.

His hands were winding her hair around her throat in the way she had always loved. There was a sort of rhythm in her head that was driving her on, driving her forward: to sit up, to wash, to get out of the bath and dry herself, to dress and put on make-up, to brush and coil her hair.

She was ready. *What else can I do?* she asked herself, as she opened the bathroom door. She must behave normally, and then he wouldn't be aware that she suspected anything. *What did she suspect?* She went through into the living-room. 'Ready?' Charles asked, dropping the newspaper on the floor, and getting up from the rocking-chair. *Ready. A little heifer garlanded for the sacrifice.* That was when she thought of what was in the wardrobe.

'Yes, I'm ready,' she said. Now he was opening the front door. *She must make it look natural.* Now, at last, her mind was moving. She went through the door ahead of him, and he pulled it shut behind them. They were halfway down the stairs when she stopped. 'I've forgotten my cigarettes,' she said. 'I'll just rush up and fetch them. Then we won't have to stop anywhere. Give me my keys.' With an irritable grimace, he gave them to her. 'Do be quick,' he said. There was an edge to his voice. But she was running back up the stairs.

Inside, and over to the wardrobe. She fumbled behind the pile of jerseys, and there it was – oh yes, her well-kept secret. Without hesitating, she pulled it out, slid it into her handbag. She was over at the door again when she remembered the cigarettes. She was sure that there was a packet in the table drawer. Yes! She snatched it up. She was waving it gaily in the air as she came out of the flat.

'Found them!' she called to Charles who was waiting by the front door. And down the stairs she ran.

fifteen

The day had grown darker as they travelled. It was raining heavily as they drove through Abergavenny, past the Angel Hotel, but it stopped by the time they reached the gates of Glan-yr-Afon, though water was falling in heavy drops from the trees. Since she had last been there, the gate had come off its hinges, was propped against one of the gateposts. The rhododendrons had crept even nearer to the drive, their unpruned branches stretching out like arms towards the car.

They had hardly spoken on the journey. Charles had stared, expressionless, ahead through the windscreen. Physical exhaustion had given Esther a feeling of fragility. Her nerve ends were twigs which she felt could snap at a word, at a sudden movement. The only thing that seemed solid in the world was her bag, firm and heavy, clasped between her hands in her lap.

Now, as they rounded the bend in the drive, Charles turned his head towards her. He smiled. 'Well, here we are,' he said.

'Yes, here we are,' she echoed, smiling back at him.

Purple stone, grey light, the sentinel towers. As Charles drew up by the porch, she said, 'I wonder where the Major hanged himself.'

'I have no idea,' Charles said. 'What put that into your mind?'

'Oh I don't know,' she said, and then, 'The spirit of the place, I think.'

He got out of the car, and came round to open her door for her. Now she stood on the gravel, clutching her bag in both hands. That might look odd – she didn't usually carry it that way. Carefully she swung it over her arm, bracing her shoulder against its unaccustomed weight.

'Let's go to the terrace,' he said, and she followed him along by the side of the house. A spray of an orange-berried plant with shiny leaves brushed her head, and a little shower of water drops dampened her shoulders.

Again the Usk was loud in her ears. The waterfall was muddy-coloured, rushing strongly down to swirl round the great flat stones. The sloping field on the other side of the

163

river was hidden by a thick veil of mist. She suddenly had a picture of Brian's little ghost flitting across the terrace.

'I feel that we shall all haunt this place one day,' she said.

'Why, that's a very romantic idea for you to have, Esther,' Charles said. 'Not at all in your usual style.'

She gave a little abrupt laugh, standing there beside him, looking down at the bubbling swirling river. The sky seemed to be becoming darker every minute. She and Charles were alone in a grey world of water and cloud.

'Well,' he said, 'the time has come to talk. We shall go to the Ring, of course.'

The time has come, she thought. 'To the Ring?' she said. 'It will be very wet there.'

'Intrepid Esther,' he said, 'surely a little wet grass doesn't discourage you. Come along now. Don't you remember the last time we were there?'

'Yes, I remember,' she said. If he had asked her that *before*, her head would have pounded, her skin would have prickled. But ever since she had seen the Star, something in her had turned as cold as stone. *He has lost his power,* she thought. But that was the most terrible thought of all.

'Come,' he said. Putting a hand on her shoulder, he guided her ahead of him across the terrace.

The lawn was a wild tangle of weeds and grass. The toppled stone bear was hardly visible through the rank, rioting green.

As they went down the slope and crossed the grass to the Ring, the wetness seeped through her jeans. Beside her, Charles's legs pushed through the growth like scythes. She stumbled on a twisted root. He put his hands on her upper arms and raised her, guided her. She felt quite helpless – as she had so often felt with Charles. But now it was different. She kept her right arm pressed against her bag, holding it to her side.

They had reached the back of the Ring.

For a second he paused by the entrance to the overgrown path, and then he started to propel her through the wet lilac branches. A twig caught in her hair. She raised her left hand to free it, and her hair fell down, from its knot, around her shoulders. Now the wet branches were soaking her shirt.

They were in the Ring, and all that she could do was stare.

A drop of water and a shiver, both ice-cold, ran simultaneously down her spine.

She stared at the two long shapes that were side by side. One was rounded with a covering of recently turned earth. The other was a pit; the soil which had been dug from it was thrown up along one side in a mound against which a spade rested.

In a single movement, freeing herself from his hands, she rounded to face him. He was smiling. She took a step back.

'Esther,' he said, 'it is time for the blood bond to be broken. It is time for peace.'

'Peace?' she said. How shrill and high her voice sounded. Her eyes darted to the earth-covered shape; she gestured towards it, looking at him.

He was still smiling. '*She*'s there,' he said. 'That girl I brought to see you. Though of course she never mattered at all. But, suddenly, how she sickened me. Ugh, how she clung. And then when I told her to get out, she tried to blackmail me. She said she loved me, and that she was going to tell Clare, to tell my little white flower. So I thought the best thing was to bring her here.' Now there was a look of contempt on his face. 'She was so despicable when she died,' he said. 'She whimpered like a puppy.' He paused. He said, 'Now you, Esther, will die quite differently, I know. You will be my aloof one. You will die with dignity. Esther, I know I can rely on you to do that.'

'You're mad, Charles,' she said. It was one of the times when her voice sounded to her just like her mother's, light and clipped. She was astonished to hear that voice coming from her mouth now.

He shook his head slowly. 'Oh no, Esther,' he said. '*I'm not* mad. It is the world that is mad, the filthy, filthy world. *Stewed in corruption*, Esther – all of you. Except my white flower. So the time has come to make an end of it. The blood bond will be broken, Esther, and Brian's tainted blood, and yours, will no longer flow with mine. There have been times, at night, Esther, when I have lain in bed, and felt that foul blood pumping through my veins. *That* could have made me mad, perhaps. But that will never happen again. Everything will be clean, and I and my pure one will be safe. The world will be as white as after a fall of snow.'

165

'So you killed Brian,' she said.

'Yes, Esther. Do you know, I felt a little sorry that I had to do that. For one thing, I'd been sure I could trust him not to tell anyone about Violet. After all, he did say to the police that I had been with him that evening. But then I saw that he was beginning to have doubts about what he'd done. So I did my best. I explained a lot to him. That was when he said what you did, Esther – that I was mad. So I knew that I couldn't trust him after all.'

He paused. Then he went on. 'He made it easy for me to kill him when the time came. When I went round there that evening, he had some vile creature there. They were upstairs. I let myself in very quietly – yes, I had a key to Brian's house, too. And when the creature had gone, I came in, and there he was, covered in paint and wearing that nightdress. Filthy, so filthy. And then I was sure that what I was going to do was right. Everything became clear to me. It was then that I realized that you and Brian were really *they*.'

'They?' she said.

He had been pacing up and down as he talked, and now the length of the open grave lay between them. He looked at his watch. 'I'm afraid,' he said, 'that we haven't time to go into all that now. It's getting late, and soon I must be getting back to London to make everything ready for my white flower. And you, Esther – you must square your shoulders, and shake back your hair, and look at me proudly. It will happen very quickly, Esther. I shall wind your hair around your throat, and you will fall asleep.'

He started to move towards her along the side of the grave. She squared her shoulders. She shook back her hair. She dragged her bag from her arm, pulled out the gun, and pointed it at him. There was a click, as she cocked the action – oh yes, she remembered. Suddenly she was brimming with power, and her finger was steady on the trigger.

He stared. She could see him not believing it, as he lunged forward. She fired to his right. To hit him, she remembered, she would have had to fire low; low and a little to the left – but she didn't want to hit him. The bullet struck the mound of earth at the side of the open grave. Mud splashed, earth spattered, and Charles leaped back.

'Don't move,' she said. The steely power that was in her

hand, that was in her head, had turned her voice, too, to steel. 'Don't move, Charles,' she said, 'or, next time, I shall aim for you.'

So his pale skin could turn paler. After a moment, he spoke. 'I don't understand,' he said. 'That gun – where did you get it, why did you bring it?'

She said, 'I found the Star, Charles. In your pocket, I found the Colgong Star.'

His hand went to his pocket. 'The Star?' he said.

'Yes,' she said. 'I suppose that it was for the Star, that you killed Lady Violet.'

He gave a sudden abrupt laugh. 'Of course you would think that,' he said. 'I knew that everyone – all the filthy fools – would think that she was killed for the Star. That was what the police thought, of course. That was why I took it.' He pulled the little parcel out of his pocket. He shook the hand-kerchief, and the Star dropped into the open grave where it glittered against the wet dull earth. 'I don't care tuppence for the Star,' he said, and then, 'I would have thought you were too much of a lady, Esther, to go through a man's pockets.'

That struck her as so funny that she burst out laughing. 'That,' she said, 'was a mistake. You should have realized, Charles, that the last thing I have ever wanted to be is a lady.'

All the time, she had been pointing the gun at him steadily. Her wrist was beginning to ache a little. With her left hand she gestured to the open grave where the Star glittered. 'Get down in there, Charles,' she said.

'Esther,' – why, he looked frightened – 'are you going to kill me?'

'Not if you get down in there,' she said. Her hand shifted on the gun, and he scrambled down into the grave, dislodging some of the mounded earth, which slid down after him. As he stood in the grave, the walls came to the height of his ribs. She stood quite still, looking down at him, allowing the gun to hang loosely from her wrist.

'And now, Charles,' she said, 'you are going to pay your debt to us all. You are going to play the Truth Game.'

sixteen

'What a ridiculous idea,' he said, and she could see that he was trying to regain command.

She said: 'You were the only one of us that never played.'

'I'm not going to play children's games now,' he said.

'Not even for your life?' she asked.

'You can't be serious.'

'I am just as serious,' she said, 'as you were, when you dug this grave for me.'

He was silent.

'Right,' she said, and then, 'What is your full name?'

'Oh, come now, Esther,' he said.

She straightened the gun in her hand, and saw him flinch. 'What is your full name?' she said again.

'Charles Henry Tibbald.'

They lived in a pretty little Georgian brick house that faced on to the large green of a Suffolk village: Charles and his mother and father. His tall beautiful mother had thick dark hair, parted in the centre, and fastened in a shining round bun at the nape of her neck. Sometimes, when she was in a very good temper, she would allow Charles to undo the bun, and play with her hair. He ran his fingers through it; he wound it around her neck in swathes. But she wasn't often in such a good temper as that.

She had a way of rising to her feet from her chair in the drawing-room, and moving, as if impelled by some sudden urgent purpose, towards the window. Several times, as a child, he had been deceived, and had followed to see what had drawn her there. But he learned that always, when she reached the window, she would halt abruptly – like a prisoner reaching the boundary of her cell – would stare out at the unbroken peace of the green, then turn and slowly return to her chair.

She sighed in a way that was different from the way other people sighed. Really, he supposed, it wasn't a sigh at all. For a sigh was an exhalation of breath, and what she did was to draw in air with all her strength, and then release it silently, imperceptibly.

She had a way of stubbing out a cigarette, half smoked. But not exactly stubbing it out. Grinding it out with a vicious little twist of her wrist, so that there was always a break in the stem, just above the cork tip. As soon as she had done this to one cigarette, she would light another. Her hands were always busy with a cigarette, in some way – pulling one out of the packet, putting it between her lips, lighting it, taking it away again. Even while the cigarette was in her mouth, she would hold it between her forefinger and her middle finger, which were pressed against her lips on either side of it, agitating the cigarette with a small perpetual tremor which made the ash fall on to the carpet – where she ignored it.

She had a way of closing her eyes, not blinking, not screwing them up, but just letting her lids drop down for a second or two. He noticed it whenever she wasn't wearing her dark glasses. He wondered if she did it behind the dark glasses. She wore the dark glasses a lot, even inside the house.

She was called Lady Belinda; that was because her father was a lord. She said she couldn't stand her family, and that they were snobs and bores. She never saw any of them except, occasionally, her cousin Violet – 'Vi,' she would say, 'isn't too bad really.' But there were times – always when she was wearing the dark glasses, and when her face, which was usually pale, was flushed, and her voice had a thick sort of sound that made him want to ask her to clear her throat – when she would talk about them in a different way. She would tell him stories about her ancestors, and fetch the big red book called Debrett, and show him the family crest and coat of arms. Sometimes she would lose her place in the book, and he would have to find it for her, or, in the middle of a sentence, she would forget what she had been saying, and he would have to remind her. That became easier and easier, because he came to know the stories by heart. He loved them. He loved to hear about her family.

About once a month, she would go away to London for a few days. He hated that. He dreaded the way she behaved after she came back: when she wasn't shut in her room, she would be silent, irritable; she would wear the dark glasses all the time.

When she was away, he would try to cheer himself up by drawing the family tree. The Debrett book was difficult to get the hang of, at first, but gradually he worked out what he wanted: the direct line through the nine earls to his mother, and then to himself.

At first, he drew it as a little diagram, but later he began to draw it as a real tree. That was more satisfying. With the diagram, his name had been right at the bottom of the page, and he didn't like that. When he drew the tree, he started with the roots, entwining among them the names of the first earl and his wife. The trunk rose, and he drew a branch across, and wrote the names of the second earl and his countess on it. So he continued, trunk and then branch through the remaining seven earls and their consorts.

He reached the top, and across it he drew a small branch, on which he wrote his mother's name – not with his father's; no, not a chance of that! Above his mother's branch, the trunk of the tree grew to a point, from which he drew two outward pointing leaves. Between them, growing upwards, a large beautiful fruit crowned the tree. He painted the fruit yellow and crimson, and then he would write his name around it in curling script, following its outline in a circle.

Really he never became tired of drawing the tree. Whenever he felt sad or lonely, he could become absorbed in that.

He took his attitude towards his father from his mother. It was easy to look at his father in the way she did. His father was such a little man – at least four inches shorter than his mother. His father had grey wispy hair and a high giggle, and he collected old keys. 'Such a damn silly footling thing to collect,' Charles's mother would comment. 'And so useless. What are keys for except to open bloody doors? What's the point of sticking them in glass cases?' (His mother said 'bloody' and 'damn' a lot, especially when she talked in *that* voice.) '*Somebody*'s been at the Mother's Ruin again,' his father would say. (What did *that* mean?) And his mother would answer, 'Mind your own bloody business. Why don't you get back to your *keys*?')

That was what happened when it came out into the open – the hostility between them which he had always recognized. His mother would talk about the keys, or she would make contemptuous reference to the fact that his father had not been fit for army service in the war, which had recently ended. 'Now if it had been TB, or something glamorous, that would

170

have been different. But *flat feet* – just like a bloody *policeman*.' Then Charles's father would say, 'Why don't you have a little rest, dear? I really think you need one.'

More often, there was silence between them, which was almost as bad. At meals, his mother would address a few remarks to Charles, and his father would bring a book to the table, and read it. 'Bloody awful manners,' his mother would sometimes mutter, and his father would put down the book, and give that litle giggle of his, and say, 'How would you like me to entertain you, dear?' To which she would reply, 'Don't worry. You couldn't entertain me if you tried.'

How useless his father was. How *silly* he was. He wasn't like the fathers in any of the books Charles had read. He never talked sensibly to Charles; he never told him anything helpful about games or machines or animals, as the fathers in the books did. He hardly talked to him at all, in fact, and sometimes Charles would catch him looking at him in such a funny way – the sort of way the farmer down the road looked at his cows.

Time passed, and everything went on just the same. Well, he supposed it was the same, only, somehow *more* the same. Until at last he had to admit that it was definitely getting worse.

More and more frequently, his mother locked herself in her room, and stayed there all day, not even coming down to meals. (On those days, Charles, as well as his father, read at table.) She went to London more often; she stayed there longer; she came back angrier. What did she *do* there?)

Of course, Charles was away for much of the time, first at his prep school, and then at his public school. He didn't mind school. Nobody bullied him – there was something about him that kept people at a distance. Then he found that there were those – soon he was able to spot them very quickly – who would do what he told them, and he became the leader of a set.

At the end of each term, he hoped that the coming holidays would be better – but they never were. There were times, now, when he hated his mother – he had learned that 'Mother's Ruin' was a humorous name for gin, but to him it seemed a terrible and true description. And yet she was so beautiful; she could still be so wonderful on those increasingly rare days when she was what he called 'herself'. At school, he thought about her often – and secretly in prep, he would draw the tree.

He came home for the Easter holidays during which he would have his fifteenth birthday. On the day he arrived, his mother was at her very best – she wasn't even wearing her dark glasses – and it was the same the next day. They were together all the time – his father kept away, in his study, with the keys.

At breakfast on the third day, his mother said, 'I'm going up to London.' She added, 'Only for a couple of days. I'll be back in plenty of time for your birthday, Charles.' How had she known that he was thinking about that? He didn't like people knowing what he was thinking – not even her. He said, 'Yes, of course. That will be fine.'

In the middle of the morning, off she went in the village taxi, to Bury St Edmunds station. Charles stood in the doorway, kicking at the iron shoescraper, as the car drove away. His birthday was in five days' time. He went upstairs and drew the tree. Somehow, he felt that doing that would bring her back in time.

But the morning of his birthday came, and still she wasn't back. At breakfast his father gave him the present he had bought: a beautifully bound edition of Shakespeare – he couldn't help being pleased with it. He liked Shakespeare, especially *Hamlet*, which they had done at school the previous term. He felt that Hamlet was rather like he was, in some ways – except that he wouldn't have been so wet: *he* would have killed that awful Claudius right away.

'I don't know what your *mother* is giving you, I'm afraid,' his father said. Charles hated him for that – but he didn't let anything at all show on his face.

That afternoon, in his bedroom, Charles drew a tree. It was a beautiful one with brown branches and green leaves and a scarlet fruit on the top. And when he'd finished it, he took a pair of scissors, and jabbed little holes all over it, and then he cut, cut, cut all along his mother's branch. He didn't touch the red fruit, but suddenly crunched the ragged sheet of paper in his fist, and then threw it into the wastepaper basket.

That evening, he and his father read their books, while they ate the cold supper that the daily maid had left for them. They were just finishing when Charles heard a car draw up outside. *So she had come!* His father heard it too, for he stood up and said, 'That will be your mother, I expect.' With his finger marking the place in his book, he left the room, and Charles heard him go along the passage to his study, and then heard the door of the study close.

Charles went out of the dining-room into the hall. There he hesitated. He could hear his mother outside, talking very loudly in *that* voice. And then she was answered by a man who was talking in the same way, who didn't sound like a taxi driver. Charles wondered if people in the village were listening, peering out from behind their curtains.

The front door was flung open, and his mother almost fell into the hall. She tripped on the mat, but saved herself by clutching at the frame of the door.

Her hair was straggling from its bun. Her face was more than flushed; it was red. Her eyes had a dull look, and she was screwing them up as if she couldn't see properly. 'Charles,' she said, 'told you I'd be back in time ... your birthday.'

She came farther into the hall, and he became aware of the figure standing behind her in the doorway.

It was a man in the kind of suit that Charles knew a gentleman wouldn't wear. It was navy blue, it was double-breasted, and the lapels were too wide. So was his shiny pink tie, and his black shoes were too pointed. He wore a nylon shirt – something that only 'spivs' wore. Everything about him was slightly crumpled, except his hair which was greased down. Charles was suddenly sure that he used a lot of something called Brylcreem. At school, to call someone a 'Brylcreem boy' was to be as insulting as you possibly could be.

The man wasn't fat, but his pale shiny face was plump, and his stomach bulged over the belt he wore to keep his trousers up – a gentleman, of course, would have worn braces. He had small shiny black eyes – like currants in a bun, Charles thought – and a horrible little toothbrush moustache. But the worst thing of all was that there were lipstick smudges all round his mouth.

'Charles,' his mother was saying, 'Charles, want you to meet Arthur. Very great friend of mine, Arthur.'

'How d'you do,' said Charles, not moving, not smiling.

'Pleased to meet you, I'm sure,' said the man called Arthur. 'Little Lindy here has told me a lot about you.'

Charles's mother was fumbling in her bag, holding it up close to her face. 'Got a present for you, but what's happened to the bloody thing? Arthur, what I do with those bloody cuff-links?' She held out the bag to Charles. 'You look for 'em, Charles. After all ... for you.'

Stiffly, he extended his hand, and took the bag from her. Inside it, there was a jumble of things: dirty screwed-up tissues, an open, spilling powder-compact, a comb with hairs in it, a purse, the dark glasses (he saw that one of the lenses was cracked), a lipstick – *that* lipstick, he supposed. He handed the bag back to her. 'They aren't in there,' he said.

'For God's sake, don't sound so *stuffy*, Charles,' she said. 'Bad as your father. That's why I'm getting out of here. Made up mind completely, haven't I, Arthur?'

Arthur mumbled, 'Whatever you say, little Lady Lindy. Just whatever you say.'

'Arthur's coming upstairs, help me pack, aren't you, Arthur?'

Arthur nodded in a dazed way.

'Well, Christ's sake come on then,' she said harshly. Arthur followed her down the hall, past Charles, who stepped back against the wall. As they started to climb the stairs, she rested one hand on the curved mahogany banister, and flung her other arm around Arthur's neck. Awkwardly – the staircase was not very wide – they ascended.

They disappeared along the landing. Then Charles heard the sound of a kiss, followed by his mother's throaty laugh. He heard the opening of her bedroom door. After that, there was silence.

It felt as if it were a very long time that he stood in the hall. Then he couldn't bear the silence upstairs any longer. He turned, and hurried along the passage to his father's study, abruptly turned the door handle, and went in.

His father sat at his desk, reading a book onto which the light from a pink-shaded table-lamp fell. Around the room were the keys in their glass-fronted cases. The cases hung on the walls, and stood on tables. Each key had its niche in a wine-coloured velvet backing, and was labelled with its date and place of origin.

174

As Charles came in, his father looked up from the book he was reading with an expression of mild surprise, an air of faint, instantly suppressed irritation. He smoothed the opened pages in front of him with an outward movement of his palms. 'Yes?' he said.

'She's going,' Charles burst out. 'She says she's going. She's packing.'

'Your mother?' His father sounded as unconcerned as if he were asking about a stranger.

'Yes,' he said impatiently – for who else could he be talking about? He hesitated. Then he said, 'There's a man with her.'

'I *thought* I heard an unfamiliar voice,' his father said.

There was a pause. His father was looking at him with slightly raised eyebrows, as if he were still waiting to hear the reason for his reading having been interrupted.

'She's not – herself,' Charles managed to say at last.

'Herself?' his father queried mildly.

'Aren't you going to *do* something?' His voice rose.

'Do something?' his father repeated. 'My dear boy, what would you suggest?'

'Stop her,' he almost shouted.

'I doubt if that would be possible,' his father said, adding, with finality, 'She'll be back. Good night, Charles.' He started to read his book again.

Charles became aware of a bumping sound. He hurried out into the passage, slamming the door of the study behind him, and through into the hall. His mother was carrying her crocodile dressing-case. With its silver fittings, it was heavy, and she was dragging it down from step to step. Behind her came Arthur, carrying a suitcase.

Charles stood at the bottom of the stairs. When she reached him, his mother put down the dressing-case. Again she opened her bag, peered into it, fumbled with its contents. 'Must be somewhere,' she said. But, after a moment or two, she abandoned the search. She held out her arms, and enfolded Charles in an embrace. It wasn't just the smell of drink, it was an added smell of sweetish staleness that made him draw back.

'Cold,' she said. 'Cold as your father. Let's get out of here, Arthur.' Picking up the dressing-case again, and followed by Arthur, she made her way unsteadily towards the front door.

'Don't go.' He was horrified by, he was deeply ashamed of

the panic that he heard in his own voice, but still he couldn't stop himself saying it again: 'Don't go. Mummy, don't leave me.'

She turned. 'Must,' she said, but her tone was kinder. 'Must bloody get away. Sorry ... the cuff-linkish. Turn up, and I'll send them. 'Bye now.' And she went out of the front door.

As Arthur, carrying the suitcase – he was sweating – passed Charles, he said, 'Well, ta-ta, sonny boy.' Charles didn't answer, just stared coldly past him.

But he couldn't help going to the door. Outside was a new shiny Morris. There were cardboard boxes stacked in the back. Arthur put the suitcase and the dressing-case in with them. He opened the door in front for Charles's mother to get in. Then he went round, and got into the driver's seat. In the light that streamed from the hall, Charles saw his mother say something to Arthur. Arthur reached into a compartment in the dashboard, brought out a half bottle of gin, and passed it to her. She opened it, raised it to her lips, took a long gulp from it, and started to cough. Coughing, she handed the bottle back to Arthur, who, in his turn, drank from it.

Charles *wouldn't* watch them drive off. He stepped back into the hall, and closed the door. He stood in the hall for a moment, heard the car start with a scream of tyres. He listened to the sound of the car until it died away, and the silence was unbroken. Then he went up to his room.

Over and over again, lying in bed, he said, 'I want her to die. I want her to die. I want her to die.' It was not until late next day that a policeman came round to tell his father that she was dead. Outside the village, on a sharp bend, the car had gone out of control, crashed through a fence, and caught fire in a field. Arthur's stock – he had been a commercial traveller – of children's chemistry sets had been highly inflammable, and identification of the bodies had been difficult.

Lady Violet came to the funeral, beautiful in black. Charles smelled her rich flowery scent as she rested her soft cheek against his. She drew back and looked at him with her blue blue eyes. 'Poor little Charles,' she said. 'Poor darling little Charles.' He gave a small stiff smile – after all, he wasn't *little* – but he could feel the corners of his mouth quivering. She took his hand lightly in hers, and she led him away, down the mossy path of the village churchyard, between the graves.

'Charles,' she said, 'don't forget that you can always turn to me if you need to. I'll give you my address in London.' Sitting on a tombstone, she wrote it on a piece of paper. 'And let me give you some money, just in case.' She gave him three pound notes. How beautiful she was – almost as beautiful as his mother.

He had a power. That was what he thought about each night, in bed. *He had a power.* He had said, 'I want her to die,' and she had died. He had been right to do it. For now she was his own once more, with her thick dark hair and her pale skin. Now, and for ever, she was herself again. And he – *he* was master of life and death.

In the week that followed the funeral, he began to notice a change in his father. His father talked more to him. He asked him into the study, and tried to interest him in the keys. And, looking up from his book, at meals, Charles would see his father watching him, with that look that was like the look the farmer gave his cows.

Also, his father, always so drily abstemious, was suddenly drinking a great deal. Not gin, but wine at meals, and, late into the evening, whisky, which made him giggle and crack silly jokes. Charles always went to bed as soon after dinner as was possible.

Four nights before he was due to go back to school, his father got drunker than usual, and Charles was in bed by nine. *I have a power,* he thought, and then he fell asleep. He woke to feel a body pressed against his.

'Charles, you lovely boy, let us be close to each other,' a voice was muttering. The voice was his father's voice, wasn't it, or was he still asleep and dreaming? A hand unfastened the cord of his pyjama trousers, and started to caress him.

He was out of bed, over by the door, switching on the light. There in his bed was his father, blinking, and looking like a little owl. 'Get out, get out,' Charles repeated over and over again, opening the door. His father, looking dazed, stumbled up, shambled past him, muttering something about 'all a mistake, dear boy'. Charles pushed the door shut before his father was properly out of the room – he felt it slam against his father's body. Then he leaned against it, panting, as he turned the key in the lock.

He sat on the edge of the bed, with the light on. He couldn't stop trembling. After about half an hour, he heard the handle of the door being rattled. His father's voice said, 'I want to explain.' He kept absolutely still, and, after a time, the rattling stopped, and he heard his father padding off down the passage.

It was six o'clock in the morning when he crept out of the house. He was carrying his school suitcase, in which he had packed everything he could think of. He had left his birthday Shakespeare on the desk in his father's study. In his pocket were Lady Violet's address and the money she had given him.

He had to wait for a long time for the bus to Bury St Edmunds, but, at last, it arrived. In Bury, he walked to the station. There was a train to London in half an hour's time. He thought that the man in the ticket office looked at him in a funny way, but he offered a cold stare in return. The man gave him his ticket, taking a long time to count out the change.

From Liverpool Street, he took a taxi. He rang the doorbell, and when a maid answered, he asked for Lady Violet. 'I'm afraid she's not up yet, sir,' the maid said, looking at him doubtfully. 'Please tell her I'm here,' he said. 'Say it's Charles: Charles Tibbald.' Perhaps she recognized the name. Anyway, she motioned him inside, and gestured to a chair in the hall. Then she went upstairs. A minute or two later, she came down again, and said, 'Please come with me, sir.'

Lady Violet lay in a great four-poster. A Pekingese nestled in the eiderdown, which was covered with letters and papers and books. Her face was pale, and faintly shiny with cream; a chiffon scarf was fastened over her hair – but her blue eyes blazed so brightly that they were the only thing he was really conscious of. Perhaps, after all, she was more beautiful than his mother.

'Why Charles, what brings you here so early?' she said.

He almost stuttered, apologizing, saying it was eleven o'clock, that he hadn't realized ...

'Never mind about that,' she said. 'Tell me what's the matter.' She pointed to a gilt chair, upholstered in pink, and he sat down on it.

He didn't know how to tell her. Then he simply blurted it out: 'My father, he – he got into bed with me.'

'Got into bed with you?' she said, raising her eyebrows.

And then, suddenly, she seemed to understand, for she shuddered, and she said, 'Oh *no*.'

Gratefully, staring down at the carpet, which was pale blue with wreaths of flowers on it, he nodded.

There was a silence, and then she said, in a very calm voice, 'In the circumstances, I feel that I should tell you that he isn't really your father.'

Not really his father. So all along, when he drew the tree, he'd been right not to put his father in. *He had known.* That must have been something to do with his power.

'Not your father at all,' she went on. 'So that makes things better, doesn't it?' She didn't wait for an answer to that. She said, 'Well Charles, I think you'd better come to live with us. Edwin will be delighted, I know.'

Edwin was her husband, who was something in the Government. He'd heard his mother say that Edwin was completely under Violet's thumb.

'Would you like that?' she asked him. 'Would you like to live with us?'

'Oh yes, I would,' he said, and then, 'Thank you very much.'

She laughed. The blue eyes sparkled. 'Then that's settled,' she said. 'We shall have great fun. There's a room on the top floor which we shall be able to make *very* nice for you.' She paused. She said, 'Should I telephone *Tibbald*, I wonder, to tell him you're here?' She stretched her hand towards the telephone next to her bed, then withdrew it. 'No,' she said, 'I think we'll let him *stew* for a bit.' The smile she gave him was conspiratorial, and he returned it. 'That's more like it, Charles,' she said. 'You're feeling better now, aren't you?'

'Yes,' he said, 'much better.'

'When do you go back to school?'

'In three days' time,' he said.

'Well, that will be all right, won't it?' He nodded, and she said, 'What about your things?'

'I brought them with me,' he said, and was rewarded by another of her smiles.

'Clever boy! Yes, I think everything is going to work out wonderfully. Though there may be one or two problems in the summer. Edwin and I are going away rather a lot. But don't worry. We'll find a solution to that when the time comes.'

When the time came, the solution had been the Children's Hotel.

A fine rain had started to fall. In the grave, the Colgong Star glittered, and Charles stood with his head bowed.

'But why did you kill Lady Violet?' Esther asked.

His face had a closed look. At last he said, 'She told me a lie.'

'A lie? What was it?'

'A lie,' he repeated. 'A filthy lie.'

'I asked you what it was.' Once more, she raised the gun, tightened her hold on it.

He said, 'It was about my real father.' And again he was silent.

'Go on,' she said.

'I went to see her. She was in a vicious mood that night. I'd gone to her for comfort after Clare left. I think perhaps she was angry that I hadn't been round there for some time. She said, "Don't you think it's time you grew up, Charles. That little wife of yours goes away, and you come running to me, like a child." That made me angry. I'd always thought that she was the one person I could trust. And then she said, "I've been thinking for some time that you ought to learn the truth about your father." She'd told me long before that he was an Italian, married and a Roman Catholic, so that there had been no question of divorce. And of course I knew – I'd always known – that he must be of a very noble family. But then she told me this filthy lie.'

'I know what she told you,' Esther said. 'She told you the truth – that he was your grandfather's chauffeur.'

His whole body tensed. 'Who told you that filth?' he said.

'My stepfather, as a matter of fact. Everybody knew about it. He was the chauffeur, and that's why they married her off to Tibbald.'

'Lies. All lies,' he said. 'I told her so, and she laughed, and I picked up the poker. She deserved to die.'

'What happened to Tibbald?' Esther said, after a moment.

Charles smiled. 'He died a year or two after I went to live

with Violet. They said it was from cancer, but I knew it was my power.'

'Your power,' she said, 'your power!' And then, 'You meant Geoff to die, didn't you Charles?'

He nodded seriously. 'Yes,' he said. 'Yes, I did.'

'But why?'

'He irritated me, and besides, I wanted to test my power. When I bounced that ball, I was testing it.'

'I see,' she said. 'Tell me Charles, what happened to your power in all the years between?'

'I was saving it for when I really needed it. Though there was a boy in my last year at school ...'

'Go on,' she said.

'He laughed at me. He said what you and Brian said – that I was mad. He said, "Tibbald, I think you're off your rocker".'

'So what happened to him?'

'He – drowned in the swimming-pool.'

'Just like that?'

'It doesn't always just happen,' he said. 'Sometimes I have to help the power along.'

'So it seems,' she said. 'You certainly had to with darling Brian, and with Lady Violet and that little Sue.'

Oh the splendour of her icy calm. *It is I who have the power*, she thought. 'Charles,' she said, 'throw me your keys.'

'My keys?' he said, and then, 'Esther, what are you going to do?'

'The keys,' she said. And suddenly he began to shake. He raised his hands to his head, and started to sob.

'Oh Charles,' she said, 'what a coward you are, and what a coward you were when you killed. *The keys*,' she repeated. 'If you don't throw me the keys, I shall shoot you.'

Through his sobs, he spoke with a wild hope: 'And if I do, then you won't.'

'No,' she said. 'No, I won't kill you, Charles.'

He fumbled in his pocket, brought out his keys, and tossed them up to her. She caught them in her left hand. 'Esther,' he said, 'Esther, I knew you wouldn't kill me. Not after all that we've been to each other.' He wiped his eyes with his handkerchief. He looked at her with the beginnings of his smile. 'Aloof one,' he said.

Twirling the keys in her hand, she said, 'What did you mean when you said that I and Brian were really *they*?'

'Why, my mother and Tibbald, of course,' he said, matter of factly.

'Yes,' she said. 'I see.'

She raised the gun and steadied it. She aimed low, aimed to the left, fired twice. He screamed as the blood poured from his shattered knees, and he sank down into the grave.

'For Geoff,' she said, 'and for Brian,' and then, 'Goodbye Charles, I'm going now.'

He screamed again. His blood was soaking into the earth. Then he started to whimper. *To whimper like a puppy*, she thought.

'No,' he pleaded – how white his face was and how red his blood; *so much blood*. 'No, you can't leave me. You can't leave me here alone.'

'Oh yes I can,' she said. She looked at him once more, and then she turned and she started to push her way through the wet lilac branches. Behind her his voice rose. 'No, no,' he was sobbing now. 'Mummy, don't go; don't leave me.' But by the time she reached the terrace, the roar of the Usk had drowned his voice.

It rained steadily. There was the tick of the windscreen wiper, and the exhilaration of her steely courage, of the point of bright steel burning in her chest. *I have inherited his power*, she thought – but that was nonsense, and she was so practical, so calm. She stopped at a garage on the edge of Ross-on-Wye to have the car filled up. Then, on she drove in the gathering darkness, with the rain falling, and the windscreen wiper ticking, ticking, '*Now anarchy is loosed upon the world*,' she murmured aloud, and the words pleased her so much that she repeated them: '*Now anarchy is loosed upon the world*.' And what was it that Charles had said? *The world will be as white as after a fall of snow*. Yes, that was exactly how it would be.

It was quite dark when she took the Mortmere turning. The gates were open, and she drove in, past the lodge. She got out of the car at the end of the drive, by the ha-ha, and walked across the gravel to the house. Three large cars were parked outside. They had visitors. But why should she care? Silently she climbed the steps to the terrace. The dining-room windows were lit up. There was a gap between the heavy curtains of one of them.

Yes, there they sat at the long polished table. Her stepfather was at the head, in his wheelchair, and, as always, her mother sat at his side, ready to help him, to take the glass from his hand if he suddenly started to tremble. There were six other people at the table: the horrible German with the duelling scar and his wife, and two other couples whom she didn't know.

Their lips moved, but she couldn't hear what they were saying. Candlelight sparkled on silver and glass.

How grey they all looked, she thought. All was greyness, except for the gleam of her mother's pale gold hair. They looked, she thought, like a gathering of vampires, risen shadowy from their daytime coffined sleep to bloat. *To drain the brightness from the world.*

She moved on across the terrace. She went in through the little side door. She tiptoed down the passage to her stepfather's study, which was in darkness. She felt her way over to his desk, and found the switch of the reading lamp which stood on it. There it was, the thick stack of paper. Yes, there were the Memoirs – how very long they were; surely they must be nearly finished by now.

She fanned the sheets of paper out across the desk till it was entirely covered with them. She crumpled three of the sheets into little balls, and put them back on the desk. She felt in her bag, under the gun, for her matches, found them, and set light to the three crumpled pages.

They didn't take long to start burning, and soon the whole of the top of the desk was a great orange flame. It looked pretty, she thought, watching from the doorway.

She would take the gun from her bag as she went down the passage to the dining-room. She would be pointing it as she opened the door, and all their heads would turn towards her. Oh, how the grey vampires would stare!

Down the length of the table, she would face her stepfather. As she fired, her mother would fling herself across the table in front of him. The bullet would make a little red hole in her mother's forehead. She would fire again. This time the bullet would strike her stepfather full in the throat.

She realized that she was smiling, and shook her head to

clear it. Flaming paper had drifted from the desk to the study floor. The carpet was burning. One of the curtains had caught fire. It was time for her to go.

As she let herself out by the side door – carefully wiping the handle afterwards with the tail of her shirt, as she had wiped the handle of the study door – she could hear their voices in the dining-room. She paused on her way across the terrace to look again through the gap in the curtains. They were eating biscuits and cheese. Soon her mother and the other women would be leaving the men to their port and cigars.

On the other side of the ha-ha, before she got into the car, she looked back. The study windows glowed with a dusky orange light.

She started the car. *Now anarchy is loosed upon the world.* But *she* must be calm; *she* must be cool. If she could organize the next few hours satisfactorily, everything should be all right.

The car was the problem. For surely, by now, the police must be looking for Charles. Brian's body must have been discovered, and his connection with Charles – the alibi for the night of Lady Violet's death – recalled.

But she would have to take the risk of the car being recognized. For she couldn't abandon it, least of all in the neighbourhood of Mortmere. Anyway, how would she get home? On a train, people might notice and remember her. And besides, she suddenly remembered, she had very little money, after having paid for that petrol at Ross-on-Wye. Certainly not enough for the fare to London. No, she would have to drive the car.

Just after she turned on to the main road, a fire engine passed her. She stopped the car, and looked back. It took the Mortmere turning. She wondered how far the fire had spread. Perhaps they wouldn't be able to get it under control. *Birds nesting in the crumbling walls.* She decided that this was a suitable moment to pick up the cloth that was under the dashboard, and to wipe every surface that she could conceivably have touched. In her mind, she ticked off the things that she would have to wipe again when she left the car: steering-wheel, gear, hand-brake, door handle.

*

She parked the car on the Embankment, by the gardens beyond Charing Cross Underground. *Steering-wheel, gear, hand-brake.* She wrapped the cloth round her fingers, and rubbed the handle as she opened the car door. It was nearly midnight. Not many cars were about, and there were no pedestrians in sight.

She left the key in the ignition and the window open – if someone stole the car, she decided, it would be an excellent thing.

She walked back to Hungerford Bridge, went halfway across it, and waited for a train. After a minute or two, she heard one approaching. She took the gun from her bag, and wiped it carefully with the cloth. When the train roared past, not even she heard the splash as the gun hit the water. She let go of the cloth. It floated down, and was carried away on the tide.

On the short journey home, the consciousness of success made it possible for her to tread lightly, as she hurried up Bedford Street, and almost to forget the extremity of her fatigue. But once in the flat – she stared round it; could she have left it only that morning with Charles? – she dropped her clothes on the floor, left them where they lay, was in bed in a moment. How she hoped that she would be able to sleep – she had a lecture at ten next morning. Almost at once, the fact of sleep overtook the wish.

She was woken at eight by a telephone call from her mother. 'I'm so sorry,' Esther said when her mother told her of the destruction of the Memoirs, and that her stepfather had suffered a second and more serious stroke. The study had been gutted, but the firemen had been able to prevent the fire spreading any further. 'The police are wondering if terrorists could have been responsible,' her mother said. 'I wonder,' said Esther. 'Perhaps you could come down this weekend,' her mother said, and she answered, 'Of course I will.'

She was much better, she told solicitous colleagues. Her temperature was normal again, though she felt a little low. 'I always think,' said an elderly lecturer called Miss Banks, 'that a summer fever is more debilitating than a winter one.'

A summer fever. The words strayed through her mind as she read the newspaper. Brian's body had not been found until Monday evening. The police were looking for a man who might be able to help them with their inquiries.

She spent the afternoon in the library, correcting essays. She wondered when what she thought of as 'Stage Two' would begin. She decided that it would start when Charles was not at the airport to meet Clare.

It was at eleven that evening that Clare telephoned her, sobbing and incoherent. Esther took a taxi to Hill Street and spent the night there. Next day, there was more of Clare's hysteria – and there were the police.

They asked Esther questions, and she answered them. No, she hadn't seen either Brian or Charles since the Sunday – she took out her diary and checked the date – when she had come back from a weekend in the country – 'at home', she said – and they had both taken her out to dinner. Yes, that had been the day after Lady Violet's murder. Yes, Charles had seemed very upset. Yes, they had told her that Charles had spent the previous night at Brian's. No, she had found nothing odd about that – Brian and Charles were old friends. No, it wasn't unusual that she hadn't seen either of them since. Often she didn't see Brian for weeks. Yes, she saw Charles more frequently, usually, but with Clare – and Clare, of course, had been away.

The policemen left at last. She stayed with Clare until six o'clock, and then she told her that she had to go. 'I'm sorry, Clare,' she said, 'but you know that I never miss my Thursday meeting.' Clare wept, but Esther remained firm. She promised to come round early next day. She made tea for Clare, gave her two sleeping pills, and saw her into bed.

She had bathed. She had put on make-up and Arpège. She wore the heavy black satin with the plunging neckline and the long sleeves, and she had fastened the ribbons of the mask under the coil of her upswept hair. She sat rocking gently. It was getting dark outside, and the darkness was even deeper behind the mask. She remembered Charles saying, 'It is called Trial by Ordeal.'

What would they make of it when they found him, when they found the Colgong Star, when they opened the other grave and found Sue's body? Whatever they thought, she could see no reason why it should involve her.

Had anyone noticed her in the car? There had been the garage man at Ross-on-Wye, but he hadn't shown any sign of interest. No, she could see no reason why anyone should ever suspect her – though there might be some factor that she hadn't taken into account at all. *He had said, 'It is called Trial by Ordeal.'*

But in the deep darkness under the mask, she realized that 'all that' was so much the lesser part of the ordeal. There she waited, in the rocking-chair – waited for what? For the police? No, of course not. She waited for Charles.

She felt certain that he wasn't dead. Surely he would find some way to reach her? For, after all, *he had his power.*

The doorbell rang.

Ted Willis
The Lions of Judah £1.25

The year is 1939 and war looms. The Nazis, at the peak of their power, hound the Jews with vicious malevolence. Kurt Reiss is Jewish, and determined to fight for his people — whatever the cost. When he is captured, after an assassination attempt on Goering, he knows his hour has come. But he is wrong. Instead, he is offered a deal he dare not refuse, and where the penalty for failure is unthinkable in its consequences . . .

'Willis is a born storyteller' DAILY MAIL

Desmond Lowden
Boudapesti 3 95p

A $1000-a-week contract for a TV blockbuster in Athens promises to bring back the good times for film editor Raikes. But something is wrong — the set-up seems weird . . . In the heat of a Mediterranean afternoon, Raikes waits for an appointment in the Greek capital. Suddenly, mayhem in the streets below — shots, screeching tyres — and there on the windowledge beside him a rifle still hot and smoking from a top-level political killing . . . for which there can be only one prime suspect.

'Bullseye expertise' GUARDIAN

Joseph Kessel
Belle de Jour 80p

The sensual story of a young woman — prostitute by day, loving wife by night — that became the sensational film starring Catherine Deneuve, directed by Bunuel.

The all too credible story of an outwardly contented and sophisticated young French housewife whose hidden cravings lead her to utter degradation.

'A moving psychological drama that plumbs the depths of being' MANCHESTER EVENING NEWS

Garson Kanin
Moviola £1.50

The Hollywood novel that tells it all.

Meet 92-year-old B. J. Farber, rich and cantankerous, a movie mogul about to sell his legendary studios. This is his story — the scandals, heartbreaks, passions and mysteries — Fatty Arbuckle's sex disgrace, Chaplin the comic genius, Garbo's tragic romance, the discovery of Monroe and her mysterious death, the trials and backroom feuds behind some of the greatest films ever made.

'More film stars' real secrets that there are footprints in the cement of Hollywood Boulevard' DAILY MAIL

Robin Cook
Sphinx £1.25

Beautiful Egyptologist Erica Baron is mesmerized by a centuries-old statue in a Cairo antique shop, believing she has found the key to a dazzling hoard of untapped treasure. But there are others, more ruthless and corrupt than herself, determined to get there first, whatever the cost. Lost in a deadly web of intrigue and murder, Erica races to unlock the secrets of a pharaoh's tomb and plumb the curse that has kept it intact since time began . . .

Jack M. Bickham
The Excalibur Disaster £1.50

Transwestern Flight 161 is a new Excalibur jet, *en route* from St Louis to New York. The 199 passengers will never step from the plane alive. The crash is a mystery. The cause — pilot error? systems failure? — lies hidden in a smoky heap of metal and bodies at Kennedy Airport. One of those bodies was Jason Baines, head of Hempstead Aviation, makers of the Excalibur. The horrible truth begins to dawn on investigator Jace Mattingly. There are other Excaliburs flying, and in each one a tiny, undetected flaw . . .

Alan Scholefield
Point of Honour 95p

It was the perfect subject for a book: Captain Geoffrey Baines Turner VC killed in action on the bloodstained French coast — and who better than his son to write the story of one man's Dunkirk? David Turner begins his research and uncovers a vipers' nest of half-truths, malicious rumour and blackmail. His father, revered by some as a hero, is branded rapist and murderer by others . . .

'Completely believable' DAILY TELEGRAPH

Patrick Alexander
Show Me a Hero £1.25

Into the 1980s, a tyranny of the left rules Britain with Saracen troop carriers, while propaganda cloaks the corpses. Backs to the wall, the Resistance plans Operation Volcano, while up at the sharp end of every strike is the man they call the Falcon — a Robin Hood with an Uzi machine-gun and nerves of steel. One of nature's heroes, temporarily useful, ultimately expendable . . .

'Probably very near the truth' YORKSHIRE POST

Colin Dexter
Service of all the Dead £1.25

Churchwarden murdered during service the headline screamed. Inspector Morse found there was more to it than that. After the second death the case was closed; everyone agreed that the murderer had gone on to commit suicide.

Everyone, that is, except Morse. He sensed that unrest still reigned over the Oxford parish of St Frideswide. He found new evidence and discrepancies; and then, another body.

'He pulls off his tricks with confidence and cunning' GUARDIAN

Arthur Hailey
Overload £1.50

His latest, greatest bestseller.
Nim Goldman, vice president of GSP&L — the corporation
feeding power, light and heat to kilowatt-hungry California.
He's got a big job, and he's got all the women he can handle.
But Nim knows the crunch is coming : soon, very soon, power
famine will strike the most advanced society the world has
known ...

'3,200,000 kilowatts, OPEC, terrorists, power thieves, hypocrisy
and paralysis in high places ... chaos for powerguzzling
California ... another blockbuster' OBSERVER

Earl Thompson
Caldo Largo £1.50

Johnny Hand is in love with life, freedom and the unbridled
pleasures of sex. In the brawling world of seagoing men, every
woman in every bed in every port is a challenge — from Lupe, who
shrugged off her marriage vows as easily as her dress, to Cehlo,
the teenybopper temptress ... A novel that swells with life and
explodes with action — the deadly perils of Cuban gun-running,
the scorching love nests of Mexico ...

'Earl Thompson is an exceptional writer — full of power, able to
expose a whole world, to create people who blaze off the page'
COSMOPOLITAN